Texas Tango

WHISPERING SPRINGS, TEXAS
BOOK TWO

CYNTHIA D'ALBA

Second Edition

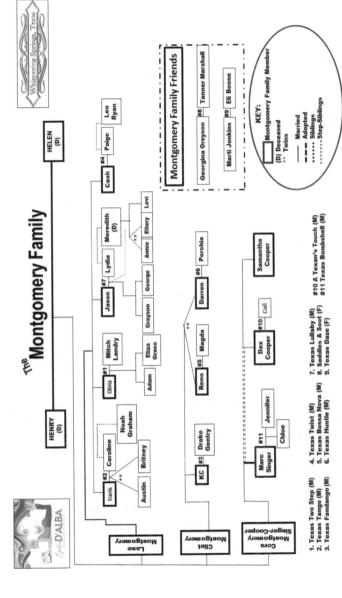

The Montgomery Family

Whispering Springs, Texas

Montgomery Family Friends

Georgina Greyson #8   Tanner Marshall

Marti Jenkins #9   Eli Boone

KEY:

☐ Montgomery Family Member
(D) Deceased
** Twins

— Married
- - - Adopted
···· Siblings
===== Step-Siblings

1. Texas Two Step (M)
2. Texas Tango (M)
3. Texas Fandango (M)
4. Texas Twist (M)
5. Texas Bossa Nova (M)
6. Texas Hustle (M)
7. Texas Lullaby (M)
8. Saddles & Scot (F)
9. Texas Daze (F)
10. A Texan's Touch (M)
11. Texas Bombshell (M)

TEXAS TANGO

By Cynthia D'Alba

Copyright © 2013 Cynthia D'Alba and Riante, Inc.

Second Edition © 2017

Print ISBN: 978-1-946899-08-8

Digital ISBN: 978-1-946899-07-1

Cover Artist: Elle James

Editor: Heidi Shoham

For Emily Milholen Reynolds. Without your legal help, the story wouldn't exist. A great big thanks for all your legal research. Any error or misinterpretation of Arkansas law is totally on me.

To Carol Graham. A lifelong friend who brings joy and sunshine into my life. Here's your story.

To Phillip. Thanks for pushing me to write, helping around the house and fixing the lawn mowers every time I break one. My life wouldn't be the same without you.

And to my fabulous, wonderful, couldn't-do-without editor, Heidi (Moore) Shoham. You always make my work stronger, tighter and sexier. Bless you for finding all those plot holes I need to fill in.

One

D r. Caroline Graham stood at the side of Angus Fitzgerald's casket, her oversized sunglasses protecting her eyes from an unrelenting Texas sun. Her gold charm bracelet clanked on the dark-grained wood as she rested her hand gently on the glossy lid. Her heart ached with a soul-deep sadness.

Until she'd moved to Whispering Springs, Texas eighteen months ago, she hadn't been close to her great-uncle Angus. She'd have never moved here without the encouragement—or should she say demand?—of his sister, Mamie Fitzgerald Bridges—her grandmother. Now she couldn't imagine not seeing his scruffy face and hearing his gruff voice every day.

"I'm sorry I didn't spend more time with you through the years, but I'm so glad we had these last months together. Mamie would have been here today if she could. She sends her love." She sniffed and wiped at the tears. "She said to tell you to prepare to get your ass kicked in checkers as soon as she joins you." She sniffed again. "I have to be honest, Uncle

Angus. I hope that's a long time away. I'm not ready to lose her too."

A hand landed softly on her shoulder. She turned her head to look into a pair of blue Montgomery eyes. Kathryn Colleen Montgomery, aka KC, squeezed Caroline's shoulder.

"I'm so sorry for your loss," KC said.

Caroline wiped her cheeks free of tears with a handkerchief. "Thanks, KC. You've been a good friend to Angus and me. I know how much he thought of you."

KC hugged her. "I loved the old coot."

Caroline laughed softly. "I know. So did I." She pulled out of KC's embrace to lay her hand on his casket again. She gave a sad chuckle. "I'll miss his cranky rants about all the politicians and—"

"Their thieving ways," KC finished.

Both women smiled.

"Yeah, I'll miss those too," KC said.

Caroline dabbed at her nose and then turned to lay a single long-stemmed orange rose on his coffin. "Rest in peace," she whispered. "You deserve it. Tell Great-Aunt Bernice I'm sorry I never got to meet her."

She stepped back and turned toward the gravediggers standing respectively to the side. "Thank you for waiting. I'm done."

The men moved in to finish the job of lowering the coffin into the ground and replacing the dirt.

"Are you sure we have to meet today?" Caroline asked as she and KC stepped away to give the gravediggers room to work. "Reading Uncle Angus's will so soon after his funeral seems so...I don't know...ghoulish."

KC nodded. "That was his request, but it doesn't have to be right this second. Take a break, go home and get some rest. You can come to my office later this afternoon if that works better for you."

She shook her head. "No, let's just get it done."

"Okay then. I'll meet you at the office."

KC turned, her leather-tooled cowboy boots grinding in the loose gravel near the grave site, her long skirt whipping around her ankles as she marched toward her battered truck.

After blowing one last kiss toward the grave of her late great-uncle who'd welcomed her with open arms, Caroline left the cemetery. The entire Montgomery clan stood in a cluster in the parking lot. She returned their waves as she drove past. Her stomach clenched when Travis Montgomery removed his hat and dipped his head toward her.

She'd been to the Bar M ranch for dinner on numerous occasions. The entire Montgomery family around a food-laden table with raucous conversations and sibling spats was an eye-opening experience.

The concept of a large family who enjoyed being together and weren't afraid of being affectionate in public was an enigma to her. She'd always wanted to be in a family like that, or thought she did. Not that she hadn't been raised in a loving home, because she had. Her parents, foreign missionaries, had worked in third-world countries through most of her life. Her maternal grandmother had raised her and loved her, but growing up, Caroline had wondered what it would be like to sit at a long table filled with family.

Dinners with the Montgomery clan always left her pondering if being a family member would feel different than being a visitor at that table. She'd never know.

The drive back to KC's law office in Whispering Springs took only fifteen minutes. She parked in front of a red-brick building sporting a gold plaque to the right of the door that identified the structure as *Montgomery and Montgomery, Attorneys-at-Law.*

She touched up her lipstick in the rearview mirror then slid from the car into the late July Texas heat.

A quick glance at the Bank of Whispering Springs clock and temperature sign made her utter an unladylike cuss word. One hundred and three, and it wasn't yet ten a.m. Everybody said things are bigger in Texas. She'd just never dreamed that would include the sweat rings under her arms.

Today would be another deadly day for heat strokes for sure. She feared the start of August tomorrow would only exacerbate the hot weather.

Dr. Lydia Henson, the other doctor in the Whispering Springs Medical Clinic, had assured Caroline the clinic could do without her today, even reiterating that at Angus's funeral. Caroline hated leaving her medical partner short-handed.

However, whether they fit her schedule or not, some things had to be dealt with today, like a will she really didn't want to hear.

Stepping into the law office reception area brought a sigh to her lips. The cool air was a welcome reprieve from the outside furnace heat.

Five more months and she was gone from this hellhole.

If it hadn't been for wanting to spend some time with Uncle Angus, she'd have never signed such an extended-temporary-practice contract here. The medical-staffing agency she used for her bookings usually found her employment where she filled in for vacationing or absent physicians from one to six months. This past two years had been her longest in a single locality since she'd finished her residency.

She had always been flexible about locations when considering work assignments, but after her first summer in

Texas heat, she'd made sure her next employment contract was somewhere cooler. Come January, she was off to Montana for two months. It might be frozen tundra during the winters, but she was absolutely melting in the heat down here.

"Good morning," a chipper middle-age woman said from behind a desk. "May I help you?"

"Yes, please. I have an appointment with KC Montgomery."

"Oh, yes, Dr. Graham. I am so sorry about your loss. Angus Fitzgerald was quite a character. We'll all miss him."

Caroline acknowledged the expression of sympathy with a nod. "Thank you."

The receptionist gestured to the seating area. "Would you have a seat please? KC just got back to the office and said to tell you she needed about five minutes. Would you like some water? A Coke? I'd offer you coffee, but from the pink of your cheeks, I think you'd rather something colder. Am I right?"

Caroline smiled. She wouldn't miss the Texas heat, but she'd sure miss the Southern hospitality. "Something cold would be wonderful. Water, please."

"No problem. Have a seat. I'll be right back."

The woman returned with a bottle of spring water. "Here you go," she said holding out the green bottle.

Caroline gave her a grateful smile. "Thank you." She took the water with an internal sigh of relief, cracked the cap and took a long drink. The cold water stung as it slid down her dry throat and splashed into her empty stomach.

Caroline took a seat and pulled out her phone to check messages. Lydia had promised to text her if there were any problems that required Caroline to head back to the clinic before the afternoon slate of patients. No emergency texts, no urgent emails. No rescue from having to hear Angus's will.

"Caroline. C'mon back. Sorry to keep you waiting."

Caroline looked up and smiled. KC's face was pulled into what Caroline called her *professional* face, sober and serious.

"Not a problem, KC," she said and stood. "The wait was just long enough to drink some water."

"Caroline." A deep voice boomed down the hall. Jason Montgomery, the second half of Montgomery and Montgomery Law Offices, took long strides toward her. "I didn't realize Angus Fitzgerald was your uncle. I am so sorry for your loss." He gave her a friendly hug.

She wrapped her arms around him to return his bear hug. "Thank you, Jason. I don't think anyone knew but KC. Angus wanted it that way."

She and Jason had met eighteen months ago when she first arrived in Whispering Springs. With his outgoing personality and take-no-prisoners approach to life, she'd developed an immediate fondness for the man. He and Lydia, her medical partner, had recently become engaged. She'd never met a pair so perfectly matched.

After collecting her purse from the floor, Caroline followed KC through the door to her office. Her travel charm bracelet jingled against the plastic water bottle. Her stomach rolled with a tsunami of acid waves. She did not want to do this today...or tomorrow...or ever really. Talking about Uncle Angus's estate made the reality of his death all the more painful.

"Have a seat." KC gestured toward one of the chairs in front of her desk. She dropped heavily into a large leather desk chair and leaned back. "That was some going away funeral for Angus."

Caroline nodded. "I bet he would have been surprised at how many people showed."

"Probably not. The Fitzgeralds have been fixtures in this community since its founding."

"Along with the Montgomerys?"

KC nodded. "Yep. Our two families go back a long way. Speaking of our families, I noticed that little tip of the head from Travis as you left."

Caroline's heart leapt at the mention of his name. Behind her bellybutton, her insides twittered. "Oh? Did Travis tip his head?" She fought to make her voice nonchalant.

KC snorted. "Yeah, right. Like you didn't see it."

"I'm sure he was just being respectful."

"Yes, that's probably it." KC sighed. "I'm sorry we have to do this today, but Angus wanted his estate closed as quickly as possible."

Caroline blew out a long breath. "I know," she said with a shake of her head. "I don't know what the rush is but..." She shrugged. "Go ahead."

KC opened the manila folder in front of her. "Okay with you if I skip reading the whereas and wherefores and go to the bequeaths?"

"Yes, please."

She smiled. "Cut to the chase. Got it." She looked back at the papers on her desk. "Okay, the bequeaths. Your Uncle—"

"Great-uncle," she corrected.

"Right. Anyway, you are aware that he left you as executor of his estate, right?"

Caroline shook her head. "No, I didn't know. I have no idea what I'm supposed to do as an executor."

Damn it, Angus. Caroline felt the emotional punch to her gut.

KC looked up from the papers on her desk. Her eyes held such a depth of sympathy and compassion Caroline almost burst into tears again.

"Your great-uncle loved you very much. The last time we spoke, he told me how thankful he was that you'd been here with him. I knew Angus my whole life. You brought out a side of him I'd never seen. My parents said that was the old Angus, the one they knew before his wife died. You were good for him."

Her vision blurred. The dam holding back her tears fractured. A large tear rolled from the corner of her eye. KC pushed a box of tissues across the desk.

"The will is quite simple and straight forward. I don't foresee any challenges or problems to closing the estate promptly." She smiled. "Trust me, Caroline. I'm a great lawyer. All the T's are crossed and I's are dotted. You'll do fine as executor, and I'll be here every step of the way, okay?"

After blowing her nose, Caroline pasted on a watery smile. "Thanks." She waved toward the papers on the desk. "Go on. Let me know what Uncle Angus had to say." Her stomach rolled with nervous energy. She wanted this done and over as quickly as possible.

KC lifted the sheath of papers again. "He left two-hundred thousand to your parents for their missionary work, or to use as they wish."

Caroline smiled. "That was nice of him. I know Mom and Dad will be thrilled."

"If you can provide me with their current location and a way to contact them, I can inform them of their inheritance, unless you want to, that is."

She shook her head. "No, that's okay. I'll let you contact

them. I'll call your secretary with that information tomorrow. I don't have it with me right now."

"I figured you'd probably want me to contact them."

Caroline shrugged. "I'm not even sure my last contact information for them is current. If not, I'll get you in touch with the missionary organization that sponsors them."

"Fine," KC said. "Going on, he left your brother two-hundred thousand for his college education. Should Noah choose not to attend college, the money will be left in a trust until he turns thirty."

"Oh." She jolted upright. Elation bubbled. "That was so nice of him. He never met Noah. I never expected this." Her back muscles relaxed at the thought of Noah's college education being funded. "I have been worried about paying for Noah's education when the time comes. There's no way my parents or I could afford to send him, and frankly I didn't want him to graduate with educational loans like mine. This is just so great."

"I knew you had a much younger brother, but you've never mentioned his age. I guess I didn't realize he was old enough for college."

Caroline smiled. "He isn't. He just turned fourteen, so it wasn't a pressing problem, but now...I am so relieved. Continue. I'm sorry for the interruption."

"Feel free to stop me any time you have a question about any of this. That's what I'm here for. He left your uncle Pat and his wife, Leslie, one-hundred-and-fifty thousand each." KC looked up from the will. "I don't understand this next one but you might. I'm going to read it just like he asked me to write it." She looked down again. "To my sister, Mamie. I've held on to this since we were kids. It's yours now. Practice up for when we meet again." She picked up a leather-covered box off her desk and passed it to Caroline.

The sun streaming through the window shot streaks of light off the jangling state-shaped charms on her bracelet as Caroline reached for the box. A sad smile crossed her lips when she looked inside and found an old, worn checkers game. "Perfect. She'll love this." She closed the box. "Go on."

"He left small amounts to the church, local library, places like that." She passed Caroline a printed sheet of paper. "Here's the list."

Caroline read down the list of bequeaths ranging from as little as ten-thousand dollars for the public library to fifty-thousand to his housekeeper. "Good. I like to see that he's remembered so many worthy causes in the community." She scanned the list again. "What about his ranch? Before he died he told me he had a great plan for it."

Surprise flashed across her friend's face before she continued. "I'm sorry, Caroline. I just assumed you knew. Angus left the ranch with the house, all its furnishings and the ranch animals to you. In fact, you inherit the remainder of the estate."

Caroline dropped heavily against the back of the chair, her mouth agape in shock. Blood rushed from her head, leaving her feeling a little faint. "What? Are you serious? I mean, of course you're serious, but why would he do that?"

KC pulled a sealed envelope from the file and passed it across her desk. "He left this for you."

"Should I read it now?"

She shrugged. "The envelope was sealed when I received it. I don't know what's in it, so I can't advise you on that. However, you may have questions for me after you've finished reading."

KC stood. "I'm going to step out and grab something to

drink. Can I get you another water or something else to drink?"

"No. Thank you." Caroline's voice was a shaky whisper. "Why would he do this?" she said to no one in particular.

Her heart raced with the emotional jolt of seeing her name written in Angus's handwriting. Caroline slid a finger under the envelope's flap. The click of the closing door barely registered as she pulled a lined piece of notebook paper from the envelope and began to read.

DEAREST CAROLINE,

If you're reading this I've gone to meet my maker. Don't be sad. I had a long life and did everything I ever set out to do. We have both known for quite some time that my end was near. Having you here with me has been one of the joys of my life. I regret not enticing you here sooner. Your parents may have given you birth, but my sister did a wonderful job raising you. You are a caring, loving woman and I prayed daily that you would find the happiness you deserve.

You may be wondering why I left you Singing Springs Ranch. Since my beloved Bernice and I could never have children, I felt like you were the closest thing to a real family I have left. I hope you will consider staying in Whispering Springs as the town can use a doctor of your skills and compassion.

If you feel you must move on, you may dispose of the ranch as you see fit. My only request is that you not sell Singing Springs to any of the Montgomery family. Since I'm gone and will never know what you do with the property, I can only hope you will use good judgment in your decision.

Please know that I loved you like a daughter.

Be happy. Love well. Build a good life.

All my love,
Uncle Angus

A LARGE TEAR rolled off her cheek and splattered in the middle of the page, smearing the ink. Seemingly out of nowhere, a box of tissue slipped between her and the letter in her lap. She jerked a couple out and blew her nose.

"Thanks," she said with a sniff. "That old coot. How dare he make me cry like this." God, she would miss him.

The chair beside her creaked as KC lowered herself into the seat. She put an arm around Caroline's shoulder. Caroline rested her head against KC's arm and took a deep breath.

"What can I help you with, Caroline?"

She sat back and looked at KC. "Uncle Angus basically tells me that I can do anything I'd like with his ranch except sell it to a member of your family. Why? I don't get it. He came to you as his lawyer. Until I came to town, he saw Jason Montgomery's fiancée as his doctor. He never said an unkind word about any of the Montgomerys. I'm baffled."

KC chuckled. "Angus and I got along fine. In fact, he got along with all the Montgomery women, even doted on us. His feud was with my great-grandfather, and even after Great-Grandpa Henry died, Angus just couldn't let go."

When KC didn't explain further, Caroline frowned. "So? What did they fight over?"

"Great-Grandma Helen."

"Are you kidding me?"

KC shook her head. "Nope. But back in the forties, there was also some deal with some water rights, which between you and me was probably the real issue. But that was so long ago that I'm not sure of all the details. I was born after his wife died. Did you never meet Bernice?"

Caroline shook her head. "No. She died when I was just a baby."

"From what I understand, he was crazy about her, so that's why my money is on the water-rights disagreement. Nevertheless, there always seemed to be a competitive disposition between our two families. But even that had waned a great deal over the past ten years or so."

"Well, I have no idea what was behind some ancient feud. I promise he never said anything to me about y'all except to complain that my medical partner snagged the only good Montgomery man before I could. Seems he really liked your cousin Jason."

They both laughed and Caroline found her tension— coiled like a stiff bedspring—easing.

"But..." Caroline handed KC the letter, "...look at the last paragraph about selling Singing Springs."

KC read it and tsked. "Still trying to control things from the grave. That is so much like something Angus would do. I know Travis has been trying to buy that property for years, but Angus wouldn't sell. Don't know why. Honestly, men can be so silly sometimes." She handed the letter back. "But he's made it clear that you can do whatever you want with the property. Should you decide to sell, I'll be glad to help you any way I can. I'm sure you can get a good price for the ranch. But let me just say I agree with Angus about you staying here. I know Lydia would be thrilled. Anyway, I think we've covered everything...unless you have questions?"

"I don't right now."

"Fine. If you think of something, you know you can call on me anytime."

Caroline stood when KC did. "Will do." She hugged her

friend, the charms on her bracelet rattling with movement. "Thanks for everything."

"Any time. Let's have dinner soon, okay?"

"Works for me."

As Caroline left KC's office, Jason called to her. "Caroline. Can you come in here for a minute?"

"Sure." Caroline walked into his office. "What's up, Jason?"

"Lydia and I are having dinner with my parents this weekend. I was just talking with my mother, and she asked me to invite you to join us. Can you?"

After talking with KC about the infamous Fitzgerald-Montgomery feud, she briefly wondered if discovering she was related to Angus Fitzgerald would affect her friendship with the Montgomerys. After seeing the entire Montgomery family at the funeral, Jason's warm consolation, and now Jackie Montgomery's invitation to dinner, she decided she was being foolish to even have such thoughts.

She smiled, warmed by Jackie's dinner invitation. "I'd love to, Jason. Tell your mother thank you."

"Great. Once I have all the details, I'll let you know."

FRIDAY AFTERNOON, Travis Montgomery pulled his truck under the only shade tree in the Montgomery and Montgomery Law Offices parking lot. He hoped his brother had some news for him about Fitzgerald's place. After ten years of unsuccessfully trying to get Old Man Fitzgerald to sell, Singing Springs Ranch would finally be his. He could feel it in his bones.

He hadn't known Fitzgerald had family, so finding out Caroline Graham was his great-niece was a tad of a surprise, but no big deal. Other than Caroline, no other

Fitzgerald family members mentioned in the obit lived here. He couldn't imagine that old tightwad leaving his ranch to any of them. And even if he did, there was no way anyone would up and move to Texas just because they inherited a rundown ranch, especially if that person knew nothing about ranching. Yup. Whoever ended up with Singing Springs would be thrilled to unload it, and Travis wanted to make sure that person unloaded it right into his hands.

He let himself in the back door of his brother's office, stopping long enough to grab a bottle of cold water from the kitchen, then headed for the reception area.

After removing his beige straw cowboy hat, he leaned over the reception desk to give Jason's secretary a wink. "Hi, Mags. Is little brother available?"

"Hey, handsome," Margaret said then sighed. "If only I were twenty years younger and not married..."

Travis slapped his hat across his heart. "My bachelor days would be over."

She smiled and nodded toward the closed door down the hall. "He's on the phone. I'll let him know you're here. I'd offer you something to drink, but you seemed to have helped yourself."

He rolled the dewy bottle on the back of his neck. "Can't decide if I want to drink this or pour it over my head. Man, it's a killer out there. What about KC? Is my lovely cousin around?"

Before Margaret could respond, Jason's door opened. "I thought I heard a reprobate out here. Stop flirting with my secretary and c'mon back. I've got a date with Lydia tonight and you know she hates when I'm late." He ducked back into his office, leaving the door ajar.

Travis groaned. "I'm coming." He looked at Margaret

and hitched his thumb toward the door where his brother had just been standing. "He been in this bad mood all day?"

She shook her head. "Nope. He was quite pleasant when KC headed out about thirty minutes ago. Your cousin's got perfect timing. She always knows to clear out and avoid the Montgomery brothers when something's brewing."

"Lucky me. Wish I knew her magic."

Travis entered his brother's office and closed the door behind him. He dropped onto the thick leather sofa running along the office wall then set his hat crown-side down on the cushion beside him. He draped his arm along the back of the sofa. "I hope you've got some good news for me. I've had a bitch of a day."

"What happened?"

"One of the Webster kids spooked a new stallion I'd just unloaded. The bastard almost trampled me, John and a couple of hands before we could get him under control."

Jason frowned. "I'd think your foreman's kids would know better than to get near a stallion, especially one I suspect was antsy to begin with. Which kid?"

Travis's mouth cocked up on one side in a grimace. "Rocky. He had a classmate visiting, and I think he was trying to impress him. But after John and Nadine get done with him, I suspect his ears will be ringing for the next week." He gave a small chuckle. "And I'm getting my stalls mucked out for free for at least a month, maybe two."

"I hated mucking stalls."

"So I remember. What's the good news?"

Jason took a seat closer to the sofa. "Well, I've got good news and bad news."

"Great. Bad news first then."

"Fitzgerald had KC prepare his will about a year ago, so his estate won't be going to the state to resolve."

Travis scowled. "I was afraid of that," he growled. "So what can you tell me now?"

"All the beneficiaries have been notified and the will duly probated. It was fairly straight forward. I don't foresee anyone challenging it."

"So don't keep me waiting. Who do I need to talk to about buying Singing Springs?"

"Dr. Caroline Graham."

Two

The breath left Travis's lungs as though he'd been kicked in the gut by a wild stallion.

He leaned forward. "Are you shitting me?" His brother flinched, which made Travis realize how loud he'd just yelled.

Caroline Graham was the first woman he'd been seriously attracted to since his wife died ten years ago. He hadn't acted on his attraction to her and didn't plan to. She was a short-timer. No reason to start something that would leave him alone when she left...and she'd made no secret of her traveling lifestyle.

And now to find out he'd have to deal with her to get Singing Springs made his insides ache. That might require too much close interaction.

He lowered the volume when he continued, but the shock of the information continued to stun him. "Solely to her? Nobody else?"

His brother nodded.

"But why?"

Jason shrugged. "Apparently, he adored Caroline."

Travis flopped against the back of the sofa and blew out a long, exasperated breath. "Apparently." Damn. So close and yet not close enough. "Did you get any other news out of our dear closed-mouth cousin?"

"Don't be pissed at KC. She was just doing her job."

"Damn woman has heard me talk about getting that ranch for years. She could have tipped me off to be nicer to the good doctor."

Jason chuckled. "Like you haven't had your eye on Caroline Graham already."

"I don't know what you're talking about."

"Right." Jason's mouth twitched as though he was struggling not to smile. "Sorry. Don't know what I was thinking to accuse you of being attracted to a beautiful woman."

Travis gave his brother his best eat-shit expression. "She's still planning on leaving at the end of the year, right? Inheriting Singing Springs hasn't changed her plans, right?"

Jason shrugged again. "Not that I've heard. Lydia has talked to her about staying on full time, but she insists she's off to Montana in January, so it doesn't appear she has any plans on remaining in Whispering Springs past December."

"Well, tell your fiancée to stop asking her to stay, damn it. Lucky for me, she's just passing through." Even as he said the words, a pang of regret at what might have been hit him in the solar plexus. He took a long draw on his water to staunch the pain. It didn't help much. If only he could have a stiff shot of bourbon... "And what are you smiling about?"

Jason made like he was zipping his lips.

"As I was getting ready to say, she'd probably be glad to leave town with a nice chunk of change in her pocket. I want to make her an offer before anyone else has the chance. Why don't you draw up a bill of sale and I'll run by this weekend. Leave the sale price blank, and I can fill it in when we come to terms."

Jason held up a hand. "Whoa there, bro. Slow down. Caroline just lost her great-uncle, and now she has all these decisions to make about the estate. Give her a chance to catch her breath."

"But what if someone gets to her before I do?"

"I suppose that's possible, but the way your holdings wrap around three sides of Fitzgerald's place, I can't see anyone else wanting Singing Springs."

"Did she say anything to you or KC about selling?"

Jason shook his head. "KC said Caroline's a little over-whelmed at the moment. Angus hadn't clued her in that she was his heir, so she's still processing the ramifications and all her options. If you start pushing her, I'm afraid she'll just shut you down. Maybe in the next week or so."

Travis scratched his head. "Okay, but no later. Go ahead and draw up a bill of sale for me to have just in case." He studied his brother's face. "What? You're looking at me strange." He grinned. "Stranger than usual."

"Nothing. I'll put together something for you. On a different subject, you going over to Mom and Dad's for dinner Saturday night?"

"Probably. You and Lydia going?"

"That's the plan."

Travis stood and collected his hat. "Okay then. I'll see you tomorrow. And for Pete's sake, keep your ear to the ground about Singing Springs though. If the good doctor even hints she wants to sell, I want to be the first to know." He reached for the door.

"Travis."

He turned back. "What?"

"Caroline will probably be at dinner tomorrow night. Lay off her, okay?"

"Yeah, sure. No problem."

"I'M DRIVING UP TOMORROW, MAMIE."

"You don't need to do that." Mamie's cough rattled through Caroline's phone receiver.

"I want to see you. I should be there about noon or so."

"How long can you stay?"

"I have to get back to Whispering Springs on Monday."

"I wish you could stay longer."

"Me too." Caroline's head rested against the back of her sofa. She unsuccessfully struggled to suppress the tears welling up. She talked to her grandmother every day, saw her as often as she could make the seven-hour drive back to Arkansas. Her grandmother was dying. Caroline knew it. Mamie's doctor knew it. And Caroline was pretty sure that Mamie knew it too.

"Is that Montgomery boy coming with you this time?"

Her heart thudded at the mention of Travis. "No. Not this time. Maybe next time."

She hadn't meant any harm when she told her grandmother she was dating Travis Montgomery. Mamie worried so much about Caroline being alone. Caroline had only meant to give her grandmother some peace of mind, but instead Mamie asked about him on every visit, with every call.

"Well, I'll look forward to seeing you tomorrow." Mamie's years as a judge had groomed her voice into a strong, authoritarian tone. The whispery, weak voice on the other end broke Caroline's heart. It didn't sound anything like Caroline's robust grandmother.

"Bye, Mamie. Love you."

Caroline dropped her cell onto the coffee table. Guilt gnawed at her. Lying to her grandmother about dating Travis was so wrong, but the idea of her beloved grandmother on her deathbed worried about Caroline's love life —or lack thereof—sliced and diced Caroline's heart. How many times had Mamie said she wanted Caroline to love and be loved by a man worthy of her affections?

Caroline pressed the back of her head into the softness of the sofa. The deception had started so innocently. When her grandmother kept asking about Caroline's life in Texas, Travis had been standing outside her office door talking to Lydia, and his name had rolled off her tongue before she could stop it. Once the idea was planted, her mind refused to let go. It was as though gasoline had been poured on her tiny spark of crush on him, exploding it into an inferno attraction.

Unfortunately, Travis hadn't expressed any interest in her, so she'd never acted on her feelings. Besides, she had no plans to settle down with anyone, much less settle in Texas.

MAMIE HAD NEVER MENTIONED anything about bad blood between her brother and the Montgomerys. She'd questioned Caroline at length about Travis and how he treated her, but when Caroline had continued to sing Travis's praises, her grandmother had seemed pleased—and relieved—that Caroline had found her true love. God, she'd felt so guilty when her grandmother used the phrase *true love*, but luckily it'd been on the phone and Caroline had been able to hide her remorse at the lie.

She dipped her chin to her chest and rolled her head from side-to-side to stretch the stiff muscles in her neck. An elephant-sized tear rolled down her cheek and Caroline swiped angrily at it. She might have overdone the "sell the idea of being in love with Travis" to Mamie. It wasn't that she didn't want to fall in love, but she was nothing if not realistic.

Mamie and Grandpa Richter's kind of love didn't happen often and certainly would never happen to her. Besides, she wasn't sure she had the capacity to produce that degree of emotional attachment to anyone other than her grandmother. Attraction to a man was a long way from love, right?

The gratitude she felt for her grandmother had no bounds, just like what Caroline would do for Mamie had no bounds. When Caroline let herself stew over the past, her guilt about crashing into Mamie's life unannounced and uninvited made her nauseous. She never doubted for a minute that her grandmother loved her, but Mamie had had to give up so much of her personal and professional life to raise Caroline and then Noah. There was no way Caroline could ever repay her.

When Caroline's parents had dropped her on Mamie's doorstep to raise, freeing them up to return to their missionary work, Mamie had greeted Caroline with more hugs and kisses than Caroline could remember in all of her five years of being alive.

Then Mamie had stepped up again to take in Noah.

She'd been more than a grandmother to both of them. She'd been their lifeline, their anchor. At least Caroline had been blessed to be raised to adulthood by her grandmother. Noah had had only nine years with Mamie.

The reality of losing Mamie swamped her. She stood and went to the bathroom for a tissue.

Get a grip, Caroline. All this navel gazing about her life

wasn't solving the problem. Her problem was how could she convince her grandmother that she was in love and happy when the exact opposite was true?

She glanced at her cell phone to check the time. Right now she didn't have the time to worry about her love life—or lack thereof. If she didn't get a move on, she wasn't going to be ready when Jason and Lydia got here to pick her up.

After drying her eyes and repairing the minimal makeup she wore, she went to work on her hair, shoving a couple of more hairpins into the French twist at the back of her head. She frowned at herself in the mirror. Was going to Lane and Jackie Montgomery's for dinner a good idea?

The Montgomery clan had always been warm and welcoming, but she'd noticed the undercurrent of tension that rippled around the gravesite when Travis Montgomery had walked up to Angus's casket to pay his respects. At the time she'd thought the reaction odd, but given her state of mind that day she'd passed it off as her imagination. She'd always found Travis to be a little aloof toward her, so maybe he was that way with many of the townspeople.

It was only after reading Angus's will and having KC explain the history between the Montgomery and Fitzgerald families that she understood why Angus had asked her to not mention their familial relationship. He'd wanted her accepted in the community without the taint of an old feud.

She pushed a pair of gold hoops into her pierced ears and picked up her ever-present charm bracelet from the dresser. Various state shapes dangled and chimed together. It was hard to believe she'd worked and lived in so many different places over the years. She made a mental note to start looking for a Texas charm to add to the collection.

Outside, a horn honked. She glanced at the clock on her phone again. Had to be Jason and Lydia. As she snapped the bracelet around her wrist, she wished they hadn't insisted she ride with them to the Bar Halo Ranch. Granted, the drive was about thirty minutes outside of town on a dark road that was mostly loose gravel, but she felt stranded without her own car. Probably too many years of being on her own.

Any lingering concerns about Lane and Jackie's reaction to her being Angus Fitzgerald's great-niece vanished the minute she walked into their home.

"Caroline," Jackie said, wrapping her in a hug. "I am so sorry about your uncle."

"Thanks, Jackie." Caroline returned the hug, relief streaming through her.

From the day she met Lane and Jackie, they'd treated her like a long-lost daughter. Jackie worried whether Caroline was eating well. Lane warned her about late nights and keeping her doors locked.

"C'mon here," Lane said, throwing a muscular arm around Caroline's shoulders. "What can I get you to drink?"

Jackie, Jason and Lydia followed Lane and Caroline to the family room. Caroline had loved this room from the minute she first walked in, loved the comfortable, relaxed feeling the room evoked. Overstuffed, well-worn leather furniture. An eighty-inch flat-screen television, perfect for watching football, which she'd done here many times last fall. Highly polished oak floors under a large Navajo rug. On the wall opposite the entry, an old oak bar from the early nineteen hundreds stood, its counter gleaming under the lights. Lydia had told her that Cash, the youngest of the Montgomery sons, had shipped the bar home after rescuing it during a hotel renovation. But Caroline's favorite addition to this room, and the one that made her stomach quiver with nerves, was Travis Montgomery.

She didn't know why the man made her knees quake and her lungs collapse. In all the months she'd been in Whispering Springs, they'd probably had twenty conversations and none of those private or personal. Their interactions were usually short and abrupt as though he were in a hurry to get away from her. She didn't understand. She'd always tried to be pleasant to be around, and she thought most people liked her.

But then Travis Montgomery wasn't like most people, was he?

The man with the ability to make lust curl like smoke in her gut stood behind the oak and brass bar, a glass filled with dark liquid in his hand. Caroline figured it was either Coke or Pepsi. Lydia had explained that after Travis's wife had died, Travis had gone off the deep end emotionally. He'd stayed drunk for almost a year then took almost another year to stay sober. The climb back to sobriety had been tough, and since then he hadn't had a drink.

Being around others while they imbibed didn't seem to bother him. Thanks to his virtual photographic memory, he could make almost any drink requested by family members. The family game was to name a mixed drink that Travis couldn't make given the supplies at hand. Stumping Travis with a drink request meant a ten-dollar donation to the church missionary fund from him. Not stumping him meant the donation came from the drink requester. On more than one occasion, Caroline had found Lydia scanning the Internet for names of drinks to baffle Travis. So far, he was batting a thousand.

"So," Travis said with a smile that made Caroline's insides quiver with longing. "What can I get for you, ladies?"

Lydia slipped onto a barstool. "Hmm. How about a little Sex on the Beach?"

Travis's smile widened, his white teeth gleaming. "Well, we aren't that close to the ocean. Plus, the parents got rid of our sandbox years ago. And my brother might mind if I slept with his fiancée. But there is some grass in the yard that might work instead." He held out his hand. "Now or later?"

Lydia laughed as she slapped his palm.

"Hands off, bro. She's mine." Jason wrapped a possessive arm around Lydia.

While Jason's action might have been done in jest, a small dart of envy clipped Caroline. She wondered what it would be like to be someone's special person.

Travis shrugged good-naturedly. "Her loss," he said with a wink before bending below the bar to open the mini-refrigerator. He brought up cartons of orange juice and cranberry juice. Then he added peach schnapps and vodka from a lower shelf. After shaking the four ingredients with ice in a martini shaker, he poured the drink over ice in a highball glass and pushed it across the bar.

"Nice try, Lydia. Maybe next time." He set an empty mason jar on the bar. "Pay up."

Lydia nudged Jason. "Pay the man."

"Why do I always have to be the one who pays?" Jason grumbled, but he pulled a ten from his wallet and shoved it into the jar.

"Because you love me?" Lydia said then gave him a kiss.

The first time Caroline had tried to stuff ten dollars into the jar after Travis made her a cosmopolitan, he'd refused to take the money, saying he only took money from family. It wasn't just what he'd said that had embarrassed her, but also how roughly and dismissively he said it. Since then, Caroline had never asked for a mixed drink from Travis.

However, she always put an extra ten in the offering plate at church.

"What can I make for you, Caroline?" Travis asked as he replaced the juice cartons into the refrigerator.

"Just a glass of white wine."

"Don't want to test my memory?" he said with a wicked smile that had her insides turning to liquid.

She shook her head. "No. Wine will be fine." She didn't need to drink much booze around him. No telling what she might confess...like her unbelievably hot sexual fantasies about him.

Travis didn't ask which white wine she preferred. Instead, he opened her favorite brand of Pinot grigio and poured. He handed the glass to her. "That'll be ten dollars."

Caroline's heart swelled with happiness. She smiled as she pulled out her purse and dropped a ten into the jar.

After all, family always paid.

Three

There wasn't much Travis loved more than riding Ransom. When his dad had asked him to check on a herd of cattle grazing near the Singing Springs property line, Travis had jumped at the chance. He crossed his wrists on the saddle horn and enjoyed the smell of fresh grass. The vibration at his hip followed by a shrill ring tone made him sigh at the interruption. He jerked his phone from its holder.

"Travis Montgomery."

"Good morning, Travis. It's Caroline Graham. Am I calling at a bad time?"

The leather saddle creaked as he settled back to talk. It was impossible to contain the rush of adrenaline that shot through his system. "Not at all. Just checking some cattle for Dad. What can I do for you?"

"I know it's short notice, but can you come by my house this evening? Say...about seven?"

"Sure. Is something wrong?"

There was a distinct hesitation on the other end of the

phone before she said, "No. Not really. I need to talk to you about something."

Did she want to talk about selling Singing Springs? Please let that be the topic of conversation. His heart elbowed his lungs at the thought.

In response to Jason's strongly worded insistence— more like an order— that Travis not bring up buying Singing Springs Ranch during dinner at his folks' house, he'd acquiesced even when he'd found himself seated beside her. Using willpower he didn't know he had, he'd even restrained from calling her all week. But now here she was inviting him over.

Granted, she hadn't mentioned the property, but what else could it be? He and Caroline Graham didn't have the type of relationship where one would ask the other to drop by for no reason, which was—in his opinion—a damn shame.

When he didn't immediately respond, she added, "I'm sorry. I wasn't thinking. Today is Friday. You might already have plans and—"

"No," he interrupted. "I have no plans for this evening. Do I need to bring anything with me?" Like a blank bill of sale in case you don't have one?

"Not a thing. I'll see you tonight then."

"Are you sure everything is all right? You sound funny."

She'd cleared her throat. "Come by about seven, okay?"

"Okay. See you then."

Now that'd she'd opened the door to his adding Singing Springs to his holdings, he planned to take advantage of their meeting to press his case. He clicked off his phone, shoved it back into the holder at his waist and smiled.

He glanced across to Fitzgerald's property. What would he do with the old house? It wasn't in the best of shape, but it was far from a teardown. With a little updating, the house would make a good home for a ranch hand and his family.

A thick dust cloud billowed behind a white Cadillac Escalade wheeling up the drive. The leather saddle creaked as he shifted for a better view. A short, balding man got out and spread a rolled-up surveyor's map across the hood of the truck. From this distance, Travis couldn't get a good look at the man's face. However, he was pretty sure he didn't know him.

The unfamiliar man studied the map then reached into the passenger side for a clipboard. He walked into the house jotting notes. Ten minutes later, the man came out, measured the exterior of the house, wrote more on the notepad and disappeared back inside.

Damn it. A real-estate appraiser. If Caroline Graham had sold that property to someone else and was planning on telling him that tonight, he'd...well, he didn't know what he'd do, but it wouldn't be pleasant.

On second thought, maybe she was having it appraised so she'd know what the property was worth when she offered to sell it to him. He smiled. That was probably the situation. His mood shot through the clouds.

It'd been a long time since he'd sweet-talked a woman into giving him something he wanted. The last time had been in the front seat of his dad's truck, and Susan hadn't really taken that much sweet-talking to give up the goods. He chuckled at the memory.

Heavens knew, he was out of practice these days. Truth be told, he was a little tired of women chasing after his goods rather than the other way around. No matter. Tonight, he'd be the most charming, best sweet-talking man in Whispering Springs.

He whirled Ransom around and headed for the barn.

After unsaddling the black steed, Travis turned him loose in the pasture and watched as his usually dignified male rolled on his back, scratching the sweaty spot where the saddle had been. A few good rolls and Ransom headed for the creek to wade in for a long drink. After a couple of more minutes enjoying his horse's antics, Travis headed to the house for a shower and something cold to drink.

His boot heels rang on the hardwood floors as he walked through the back door into the kitchen. As usual, the counters shined. Not a dirty dish in sight. He'd reached for the refrigerator door when a florescent orange sticky note on the door caught his eye.

TRAVIS—IF you get my clean floor dirty, I'm going to put poison in tomorrow's dinner. I've left a casserole in the refrig you can microwave.

> *Love ya*
> *Henree*

TRAVIS LAUGHED as he turned his head to check for dirt. His laughter turned to a groan. He'd splashed water on the ground while refilling the horses' trough, and apparently, he hadn't noticed where he'd stepped. A trail of mud splotches tracked his progress from back door to refrigerator door. Henrietta Webster, wife of his foreman, John, kept Travis's house for him, left him nutritious meals and kept him in clean clothes. And she was going to kill him.

John and Henrietta Webster had come into Travis's life the last year of his wife's illness. Travis had spent every day with Susan, not caring about food, sleep or clean clothes.

His ranch would have failed if not for his parents' intervention and the Websters' employment.

During that year and the one following, he doubted he'd given the Halo M more than a passing thought. After Susan's death, he'd lost himself deep inside any bottle of booze he could find. Thank God, his parents had recognized his downward spiral early. They'd hired the Websters to give Travis a hand. Eleven years later, they were still giving Travis a hand, except now the ranch had doubled in size, the cutting-horse breeding and training operations had grown to national prominence, and the Websters' single-child household now sported four children, the oldest being Amy at age fourteen. At times, Travis felt like child number five...like now.

He removed his boots and carried them to the laundry room where he picked up a wet mop. He adored Henree and would do anything to keep her happy. If he left that mess, those feelings might be definitely one-sided in the morning. So it was mop tonight or learn to do his own cooking and laundry tomorrow. Having tasted his cooking and wearing underwear accidently dyed pink, he figured a little mopping tonight was a better plan.

After reviewing his sure-fire strategy to convince Caroline to sell Singing Springs to him one last time, Travis headed for her house. Continuing to grow the Halo M ranch rested with adding the acreage from Singing Springs. The sooner she sold, the sooner he could move ahead with his expansion plans.

He pulled into her drive a little early, but he wasn't worried she wouldn't be ready. Lydia had mentioned how fastidious Caroline was about appointment times at the office, so surely early was better than late.

. . .

CAROLINE CLICKED off her phone after speaking with her parents, a real accomplishment considering they were in Rwanda on an extended missionary trip and phones weren't readily accessible. As she'd expected, her parents were thrilled with their inheritance, which they mentioned would immediately go back into their ministries. She had to respect their dedication to their work, but a part of her would always resent family being second in their priorities.

On more than one occasion, she'd questioned if family ranked even that high. She loved Mamie, had loved being raised by Mamie, but she often wondered about her lack of understanding about families. A piece of her resented her parents for not being the parents she saw on television shows. Growing up, she'd always wondered if families were really like that.

Being around the huge Montgomery family was her first life experience with a mother and father and all the children around a table. Growing up, she'd visited friends and observed their family interactions, but that had been nothing like being at the Montgomery table.

She studied the fizz bubbles in her Diet Coke, watching as one by one they floated to the top and popped. A week had passed since her dinner with the Montgomery clan, and she was still enjoying the feeling of being considered part of the family, even if it were a tad tangential.

When Dr. Lydia Henson had offered the twenty-four-month contract to work at the Whispering Springs Medical Clinic, Caroline had taken it because Mamie had wanted her to spend time with Angus. The other advantage was that the Texas location also put Caroline closer to Mamie in Arkansas. Caroline had never expected Lydia's fiancé's family to adopt her, but they had, all except Travis. He'd kept his distance, always polite but distant, as though he preferred watching life pass as an observer rather than a participant.

When she'd first met Travis, she'd been a little awed. The oldest son of one of the oldest and most established families in the area. The Montgomery roots ran so deep in this area of Texas that she sometimes wondered if the family felt pain when a tree was cut down.

The other thing about him that tied her tongue was his looks. He was a total knock-out. Tall and lean, not an ounce of fat to be seen anywhere...and she'd looked. Silver hair clipped short. Ice-blue eyes. Strong jaw. Flat stomach. Tight ass...and that described both his physical attribute and his attitude.

She was aware of his wife's death from breast cancer. For a twenty-six-year-old man to go through such a traumatic loss had to be a crushing blow to his world. For a while, Caroline had cut his priggish attitude some slack. In her own practice, hadn't she witnessed how tough cancer can be on a family?

Still, ten years had passed. Surely he'd moved on, right? How long could he play the widower card as an excuse for detached behavior?

Then she smiled as she thought about stuffing ten dollars into the bar kitty for her drink last Saturday. In her opinion, that was a sure sign he was getting comfortable being around her. And she did want him at ease around her. She needed a favor from him...a huge favor.

This morning when she'd called him and asked him to come by her house, she'd been so nervous, sure he could hear the quiver in her voice. Shivers marched up and down her spine as she relived his deep Southern voice asking if he needed to bring anything with him.

Her first thought had been a condom. Then she'd chastised herself and said no. This Friday-night meeting was neither a date nor a hook-up. It was a plea for help.

A cuckoo bird popped from behind the door on his clock to crow five times. Because she moved so often, Caroline didn't have much personal furniture, opting to rent most of what she needed during the terms of her contracts. However, the old-fashioned cuckoo clock from her Grandpa Richter had a place of honor in every temporary residence.

She glanced toward the Swiss clock to make sure she'd heard the bird correctly. Five o'clock. Time for her daily chat with her grandmother. She reached for the cell phone on her coffee table just as it began to vibrate. She leaned back on her sofa, checked the incoming call name and answered. "Hi, Mamie. How are you feeling today?"

"Bah," her grandmother said. "This hospital is gonna kill me before I can die on my own."

The shaky and feeble tone of her grandmother's voice settled deep in Caroline's gut. She wrapped one arm around her abdomen and shut her eyes, rocking slightly in despair. Both of them knew the end was not far off. Jokes were the way Mamie was handling the realization that the end of her life was close, but Caroline couldn't find humor in something so painful.

"Now, Mamie—"

Mamie exhaled a long sigh. "This hospital isn't gonna kill me before God does. I don't have long. You and Dr. Stewart can continue trying to find some good news in all those lab tests he does, but there ain't nothing gonna heal an eighty-two-year-old heart when it's decided it's done."

Caroline's chin dropped to her chest and she fought the tears filling her eyes. It wasn't Mamie's age that was killing her. It was a lifetime of cigarette smoking taking its toll on her organs. "Oh, Mamie. Do you know how much I love you? How much I'm going to miss you?"

"No more than I adore you, my precious child. Raising you and your brother was a gift from God, right there with your mother and Pat."

Large wet tears rolled down Caroline's cheeks as she glanced at the picture sitting on the nearby bookshelf of her and Mamie at her medical-school graduation. "I was a burden. It was so unfair of my parents to dump me on you to raise, not to mention taking on Noah too."

"You're wrong, my dear. So very wrong. You and your brother filled a hole in my life I didn't even know was there until it was gone. But I'm worried, Caro."

"About?"

"You. I'm worried about what will happen with you when I'm gone."

"Me? Mamie, you don't have to worry about me. I'm thirty-two. I'm a doctor. I can fully take care of myself. We need to be talking about Noah."

A violent cough rattled through the phone. Mamie cleared her throat before she continued speaking. "Noah's been taken care of. Pat and Leslie have moved into my house. We thought it best to keep him living at home. He's going to be fine."

Caroline closed her eyes again. Her jaws tightened. At the moment, guilt chewed at her soul. She knew she should offer to take Noah, give her little brother a place to grow up. But seriously, what kind of life could she offer him? Moving every few months to a new job? A new location? Wouldn't it be much better for him to have the stability of staying where he'd lived for the past nine years rather than uprooting him again and sending him to live with a sister he barely knew?

Even if she settled in one spot, her long hours of work would be a deal-breaker. He'd be alone too much and too often, and that could spell disaster for a fourteen-year-old boy who already had a propensity for attracting trouble.

No, he needed to be in a home where there were two adults—adults who would make sure he got to school, did his homework and ate a good dinner. She wasn't the right person for that. What did she know about teenage boys?

"Yes, I'm sure that's the right place for him. Aunt Leslie is a little strict, but he'll be fine there," Caroline said, hoping her voice didn't sound as guilty as she felt.

Fine. What a glowing endorsement she'd just given the home she was allowing her little brother to be raised in. Poor Noah. Dumped first on Mamie and then on Uncle Patrick and Aunt Leslie.

Shouldn't she be doing more for him? Could she do more for him?

No, she couldn't. She wasn't the best solution for her little brother. Pat and Leslie were.

Truth be told, she didn't really know Noah very well. She'd been off to college when he'd been born and in graduate school when their parents left him with Mamie while they returned to whatever country they were doing their missionary work in at the time.

"My darling, Caroline. It's you I'm worried about. You work too hard. And you haven't ever brought this man you're seeing to meet me. After all, he is a Montgomery. I need to see for myself if he's good enough for you."

She smiled at the mental picture of Mamie putting on her judicial robes, swearing Travis in on a Bible and having him take the stand where Judge Mamie Bridges could interrogate him. "I told you, Mamie. Travis's ranch keeps him going day and night. It's just too hard for him to get away for any length of time." Chewing guilt took a big bite of her gut, and the smile dropped from her lips. She hated the lying, even if she believed it best for her grandmother's peace of mind.

"Even for a honeymoon?"

Caroline licked her lips and dug deep into her soul to perjure herself to her grandmother. She forced a lighthearted chuckle. "Of course he'll take off for the honeymoon. Why, we were just talking about that last night." She clinched her eyes shut with the falsehood.

"Oh, that's wonderful. So you've set a date then?"

Caroline was the world's worst liar. Her blotchy face and shifty eyes betrayed her, but on the phone? She was getting to be an expert. Now if only she could keep up the deception. If a little white lie could make Mamie's passing easier, then so be it. Caroline would take that issue up with the Lord when she was standing at the pearly gates. Until then, let Mamie have her peace.

"Well, not a firm date. We're still looking at schedules, visiting available chapels and such."

"You want to make this old woman happy? Get married here...while I can still see you marry the man you love." Her raspy breathing made her words hard to understand, but Caroline suspected where her grandmother was headed. "We both know I don't have long. I've dreamed of signing your marriage license all my life. After all the ones I signed as an officiating judge, to sign my own granddaughter's would be like leaving a part of me behind with you."

Mamie coughed and Caroline could hear the chest congestion rattle over the phone. The last time she'd talked to Mamie's doctor, he'd confirmed that pneumonia was setting up house in Mamie's already weakened lungs.

"I love you, Mamie. You need to get your rest. We can talk tomorrow."

She disconnected the call knowing Mamie was right. She probably didn't have long to live. Whether it was weeks or months, no one could say with confidence. What seemed certain was that Caroline's beloved grandmother would not be around to see the Labor Day fireworks. At the rate her body was failing, she might be lucky to see next week.

Her grandmother was nobody's fool and nothing about her illness had dulled that smart mind. She might have been raised in the back hills of Arkansas, but she'd been a lawyer and a circuit judge before retiring. If she wanted to sign Caroline's marriage license, she was suspicious of Caroline's tale of love at first sight.

There was nothing Caroline wouldn't do for her grand-mother. Nothing. If Mamie wanted to see a wedding, then Caroline would find some way to make that happen.

The next step was to convince Travis to do her a huge favor...marry her.

Since she'd talked to Travis this morning, she'd run a million different scenarios on how to ask him to stage a fake wedding. Good God Almighty. It sounded crazy even to her.

The trick would be to keep him from running out the door and calling the guys with the white coats to come lock her up. She had to make him understand she needed this for Mamie and not for herself.

Caroline did not need—and frankly, did not want—a husband. Her life was as she wanted it...uncomplicated. Sure, she was lonely sometimes, but she could handle that. She never wanted to be a burden on anyone ever again.

She curled on her side on the couch and studied the African fertility masks on the wall, a gift from her parents last December when they couldn't make it back from

Uganda for Christmas. Would she store them when she left Whispering Springs for her next job or sell them? As if anyone would want them. She lowered her eyelids for a minute to fight the exhaustion headache building behind her eyes.

A car door slammed outside. Her eyes flew open in time to catch a shadow as it passed the front window. Dressed in her favorite pair of jean cut-offs, a T-shirt with an anatomically correct drawing of the male reproductive system and no shoes, she wasn't dressed for company, and her appointment with Travis wasn't for another ninety minutes.

If this was the people from the church down the street trying to convince her that their brand of religion was the only one that would get her into heaven, she was going to give them a huge piece of her mind. She did not need that kind of grief right now. The last thing she wanted was somebody telling her every Sunday what a sinner she was and how she was going to hell if she didn't change her ways. Those people had no idea who she was and what she did. They certainly didn't know if she was going to hell.

Besides, she was a doctor. That would probably get her a get-out-of-jail-free card when she got to heaven, right?

She pushed up from the couch, ready to run off whoever was there. She was tired and cranky and wishing she hadn't made an appointment to meet Travis tonight. Plus, she was having second thoughts about this whole fake-wedding idea. What other excuse could she dream up for inviting Travis over before he got here?

Chimes rang from somewhere down the hall. Flinging open the door, she drew in a breath and got her prepared speech ready to run off the religious zealots. Her breath left in a gasp when she stared at Travis's tanned, chiseled face.

He held a straw cowboy hat in front of his body like a

gladiator's shield. A blue polo shirt stretched across wide shoulders, the color drawing attention to his incredible azure eyes. The stiff crease in his jean legs was laid flat by his thick muscular thighs. Brown cowboy boots—cleaned and polished to a high shine—peeked out from the hem of his jeans.

She let her gaze make the pass up and down his body once more. Holy moly. He did pack a punch to a gal's midsection.

He gave her a dangerously sexy smile. "Hey, Caroline."

Her stomach gave a nauseating quiver as it did a back flip. She gulped back in the breath she'd lost and tried to steady her now quivering knees.

"Travis?" She looked at her watch. Where had she lost an hour? "I'm sorry. I guess I lost track of the time."

She struggled to keep her fingers from running through her hair in an effort to arrange it into some type of coiffure. Then she remembered she'd washed off her makeup when she'd showered, meaning to reapply a light coat before he arrived. That meant she was getting ready to request the biggest favor of her life while sporting ratty hair, no makeup, old clothes and barefoot.

She was pretty sure that if she dropped dead right now, God would feel so sorry for her that she'd sweep right through those pearly gates.

"Can I come in?" Travis asked, the corner of his mouth continuing to twitch in a smile, as though he knew something she didn't.

She knew he'd spoken. She'd seen his lips move, but apparently mortification made a person become immediately deaf.

"Caroline? You asked me to come over about seven. It's..." he checked his wristwatch, "...almost seven. Sorry.

44

I'm a little early. Are you going to let me in? Unless you want to have a conversation with me on your porch and you standing in the door."

"What? Sure. Sorry." This time, she couldn't stop her hand from trying to fluff her flat hair. "I wasn't expecting you for another half-hour."

He chuckled. The deep-throated sound rattled out of him and into her, igniting a warm glow that started in her middle and radiated out like concentric circles from a rock dropped into water. Her blood began to boil from all the heat emanating from the sexiest cowboy in a tri-county area. Caroline felt beads of sweat pop out on her upper lip as a flash fire burned from head to toe.

"Sorry to catch you off-guard, but you look great. Educational shirt you've got on." He grinned then tapped his hat on the end of her nose. "No reason to dress up on my account."

Crap. Not a good sign when the guy you want to impress enough to talk into the huge favor doesn't care if you look like a street person.

She sighed. "Uh-huh. Right. C'mon in."

He stepped into the living room and glanced around. "Nice place. Love those African masks." He walked over to study them closer. "There must be a great story behind those."

Caroline shrugged. "Not really. Just a present from my parents. You want something to drink? I have diet soda, water, iced tea, fruit juice."

"Water would be great. Thanks."

She headed for her kitchen, trying to figure out if she could do anything about her appearance before she returned to the living room. Unless there was magic in that can of Crisco, she was doomed to her homeless hobo look for

45

tonight's appointment. She vowed to stock emergency makeup and a change of clothes in the kitchen from now on.

Straightening after pulling a bottle of water from the back of the refrigerator, she backed into a solid wall of hot male muscle. Strong hands grabbed her arms to keep her from falling at the same time the scent of raw male teased her senses. Sexual tension tightened every muscle. The area between her thighs throbbed with carnal lust.

"Oops," Travis said.

She whipped around and smashed the cold bottle of water against his chest. A dark wet spot spread on his shirt. "Here." Her heart jumped into her throat. Heat flared on her face. She had to curb the impulse to press her flushed cheek to his shirt.

Crap. Tonight was going to be a disaster.

"Thanks." He uncapped the bottle, drank about half in one long gulp then wiped his mouth with his hand. "Man, I needed that. The heat today was a killer, but then I guess you know that."

Her lower back tingled as a sexual itch expanded throughout her heated body. She needed a little physical distance to regroup. "Let's go back to the living room. I'll try to explain why I asked you here."

"Great. I'm hoping you've given some thought to selling the Fitzgerald property."

Caught off-guard by his comment, she stumbled over her feet. Lucky to not fall, she decided no response would be the best response. She'd had Uncle Angus's ranch appraised this week for tax purposes. Selling the ranch wasn't even on her radar at the moment, although she didn't have a clue what she would do with the place.

She returned to the living room with him following on

her heels and retook her seat on the couch. He took the other end. She turned toward him, leaned against the armrest and crossed her legs in yoga style. They sat there for a couple of minutes. Caroline couldn't take her eyes off the movement of his Adam's apple sliding up and down in his throat as he drank the water. She found herself swallowing in concert with each of his swallows.

No doubt about it. Travis Montgomery was an excellent male specimen. Too bad she didn't need a husband...at least not a real husband.

He leaned toward her. A clean soapy scent wafted down the sofa toward her.

"Look, I know how hard it must be to consider selling your great-uncle's property, so I'll make this easy for you."

She frowned and braced herself for his reaction. She held up a hand. "Wait a minute, Travis. I didn't ask you over here to talk about selling Angus's property."

He returned her frown. "You didn't? Then why am I here?"

Caroline drew in a deep breath. "I need a husband and I need one fast."

Four

Travis pushed back into the sofa's overstuffed padding as the shock of her words rattled through him. Husband? Caroline Graham wanted to marry him?

"What?" His eyes opened so wide he could feel them drying in the cold air conditioning. "I mean...I'm flattered, of course, but...but...are you pregnant?" Oh good Lord. She was a doctor. Surely she knew how to avoid pregnancy? Besides, he couldn't be the father. Hell, he'd never even kissed her. Where—

"Calm down, Travis," she said with a shake of her dark hair. "I'm not pregnant."

"But—"

"And," she interrupted, "I'm not in love with you or anything like that."

The air in his lungs left in a rush. "Then what the hell are you talking about?" Her calmness irritated him. Suspicion colored his view of the situation. "Is this some elaborate joke you and Jason dreamed up to jerk my chain?"

"What? No. No. Of course not." Caroline stood and waved her hand for him to remain sitting.

He couldn't say he minded remaining seated. His position put him on a perfect level to enjoy the left-right swish of her tight butt as she walked around in a pair of shorts that might get her arrested in downtown Whispering Springs for indecent exposure. He wished he were in a better mental state to enjoy the view. Or let her compare his male anatomy to the drawing on her shirt.

"Stay put. I'll explain, but I have a tendency to pace when I'm nervous." She glanced toward him, a pink tinge of embarrassment coloring her cheeks. "And trust me, I'm nervous."

She's having trouble speaking because she's nervous? Of him?

Travis nodded then settled back and crossed a boot-covered ankle over a knee. He'd played enough poker to know when to stay quiet and study the competition, and now was that time. He put on his poker face. He may not know what to say, but he hoped whatever was going on ended with her selling him Fitzgerald's place.

"Fine. Explain."

She sighed and walked over to the cowboy hat he'd left upside down on a floral armchair. After stroking the chair's fabric for a moment, she faced him. "I don't want a husband. Not you. Not any man really."

"Oh. I see. I didn't know you were gay...not that I have any problem with that," he added. Okay, he was a little shocked. Not that he had anything against girls who played on the same team, but he'd have sworn she had a touch of lust in her eyes in the kitchen.

"What? I'm not gay. Good Lord, Travis." Then she started laughing. In fact, she doubled over, wrapping both arms around her waist. After a couple of minutes, she wiped her eyes and chuckled. "Thanks," she said and sucked in a deep breath. "I needed that." She snickered a couple of more times and then sighed as she rubbed both hands over her face. "Okay. I'm better. Now, like I was saying, I don't want a husband, but I need one. Temporarily, I mean." She looked at him. "Let me make a long story short. My grand-mother, the woman who raised me, is dying. She wants nothing more than for me to be married before she dies." A rueful smile crossed her full, luscious lips. "It doesn't matter how old I get, she worries about me being alone. But I guess it's kind of nice that someone cares that much about me."

"But you still have your parents, right? Somewhere over-seas, if I remember correctly." The thought of his parents being gone from his life brought a swell of sadness. He feared that would be as hard on him as Susan's death had been. He wasn't sure he could survive another emotional blow like that, and he'd spent the last ten years making sure he didn't have to.

Her responding snort was unexpected. It wasn't an expression of humor like her laughter and chuckles. This sound clearly conveyed an underlying tone of something else...anger? Disgust?

"Yeah, alive, but they haven't been in my life in a long time." She pointed at the African masks. "Christmas last year. They're Christian missionaries. They've traveled all over the world and don't make it back to the US much."

This time her snort didn't surprise him, but her under-lying hostility toward her parents, or maybe their chosen profession, came through loud and clear. Her shoulders slumped for a second before she pulled them back and stood as straight as a fence post. She appeared to be collecting herself, so he didn't speak. Frankly, now that he was over his flabbergasted state, his curiosity had been stroked. His mother had always said his curiosity had been overdeveloped and would surely get him into hot water one day. Was his pot of water simmering?

She picked up his hat and tried it on. It slid down to the top of her pert nose. She laughed.

He smiled, picturing her wearing his hat and nothing else. The mental image made his heart quicken and the blood drain from his brain to his crotch.

All her flitting around the room had his mind drawing erotic pictures instead of paying attention to what she was saying. The way she tilted her chin and cocked her hip to one side was so damn sexy and...his lungs froze up as a band around his chest tightened, making it difficult for him to catch his breath.

Slow down, bud. This was Caroline Graham, not some bar chick he was picking up for a night of hot, sweaty fucking. He didn't need—or want—the complications of sex with a family friend.

Besides, finding a gal for a couple of hours of sex was, well, easy. One town over was Long Branch Roadhouse, better known as the Love 'Em and Leave 'Em bar. There was always a willing gal or two ready to party for a few hours. Then it was home again. No commitments. No ties. No heartache.

And no fucking in his own backyard. He'd learned that lesson the hard way with a local divorced debutant who had him on her radar for husband number three. It was a die-hard rule he almost never broke and he wasn't going to break it now...even if the idea had its appeal at this moment.

Setting the hat back as she'd found it, Caroline rubbed at an invisible smudge on the dark-wood side table before turning back to him. "I owe my grandmother everything."

She'd been quiet so long her words jarred him back to the situation. "Your grandmother," he repeated just to let her know he was still listening, not that he had been, but he would now.

"Right. My grandmother was the one who was there for me. Loved me. Supported me. And now she's dying." Her emerald-green eyes glistened. She turned away and tried, unsuccessfully, to surreptitiously wipe her eyes. "And the worst part is that I've been lying to her."

Now that got his attention. He lowered his foot to the floor and leaned forward to rest his forearms on his thighs. "Really? Lying about what?" For some reason, a warning siren began to wail in his mind like a female cat in heat.

Caroline wrung her hands and a red flush colored her throat and face. "My last serious relationship ended before I moved here. In fact, it ended about six months before that."

"Why? I mean, why did you break up with your boyfriend? All the moving around?"

She chuckled, but the sound was tinted with discomfort instead of humor. "Not hardly. Let's just say I didn't break up with him. And before you feel sorry for me that I got dumped, don't. It was for the best." After a quick glance in his direction, she shifted her eyes to the African masks. "Anyway, Mamie—my grandmother—was more upset than I was. I think she had high hopes I'd marry him and she could quit worrying about me. And no matter how many times I told her not to lose any sleep over my marital status, she was still concerned about me being alone. Nothing I said convinced her I was content with my life as it is." She traced a finger along one of the carved designs in the mask. She cut a quick glance his way then whipped it away. "Don't kill me when I tell you this next part."

He'd been listening and had enjoyed watching the

tensing and relaxing of her thigh muscles while she walked, but now she had his undivided attention. Kill her? What had she done?

"One night..." She slanted another look his way. "I swear I don't know what came over me. One night when Mamie kept going on about me being alone and she sounded so sorry for me and—" The muscles in her face bunched and her lips pulled tight. "I don't want anyone to feel sorry for me...ever. That night I just blurted out that I was dating you. I am so sorry. I swear I didn't do it on purpose." A frown creased her brow. "I am so sorry, Travis."

He'd been confused at the beginning of the conversation, now he was truly baffled.

"Me? Why?"

Her cheeks took on a rosy color. "You happened to be standing outside my office door that day talking to Lydia. You were handy. That's all."

He shrugged. Made sense. "Okay. You lied to your grandmother. Told her we were dating. Got it." When she couldn't meet his gaze, an acid bomb exploded in his gut. "What is it, Caroline? What haven't you told me?"

Caroline murmured a very unladylike cussword. "I sort of said a little more than dating."

An inconceivable thought formed. A sharp cold ran through him, followed by a flash of red-hot fury. "You told her we were married, didn't you?" He slapped his thigh.

"*No*. I didn't. I, um..." She hurried back to the couch and sat. "No, I didn't. But maybe I exaggerated our relationship a little more than I'd intended."

"Exaggerated?" Disbelief and amazement flowed like beer at a frat party. His left eyebrow arched. "What the hell are you talking about? You're a friend of my family's, but we —you and I—don't have a relationship beyond that. What were you thinking?" He ran his hand across his short cropped hair. "Hell's bells, Caroline."

She flinched. "It gets worse. I, um, oh God, Travis, I told her we were getting married, and now she wants us to get married before she dies." She shut her eyes and hung her head. "I am so sorry. I just don't have the heart to tell her I was lying, or even that we broke up. She'll just feel sorry for me that another guy dumped me, no matter how I try to spin the break-up." Speaking directly to the floor, she added, "What can I do to get you to pretend?"

"Pretend what? To be in love with you?"

She shook her head. "Pretend to marry me."

"Are you crazy?"

"Maybe, but..." She dropped her hands on the sofa cushions and stared him straight in the eye. "Hear me out. If you say no, fine, but at least listen to what I have to say."

He waved her on and leaned back.

"Here's what I was thinking. We fly to Crystal Lakes, Arkansas. There's a direct flight from Dallas to the local airport there. We take out a marriage license, go to the hospital, let Mamie watch us go through a wedding ceremony, she can sign the danged thing and then we fly back to Whispering Springs. We'll never file the license, so there'll be no marriage. I mean, think of all the times people get a marriage license and never go through with the wedding. That's what the clerk's office will think. This would give Mamie so much peace." She leaned forward and placed her hand on his knee. "Please, Travis."

The palm of her hand heated his flesh, even through the thick denim of jeans. He'd never noticed how long her fingers were, or that her nails bore a professional-looking manicure.

He mentally thumped his head. *Get your head in the game.*

"Forget it, Caroline. That's nuts. No way am I going to con what is probably a nice old woman. First, it's beyond dishonest, and second, I believe in marriage."

She dropped her head heavily against the back of the sofa and pulled her hand away from his knee. The heat from her touch quickly dissipated in the air-conditioned room. He immediately missed her touch.

"Will you at least think about it?" She looked at him with pleading eyes and he felt his firm resolve faltering.

"Look, since this is all a sham anyway, why not just get someone to play my part? Get some other sucker to pretend to be me pretending to marry you."

She chewed the inside of her cheek. "I would if I could, but I can't."

He gritted his teeth. "Why not?" he asked in a sharp tone.

She drew back. "Remember last Christmas when your parents were snapping pictures right and left? There was one of us, me and you. I, um sort of sent that to Mamie."

"What?" He exploded off the couch and stomped across the room to snatch up his hat. "You're insane, Caroline. No wonder your last boyfriend ran. He must have seen this bizarre streak and got out while the getting was good." He pounded his hat on his head. "I am not going to have a pretend wedding like a couple of kids playing house. Forget it." His eyes squinted in a threat. "Maybe you should think about leaving Whispering Springs a few months early. I'll cover any buy-out on your contract. Hell, woman, I'll hire a moving company to get your ass out of town." He grabbed the door handle but her next words stopped him dead.

"I'll give you Singing Springs Ranch if you'll do this."

He dropped his hand from the door handle and turned toward her. "No. I'll pay you a fair price for Singing Springs." He quoted a seven-figure number that was high but fair.

She shook her head. "I can't sell you Singing Springs."

"Why the hell not?"

"Uncle Angus asked me not to sell the ranch to you, so I won't. But he never said anything about trading it to you."

"You are either the most peculiar woman I've ever met or the dumbest. That ranch is worth a hell of a lot of money."

"You don't understand. I don't give a flying fuck about money."

Her foul language shocked him. He didn't think he'd ever heard her say anything worse than shoot or darn it.

Her shoulders sagged like a deflated balloon. "I only want—no, make that need to give my grandmother what she wants before it's too late."

"No, Caroline. I won't do this, not even for Singing Springs."

SATURDAY MORNING, as Travis drove along the property line separating Singing Springs Ranch from Halo M Ranch, his desire for the property was so strong he could taste it. He'd been prepared to drop some serious cash to get it, but to stage a fake wedding, to play a fake groom to get the property felt, well, it felt dirty. Like he was a flim-flam artist selling worthless stock to an old woman. It wasn't right.

But on the other hand, who would they be hurting, the imp who always got him into trouble asked. It was obvious that Caroline adored her grandmother and would do nothing that would ever harm her. Maybe he was overreacting. He just didn't know if adding the Singing Springs acreage to his ranch holdings was worth the guilt he'd feel at deceiving an old woman.

The phone on his belt vibrated.

"Travis Montgomery."

"Well, good morning to you, sugar." The voice on the other end was female, Southern and sweet enough to send him into a diabetic coma. Elsie Belle Lambert.

"Mornin' Elsie Belle." He'd briefly dated Elsie Belle Lambert six months ago. After three dates, she'd begun pushing for something more permanent, like marriage. Even though he'd made it clear from the start that he had no interest in any long-term relationship, the woman never gave up. No amount of discouragement deterred her, so he didn't waste his time trying. "What can I do for you?"

"You can go to the End of Summer dance at WSCC with me. I've got the most wonderful dress that'll match your eyes perfectly."

Ah. Damn. He should have remembered the annual dance at Whispering Springs Country Club. It marked the end of summer vacation and the return to school for students and teachers. A huge fundraiser for the high school football team, his family always attended to show their support for the local team.

Think, damn it. Think. Elsie Belle would not take no for an answer.

"I'm sure any dress would be lovely on you, darlin', but I've already got a date for the dance."

His announcement was met briefly by stunned shock. "Really? This far out? How nice. Who's the lucky woman?"

He opened his mouth to say, "No one you know," but what came out was, "Caroline Graham." *Damn.* Why had he said that?

"Dr. Graham. How...nice. I'm sure I'll see you both there then."

"Of course you will. Good to talk to you, Elsie Belle."

When she clicked off without saying goodbye—and without asking him to take her to dinner—he snapped his phone back into its holder. What was he thinking? How could he have blurted out Caroline's name without thinking?

She had been on his mind. Maybe it was natural that her name would be the one on the tip of his tongue.

Had he just done the same thing Caroline had done when she told her grandmother about him? Well, hadn't he just landed in a big old pile of steaming horse manure.

He finished his morning ride still unsure how to untangle the knot he'd just tied with his lie. Maybe Caroline didn't have a date and he could ask her to go...as friends, of course. That'd make his lie not so much a lie and more of a prediction.

Before he headed to the barn, he turned Ransom toward Singing Springs. He opened the adjoining gate and rode onto Fitzgerald's property. The grass was still green and high. The creek running through the back end of the acreage bubbled, fed continually from the underground spring. He slipped from Ransom's back and allowed the horse to drink his fill of the fresh water. He wanted this property. Needed it to secure Halo M's future and build the ranch he dreamed of. He'd always told himself that he'd do whatever necessary to get his hands on Singing Springs, and now it was being handed to him on a silver platter. He'd be a fool not to grab it.

He scrolled through the stored directory on his phone until he found Caroline's number and then hit send. As the phone rang on her end, he paced and practiced what he would say when she answered. For just a moment, he felt as though he were fifteen again and calling a girl for their first date.

"Dr. Graham."

"Hi. Caroline. It's Travis. Travis Montgomery." He flinched at how nervous he sounded. It was worse than when he was thirteen and going through the nightmare voice change of adolescence.

She laughed. "Yes, Travis. I got the Montgomery part. What's up?"

"I was wondering if we could get together after church tomorrow. To talk...about Singing Springs. I'll buy your lunch. We can drive over to Tuckerville. There's a great Italian place."

"Tuckerville, huh? Hiding me from the locals?" She chuckled. "Lunch would be great, but why don't you just follow me home and I'll cook. We can even hide your truck in my garage so nobody will know you're here."

This time he laughed.

"Besides," she continued. "My house will give us some privacy to talk. Tell me you've given my offer some thought."

"Some, but I have to be honest. I still have some major reservations, but I'm willing to discuss your offer a little more."

"Good." She sighed into the receiver. "I'm not crazy. Desperate, yes, but not crazy. Fried chicken work for you?"

"Oh, hell yeah. One other thing though. You realize how small Whispering Springs is and how fast news travels. If I follow you home for lunch, it'll be all over town by two o'clock, so as bad as this may sound, I do want to park in your garage."

"I'm fully aware of how quickly news can fly in this

town. Why, I've already heard I'm your date for the End of Summer Dance at the club."

He groaned.

She laughed. "I'll see you tomorrow."

MAMIE BRIDGES HAD BEEN RAISED in the Superior Avenue Methodist Church of Crystal Lakes, Arkansas. From the day Caroline moved into her grandmother's house, she'd attended the Methodist church every Sunday with Mamie. While in college, then medical school, and finally during her residency and contract work, she'd always made it a priority to find a Methodist church in the area to attend. Before she moved to Whispering Springs, her biggest issue had been deciding which Methodist church to attend. Not a problem here.

Being a small community, Whispering Springs offered limited religious options. Southern Baptist, Catholic or Methodist. Worshipers could choose one of those or drive thirty or more minutes to Tuckerville to attend church. Most townspeople and ranchers were divided between Baptist and Methodist, with Catholic mass only being offered every other Sunday due to low attendance and the lack of a Catholic priest to conduct services without bringing in one from Dallas.

Sunday morning, Caroline walked into the Whispering Springs United Methodist Church as she had every Sunday since moving there. However, today she felt as though every eye was on her. The usher who handed her the morning bulletin grinned a little too broadly and his, "Good morning, Dr. Graham," was a little too jolly, as though they shared a secret.

Paranoid much, Caroline? There was no way anyone

knew she and Travis would be having lunch today. She was reading too much into the usher's greeting.

Caroline entered the sanctuary. The entry aisle bisected the rows on the right into the front portion of twenty rows and a back section of four rows. It didn't take but one visit to discover mothers with new babies sat in the back section for easy access to the fellowship hall in case of cranky ones and dirty diapers that needed attention. The left side of the worship area had twenty-five rows. Where new mothers and babies claimed the back of the right side, teenagers claimed the last five rows of the left side.

Interestingly, the congregation referred to the left side as Fitzgerald side and the right as Montgomery side. Apparently, the two families had contributed equally to build the church in nineteen-nineteen. Caroline usually sat on the Fitzgerald side but only out of habit. She'd grown up sitting on the left side of the Superior Avenue Methodist Church's in Crystal Lakes, Arkansas. Today, Jackie Montgomery waved to her from the third row of the Montgomery side and pointed to the seat beside her. Manners dictated that Caroline had to at least acknowledge the invitation, but she didn't need to do more to stir up the rumor mill.

Caroline stopped beside the pew. "Good morning, Jackie." She leaned forward until she could see the two women on the other side of the Montgomery matriarch. "Morning, Lydia. Hi, Olivia. Been a while since I've seen you. Hey, Adam."

Olivia Montgomery Gentry was Travis's only sister. From what she'd heard from Lydia, after a nasty break-up with the father of her son, Adam, Olivia and Mitch had only recently reconciled. Adam, a cute kid with curly dark hair, sat beside his mother swinging his legs as he drew horses on today's service bulletin. He gave Caroline a lop-sided grin that she knew would break hearts some day.

After the greetings had been exchanged, Jackie pointed once again to the empty spot on the pew next to her. "Sit."

Caroline chuckled. "Yes, ma'am. Sitting."

Jackie laughed. "Can you tell I'm used to dealing with hard-headed cowboys? Not to mention a hard-headed daughter."

Caroline smiled. "That I can." She glanced around. "Where's Lane and the boys?"

"They'll be along in a minute or two. Last I saw them, they were having a heated discussion about water rights with Judge Devlin."

"I know nothing about ranching, but it seems like water rights come up a lot around here for discussion."

"With this latest drought, even more than usual. So Lydia tells me you only have a few months left with us."

Caroline nodded. "Right. Five. My contact with the clinic is up at the end of the year."

"Have you given thought to staying on? We sure could use you around here."

"Thanks, Jackie. I'm flattered, but I've already made commitments for next year."

Olivia leaned forward. "Where to next?"

"Montana for a couple of months then to Utah in the spring."

Jackie touched Caroline's hand. "Will you be back here some day?"

Caroline shrugged. "I don't know. I doubt it. I've never gone to the same place twice."

"But you have a home here now. You should think about that."

Before Caroline could answer, a large, rough hand settled on her shoulder. "Good morning."

She turned and looked over her shoulder into Lane's blue eyes. From the shape and color, she knew where Travis had gotten his sexy stare.

"Morning, Lane." She stood. "I was just saying a quick hello. Here. Take this seat."

"No. Sit. Sit."

The pew behind the Montgomery clan had already filled with Elsie Belle Lambert and her parents. If Lane didn't take her seat, he would be separated from his family.

As Caroline stepped into the aisle, Elsie Belle gave her a hostile stare, which she found odd. She'd done nothing that should upset that gal.

"Sit, Lane." Caroline tilted her head across the aisle. "I'll grab a seat there." She leaned into the pew. "Nice to see you all this morning." She stepped into the pew directly across the aisle and sat. She watched as Lane slipped in and took the seat next to Jackie.

The choir leader motioned for the congregation to stand and Caroline stood.

"Scoot over," a male voice whispered into her ear.

An army of goose bumps sprang to attention on her arms.

"Scoot over," Travis repeated with a gentle jab with his elbow. "There aren't any seats left."

Caroline glanced around. He was right. There were a few seats in the sanctuary, but most of them were in the new mothers and babies section. No surprise he didn't want to sit there. Still, to sit by her in church might send the wrong idea, but she stepped to the side and Travis slipped in.

"You know you're going to feed the rumor mill sitting

here by me," Caroline whispered while the rest of the worshipers were singing the opening hymn.

"I can't help it. It was here or in the crying-babies section and that wasn't goin' to happen. Now, hush," he whispered with a nudge. "I'm singing."

She hushed and listened as Travis's deep bass voice sang "Amazing Grace." The low hum of his voice had her insides vibrating like guitar strings and her knees going soft. The man could sing. How did she not know that? If he hadn't been a rancher, Nashville would have come calling for his talents. As the hymn came to a close and she bowed her head for the opening prayer, she realized she'd never sung a note.

They sat as Reverend Berry made his opening announcements. Hot waves from Travis's body heat surrounded her in his woodsy cologne. She tried to concentrate on the sermon, but her mind refused to stay in Whispering Springs United Methodist Church and instead took off on its own trip down the road to fantasy town and some totally inappropriate scenarios for church.

TRAVIS HAD DONE some dumb things in his life. Sitting by Caroline Graham during church might rank up with some of his biggest mistakes, but it wasn't as though he'd had much of a choice. Sitting on the Fitzgerald side of the nave wasn't a big deal. He'd sat there a lot during his teenage years. Sitting with crying babies and breastfeeding mothers made him squirm regardless of the location inside the church. But pressed up next to Caroline's curves presented two potential dilemmas.

The first was sitting directly across the aisle, if the look on Elsie Belle's face was any indication. Three dates. No sex. That was their total history, if you didn't count a couple of hot, steamy kisses and some very heavy petting in high school some twenty years ago. Why the woman thought she had a claim to his time left him baffled. But honestly, the way most women thought left him baffled. However, the glare she gave Caroline made his balls pull up tight for protection.

The other potential problem was directly to his left. Dr. Caroline Graham. He didn't like the change in his thinking of her as a sexy, desirable woman instead of his future sister-in-law's temporary medical partner or a sweet family friend. When had he stepped over the line and given thought to breaking his never-fuck-where-you-live rule? Of course, he wouldn't actually be breaking his rule, more like bending the rule since she didn't actually live here and would be gone in just a few months. Hmm. A loophole perhaps?

He ventured a subtle peek at Elsie Belle. This might be a little wrong of him, but maybe Caroline could be useful here. How could he convince Elsie Belle that he and Caroline were a couple without conveying that message around town? Tricky, sure, but doable. As the closing hymn began, he promised to think more about that.

As soon as services were dismissed, Caroline slipped past him with a quiet, "See you later," and was gone. Making his way to the exit resembled running a gauntlet. Hands to shake. Backs to slap. Promises to make for a lunch or dinner with friends. When he finally pulled from the Whispering Springs United Methodist parking lot twenty minutes had passed, but that worked to his advantage. Most of the parishioners had had time to make it to the Lone Star Diner for lunch, making his drive to Caroline's house more discreet. Thank you, Jesus.

Once he could have sworn he saw Elsie Belle's black Porsche behind him, but when he turned, the car traveled on straight. The thought of Elsie Belle following him to Caroline's house made him antsy. After her divorce, the damn woman had set her marital sights on him. Getting her off his back was going to be as hard as removing a burrowed tick off a dog. She needed to set her marriage aspirations on someone else...the poor bastard.

He pulled into Caroline's drive and into the gaping mouth of her garage and parked alongside an ancient Honda. The aroma of fresh fried chicken assaulted him as he exited his truck. He licked his lips. He had no way of knowing if Caroline was a good cook, but the smells were making his mouth water.

After knocking on her door, he hit the remote on the wall to lower the garage door. The sense of cloak and dagger by sneaking into a house made him feel sixteen again. He smiled at memories of his teenage years and some the antics he and Jason had gotten away with.

"Come on in," Caroline hollered from the kitchen.

He walked in and drew in a deep breath. "I hope your cooking is as good as it smells."

Caroline smiled over her shoulder. "It's better. Mamie taught me good old Southern cooking. Won't swear it's heart-healthy, but I can promise it's tasty."

In the time since she'd left church, Caroline had changed into a pair of knee-length khaki shorts and a white sleeveless top. Ten red-tipped toes tapped on the floor in time to the country music filling her house. She looked relaxed and at ease, which should have made him relaxed and at ease. Instead, thoughts of a naked Caroline with her long legs wrapped around his hips while he drove deep made him twitchy, not to mention horny.

She frowned. "Everything okay? You're a little flushed."

"No, no. I'm fine. Starving though." He resisted the

impulse to wipe at the sweat he felt popping out on his brow. He was glad neither of his brothers were present. They'd be poking him and whispering, "Horny sweat."

She smiled. "Glad you're hungry. You know we Southern gals have a tendency to cook too much." She pushed a plate of fried chicken at him. "Put this on the table. I'll get the rolls out of the oven and we'll be ready to eat. What can I get you to drink?"

He brought the plate closer to his nose and sniffed. "Oh man. That smells wonderful. When did you have time to cook all this?"

A sparkle winked from her eye. "An old trick my grandmother taught me. Do all the cooking before church and leave it in the oven on low. It's ready when you get home. Drink?"

"Water or iced tea would be great."

He carried the platter of chicken to a well-set table of china and cloth napkins. He wasn't surprised but flattered by her obvious attention to detail. Were cloth napkins a given for her or only used for special occasions? Was she raised to eat meals like this every day or did she only put out a spread like this for holidays and guests? With every question, he realized he didn't really know Caroline Graham very well.

Would she have had a glass of wine if he weren't here? He hated the thought that she might have wanted wine but wouldn't because of him. He must have stood a little too long, because when she walked into the dining room she set the hot rolls on the table with lift of her eyebrow.

"Everything okay, Travis?"

He smiled. "Just knocked out by your table." After setting the platter of chicken on the table, he hurried over to pull back Caroline's chair.

"Thanks." She gracefully slid onto the seat. "Sit," she said with a gesture toward the only other chair at the table.

The food was as delicious as it'd smelled. The chicken was crispy. The rolls hot and buttery. The mashed potatoes smooth and thick. A meal designed to go directly to a man's heart.

"So," Caroline said. "You called this meeting. What's on your mind?"

He laid his knife and fork on his plate then wiped his mouth with the soft white napkin. Leaning back into his chair, he tried to find the right words. Finally, he decided to jump in. "I've thought about your offer."

"And?"

"It's obvious you love your grandmother very much."

"True."

"And that you'd never do anything that would hurt her."

"True again."

He drummed his fingers on the table, a nervous habit he'd never been able to break. "Are you sure you won't just sell Singing Springs to me? I've made you a very generous offer. Hell, probably more than it's worth."

She smiled. "No. It's a trade or nothing. Take it or leave it."

He sighed. "So what's your plan?"

Now that he appeared to be resigned to her crazy plan, the smile on her face lit a twinkle in her eyes.

"Quite simple actually. We fly to Crystal Lakes. There's no waiting period so we can get a marriage license the same day. We go to the hospital, see my grandmother, let her do a wedding ceremony and sign the license and we fly back to Dallas. We never file the marriage license. No filing. No marriage. It'll be a quirky souvenir. That's all."

He hated to ask about the Singing Springs deed, but that was why he was here. "And Singing Springs?"

"We execute a quitclaim deed that you won't file until I leave town. Once I'm gone, it won't matter how you got the land, but I'd rather not answer any questions or have to lie to people."

He lifted an eyebrow. "You mean lie to people other than your grandmother."

She flushed. The pink of her cheeks along with her hooded eyes produced a different expression from what he was used to seeing from her. For one moment, he wondered if this was how she looked during the heat of sex. And no, he shouldn't have been thinking about sex with Caroline Graham. Dangerous waters for sure.

"I love my grandmother, and trust me when I tell you if there were any other way to make her happy, I'd do it. But my happiness is all she asks about. Let me give her the one thing she wants, the one thing I can give her...peace at knowing I'm in love and settled."

"When would you want to do this?"

"As soon as possible."

"Do you mean this week?"

"Tomorrow if I could, but that's short notice for you to get away from the ranch and to make sure Lydia can cover my shift. Can you get away this week? Like maybe Tuesday?"

A cold sweat broke out on his brow, only this time the sweat didn't have anything to do with his sex drive. A bead of perspiration rolled down the side of his face. Married. In forty-eight hours from now. Even if it was a staged wedding, his gut roiled with nerves.

"I can probably get away for the day on Tuesday. But..."

He pumped his eyebrows. "What about the wedding night?"

She laughed. "I'm picturing me at my house and you at your house."

"Tuesday it is."

"I'll make all the arrangements and call you tomorrow, okay?"

"If this is the only way for me to get Singing Springs, then..." He sighed. "Talk to you tomorrow."

Five

True to her word, by Tuesday morning when they met at Dallas Love Field, Caroline had everything in order, including a legal document she had drawn up that spelled out their arrangement. He wasn't sure whether to be impressed by her attention to detail or agitated that she found him so predictable she might have already had all these documents ready to go.

She'd arrived at Dallas Love Field wearing an off-white suit and a silky-looking cream-colored top. He couldn't help but admire her shapely calves and trim ankles as he allowed his gaze to roam. Her red-tipped toes from Sunday were encased in a pair of low-heeled off-white shoes. She'd fixed her hair in a fancy twist of some sort at the back of her head, like she'd done the last time they'd eaten at his parents' house. All he could think about was pulling out the pins holding it up and running his fingers through her long hair.

And no. He shouldn't have been thinking about that.

"Okay, here's your boarding pass," she said, handing him a strip of floppy paper. "And before you get off on some testosterone-driven rant about how I shouldn't have paid for your ticket, chill. It was only sixty bucks roundtrip and you're doing me a huge favor."

He shrugged but played along with her lie. He'd checked ticket prices and knew she'd paid quite a bit more. Plus, she'd nailed his discomfort with her paying for everything. The man should pay, or at least that's how he'd been raised. The women he did date—on those rare occasions when he did go out—expected him to pay for everything. He couldn't remember the last time a woman had picked up the bill.

"I'll try to rein in my testosterone surges." He smiled when she chuckled. He was beginning to love to hear her laugh. "But you know I would have paid for the airfare or anything else."

"I know. It was nice of you to offer, but this is my trip." She paused when the agent at the desk announced boarding. Caroline drew in a deep breath. "Okay. Let's go."

As passengers began filing onto the plane, he allowed Caroline to walk ahead of him while he, once again, enjoyed the view of her swinging hips. Lord, the woman could walk. As the thought crossed his mind, the heel of her shoe caught on a metal plank of the jet bridge, causing her to stumble. He grabbed her elbow to steady her.

"You okay?"

She straightened and smoothed a non-existent wrinkle from her skirt. "I'm fine. Thanks."

Was she as nervous as he? Hell, even if she wasn't nervous about today, he was. Thinking about saying those words, taking those vows, even when he knew neither of them were serious, was making him squirm. He believed in the sanctity of wedding vows. He'd only said them once and had meant each syllable with every fiber of his being.

Damn Fitzgerald for putting him in this spot.

He had to make himself believe this was like taking a role in a play...that was all. Playing a role didn't make the words less powerful, but maybe he could make it okay for him.

The plane was small, three leather-covered seats for each of the twenty-five rows with an aisle dividing the seats, two on the right side and one on the left. Out of the seventy-five available seats, only forty were occupied. He slipped into seat 5B with Caroline beside him in 5C. There were no passengers in row four or six, which gave them a great deal of privacy.

As the plane taxied, Caroline stared out the window and tapped her fingers on the armrest between them. Once the small jet reached cruising altitude, the tapping stopped, but there was a distinctive nervous jitter to her hand.

Travis placed his hand over hers. It was ice cold. He laced their fingers to warm hers. "We don't have to do this, you know. We can still visit your grandmother. Tell her I got cold feet. Put the blame solely on my shoulders. I'm sure your grandmother would believe that a Montgomery would leave a bride at the altar...literally and figuratively."

She looked at him, slowly closed her eyes for a moment then opened them to meet his gaze. "No. This is truly the only thing I can do for her before she's gone. If she wanted anything else, I'd get it for her. You must understand. When your wife was ill, didn't you feel the same?"

At the mention of Susan, Travis's chest squeezed and all the breath rushed from his lungs. She was right. The memory of those final days flashed through his mind. The sorrow. The desperation. The days of trying to prepare himself for something there was no preparation for. He gave her hand a little squeeze.

"Near the end, when I knew we'd done everything medically we could for Susan, I would drive sixty miles every other day to buy her a particular ice cream I could only get at one store. Sixty miles there and sixty miles back." He smiled at the memory. "I even bought a specially equipped freezer to keep in the truck so the ice cream wouldn't melt before I could get it home. A couple of weeks before I lost her, I bought her a white mare. We'd always talked about raising pure white horses." He dropped his gaze to their interlocked fingers. "It was silly, but I thought if she saw the horse that maybe..." He shook his head. "I don't know. That seeing the horse from our plans would give her the will to live. Desperate thinking by a man too young to experience that kind of loss." He squeezed her fingers. "I think now I finally understand why I agreed to your crazy plan. I understand your need. I do."

She sighed. "Thank you."

When she began to pull her fingers from his, he stopped her. "You have to get used to me touching you for this to be believable."

"You're right." She resettled her fingers between his.

His gut pulled taut at the sight of their linked hands. He'd spent more intimate time with Caroline over the past five days than he had in the past five months. He'd always found her physically attractive, but now he was drawn to her on an unanticipated emotional level also. An unexpected heat flared in his chest and he found his breathing picking up speed. "So, you're going to go ahead as planned?"

She nodded.

He squeezed her fingers before pulling his hand free. "Then I have something for you."

He stood and rummaged in his flight bag stored in the overhead bin until his fingers touched a velvet box. He pulled it out and retook his seat. Caroline gave him a quizzical look. He popped open the box and displayed three rings. The middle ring supported a large emerald-cut diamond solitaire highlighted on each side by two rows of diamond baguettes. It was flanked on the right by a gold man's wedding band and on the left by a complimentary wedding band with two rows of baguette diamonds. The wedding band was designed to fit under the diamond solitaire to complete the set.

"You just happened to have these lying around your house?" Caroline asked, incongruity tempering her tone.

"Well, my safe actually. The rings belonged to my dad's mother. I inherited the set, but Susan didn't like them. Thought they looked too old fashioned, so I locked them away. Hadn't looked at them for years. I'd forgotten how much I liked the engagement ring."

"It is beautiful." She took the ring box from him. Turning the box from side-to-side, she admired the rings from every angle. As the sun streamed through the small porthole window and shot through the diamond, primary colors sparkled off the bottom of the overhead bin. "Absolutely stunning." She looked at him. "Are you sure you want to use these?"

"Did you bring rings?"

"No. I ran out of time with getting everything else done before leaving."

"Then..." He pulled the engagement ring from the box. "Give me your left hand." When she did, he slipped the ring on her fourth finger. It fit as though it'd been made for her. For a moment, the view in front of him swam. The hollowness inside he'd felt since Susan's death was filled by a deep-seated sense of calm. He drew in a long, satisfying breath.

"Travis." She held her hand out in front of her to study

the ring. "It's truly beautiful." She leaned over and brushed his cheek with her lips. "Thank you."

CAROLINE STUDIED THE RING, stunned at Travis's generosity. She'd only be wearing it briefly, but for him to have brought it had her insides tangoing in pleasure.

He'd been right when he'd asked if she was having reservations about this staged wedding. She was. Like every little girl, she'd dreamed of her wedding day. Never had those dreams included marrying a man she barely knew while standing at the bedside of her dying grandmother.

As she'd grown into adulthood, the vision of being married and settled in one spot had faded like all childhood fantasies do in the light of reality. Marriage meant being dependent, a loss of freedom, a loss of control over your own life. No thank you. That wasn't for her.

As the pilot announced immediate landing, Caroline touched Travis's arm. "Thank you again."

The white stretch limousine she'd reserved awaited them when they arrived at baggage claim. The driver stowed their overnight bags into the trunk as they slipped into the rear seat. Her gaze slid over to him. "Sorry the return flight for today got canceled and we couldn't do this as a one-day trip like I'd promised."

"Not a problem."

She drew in a deep breath. "Ready?"

He smiled. "I am." When she began tapping on the armrest, he frowned. "What's the problem? Having second thoughts again?"

She reached down and pulled her purse into her lap. "No second thoughts. I just... Well, I wasn't going to give you this until we were on the way home, but I realized on the flight here I have to trust you. No, not *have* to, but do trust you." She pulled an envelope from the large tan bag. "Here," she said, setting the clasped envelope on the armrest. "It's the quitclaim deed for Singing Springs."

He looked at the envelope as though it were radioactive and made no move to take it. "Why?"

"Why? That was our agreement."

"True, but I could take this deed and run."

She smiled. "But you're not going to do that."

He huffed out a breath. "Of course not."

"Exactly." She reached across the car and laced her fingers through his. His hand was warm and the skin tough and callused. It felt like a man's hand should feel. Work-hardened but still capable of a gentle stroke. "I trust you, Travis." She squeezed his hand. "And I can't begin to thank you. If you could have heard the excitement in Mamie's voice when I told her... Well, it was the happiest I've heard in a long time. For that alone I owe you."

The limo rolled to a stop. The driver sprang from his seat and whipped the rear door open. Travis stepped from the back seat and reached his hand back in to assist Caroline's exit. The old county courthouse stood in front of them.

"We'll be a few minutes," she told the driver.

He pulled a card from an inside pocket of his jacket. "Yes, ma'am. The parking is a little tight around the courthouse. Give me a call when you're ready to go. I'll be just up the street."

Travis took the card and shoved it into his pocket. "Will do."

The driver climbed back into the limo and pulled from

the lot. Travis turned toward the old building. "Where do we have to go?"

"County clerk's office on the first floor," Caroline replied, but she didn't move.

"Caroline." Travis grabbed both her shoulders and turned her to face him. "It's not too late to change your mind."

She shook her head then smiled. "No. It's not that. I was just remembering the time Mamie arranged a courthouse tour for my Girl Scout troop. The jail was located in this building then." She pointed to a far corner. "Over there. The prisoners would yell things from those windows." She laughed. "I learned a few new words that day. Some of the mothers were not happy with Mamie." She took his left hand. "Come on."

The county clerk's office was obviously having a very slow day. No one was waiting to be served, and behind the desk, many of the staff stood looking at some pictures. A short, well-endowed woman waved a hand. "Be right with ya." She pulled away from the group and took a seat behind the desk. "Now, how can I help you folks?"

"We need to get a marriage license," Caroline said.

"Well, good for you. Congratulations to you both." She pulled two clipboards from under the desk, clipped a form onto each of them and slid them across. "I need each of you to complete an application. If you've been married before, I'll need to see a divorce decree or a death certificate. The fee is fifty-eight dollars. We only take cash."

Caroline and Travis moved to the chairs along the wall to complete the paperwork. Travis wrote quickly and finished first.

"Done?" he asked

"Just about." Caroline signed the form. "Finished."

Travis took both clipboards and returned to the counter. He pulled a folded piece of paper from his jacket, placed it on top of his form and handed both to the clerk. She took them, unfolded the paper and nodded. Caroline could read the large bold print at the top. *Death Certificate.* She hadn't even given a thought to his being a widower.

"Good thing you remembered this," the clerk said. "Have to have it. Okay, let's see what we've here." The clerk's fingers began flying across her keyboard as she entered Travis's information. It didn't take long before she refolded the death certificate and handed it back to him. "You're done. Let's get your bride in there." She lifted Caroline's clipboard and read the name. "Caroline Graham. You related to Joshua Graham over on Maple?"

Caroline shook her head. "No, ma'am."

"Just as well. He's an old bastard anyhow. Okay, let's see. Never married, so I don't need anything there." She continued to talk to herself as she rapidly entered Caroline's information. "Okay, that's it." She looked at Travis. "If you and Ms. Graham will have a seat, it'll be just a minute."

In about five minutes, the clerk waved them back to the window. "Okay. Here is your license. Remember that you need to have it signed and back to this office within sixty days. Good luck to both of you. I wish you many years of happiness." She smiled as she passed the legal document across the counter.

Travis took the license, folded it and slipped it into his jacket pocket. "Thank you."

After retrieving her purse from the chair, Caroline looked at the clerk. "So we're done?"

"Yes, ma'am. Good luck."

"Thank you."

Caroline was amazed at Travis's calm exterior, in

contrast to her quivering insides. Once they reached the exterior door, Travis dialed the limo, which pulled up not more than a minute later. They climbed in, the air vibrating with tension. Or maybe it was just her. She didn't know.

They pulled into the circle drive that fed St. Michael's Hospital visitor entrance. As before, the driver slipped from the car before Travis or Caroline could reach for the door release and opened the rear passenger door.

"We will be a while in here," Caroline told the driver. "I'll call when we're ready to go."

"That's fine, ma'am."

As the car pulled away, Caroline's stomach rolled and pitched like a ship at sea. Travis's hand at the small of her back as they entered the hospital did little to calm her nerves. If anything, his touch was stirring up emotions she had no right to feel about him. In the lobby, she paused.

"You okay?" Travis asked. He turned and looked into her eyes.

"No second thoughts, not about what we're doing. I just wish...I mean..." She let out a long breath. "I just wish this wasn't a fake wedding." As though realizing what she'd said, she added in a rush of words, "Not that I'm saying I want to marry you. I mean, you're great and all that, it's just that I wish I was really in love and—"

Travis chuckled. "I'm great and all that?" Then he let out a laugh. "Way to flatter your groom."

She pulled him off to the side. "That's not what I meant."

He smiled and captured her chin between his thumb and forefinger. "Caroline. You are a wonderful woman any man would be lucky to have as a wife. If I were looking for one, you'd be at the top of my list."

Her heart leapt into her throat at his words. The air

whooshed from her lungs. The heat of an oncoming blush warmed her cheeks. She jerked her head, pulling out of his grasp. "I'm fine. Let's just get this over with. I get a husband for a few hours and you get a chunk of land forever. Works for me."

Whipping around, she marched for the elevator.

Like I'd want to really marry him. Ha. Give me a break.

Thoughts that hit a little too close to the truth deserved to be laughed off, so ha-ha.

The elevator opened on the third floor and they stepped off. Immediately, Caroline's olfactory senses were assaulted with the smell of industrial-strength disinfectant mingled with the aromas from the lunch food cart delivering patient meals.

"Man, I hate that smell," Travis groused.

Caroline put her arm through his. "I'm sure you do. Most people do. Believe it or not, most hospital personnel learn to ignore it, along with a lot of other unpleasant odors." She placed her other hand over his. "Ready."

He snuggled her closer. "Let's do this."

As they neared Mamie Bridges's room, the sound of happy voices filtered out and into the hall. Caroline frowned. What was going on?

She knocked gently and pushed the door open. Her eyes flew open in surprise. "Oh, no."

The drab hospital room had been transformed into a makeshift wedding chapel. White ribbons and hearts draped the window. Lengths of white silk decorated the dingy-yellow walls in flowing swags. Soft music floated from a box in the corner. And flowers. There were flowers everywhere. White roses. Cymbidium orchids. Baby's breath. Calla lilies. White peonies.

Caroline's breath rushed out in a loud gasp. "What in the world?"

The chattering halted and the people in the room turned toward the door.

"Caroline. Come here, child," her grandmother said from the bed, her arms stretched out for a welcoming embrace.

Caroline rushed across the room. "Mamie. It's so good to hear your voice." She gently hugged her grandmother's frail frame, the old-fashioned rose scent of Mamie's cologne filled Caroline's nose, bringing unwelcome sentimental tears to her eyes. She pressed her cheek against her grandmother's soft, but parchment-textured cheek then stepped back to clasp her grandmother's hands, careful not to hold her fragile fingers too tightly. "You look wonderful, like you're ready to take on the world."

Mamie's white hair had been curled, teased and sprayed stiff, like many women of her generation. Her normally pallid cheeks sported red slashes of blush. She wore eye makeup and mascara. Instead of one of those horrid hospital gowns, she wore a blue suit jacket with a pink silk blouse.

Mamie squeezed Caroline's fingers. Granted, it was a weak squeeze, but it felt so good to feel her grandmother's fingers in hers. "Of course I do. I couldn't let you get married with me looking like an old dying woman, now could I?"

Caroline leaned over the bed and hugged her grandmother again. "I miss you so much." Tears formed in the corners of her eyes. "I am so sorry I don't get up here enough to see you."

"Now, don't start that," Mamie chastised in a weak voice. "This is a happy day. One of the happiest days of my life." She looked around. "Now, where's my grandson-in-law-to-be?"

Caroline turned, expecting to see Travis standing in the door. He wasn't. Her heart skipped. Where was he?

"Over here, Judge Bridges," Travis's deep voice drawled from the corner.

Caroline shut her eyes briefly as the fear that he'd left crumbled. She drew in a quick breath and turned in the direction of Travis's voice. She'd been so nervous all day. She hadn't really looked at him. Dressed in a dark suit with his boot tips glistening under the room's florescent lights, he looked more handsome than she'd ever seen him. He smiled when she turned. "Be right back," she said to Mamie and crossed the room to where Travis stood talking with her brother, Noah.

"Hi, Noah. You have really grown."

"Yeah," he snarled. "People do that when you don't see them very often."

Travis's head snapped toward Noah. "Now, son, I'm sure you don't mean to speak to your sister on her wedding day in that tone of voice. I think you owe her an apology."

Caroline touched his arm. The muscles were tight with tension. "It's okay, Travis. I'm sure he didn't mean it." Travis had always had his parents, had known his parents loved and wanted him. He couldn't understand what it was like to be dumped on your grandmother's porch to be raised, whether she wanted the task to or not. She understood though. Noah deserved a break. He sure hadn't had one in his short fourteen years.

Travis looked at her. "No. It's not." He turned back to Noah. "Don't you have something to say, son?"

"Sorry, Caroline."

Caroline pulled Noah to her for a stiff hug. His arms

hung like paralyzed limbs at his side during the embrace. She understood better than anyone how he was feeling. The only real parent he'd ever known was going to die. Their biological parents were far away, and while it was possible he could go to live with them, he hardly knew them. And if she were in his shoes, she wouldn't want to go live in a third-world country.

"I'm glad you're here," she said, but in reality, she was more surprised than happy to see him.

"Caroline. Darling. You look wonderful." A pair of female arms surrounded her.

Caroline twisted to face her aunt. "Hi, Aunt Leslie." The two women embraced. "What a surprise. I hadn't expected you and Uncle Patrick to be here."

"Of course we're here," her uncle boomed. "Do you think I'd let my only niece get married without her family around her? No way."

Her uncle enfolded her in his arms. "I'm so happy for you, Caro," he whispered quietly enough for only her to hear. "I spoke with your mother yesterday. She was so sorry they couldn't be here. But the expense to get back to the US plus the amount of time they'd be away from their work was just too much. She didn't feel they could leave right now."

"No sweat," she replied. "I know how important their work is to them." They were dedicated to their work. Every dime they earned or inherited would go into their ministry.

In her carefully constructed plan, only Travis, her grandmother and she would be here for this wedding ceremony. Arkansas law didn't require witnesses to legalize a marriage. So with her grandmother's inevitable demise, only she and Travis would have remained with the knowledge of the wedding. She hadn't planned on Mamie spreading the word. However, this late in the game, she had no choice but to go forward with her plans, extra witnesses or not. She could always stage an annulment later if necessary, sure that her family would understand her commitment to her work. She sighed.

Oh, what a tangled web we weave when first we practice to deceive.

Six

After proper introductions with her uncle and aunt, Caroline took Travis's hand and led him to Mamie's bedside. Her gut whirled at the feel of the work calluses and tough skin of his fingers on hers. As if acting independently of her brain, her thumb stroked the rough flesh along the side of his. His fingers squeezed hers and her gut whirl became an F-5 tornado.

"Mamie, this is Travis Montgomery. Travis, my grandmother, Mamie Bridges." Her voice quaked with nervous energy.

Caroline could see her grandmother's stamina was beginning to sag. The blush on her cheeks provided the only hint of color. The years of cigarette smoking had taken their toll. Her lungs labored to draw in air. She rested heavily against the pillows behind her. Mamie really should be on oxygen, but knowing her grandmother, Caroline suspected Mamie had taken it off so she'd look better. No telling how long Mamie had been putting on her aren't-I-doing-great routine for Patrick and Leslie. It was time to get this show on the road and more oxygen back in Mamie's system.

Travis grasped Mamie's limp hand. "Nice to meet you, Judge Bridges."

Mamie gave him a gentle pull. He leaned in closer. "That's no way to greet your grandmother-in-law to be," she said, her voice now distinctly weaker than when they'd first entered the room. "Family hugs, not shakes."

Travis chuckled. "Yes, ma'am." He hugged Mamie then stood. "I see where Caroline gets her good looks."

Mamie pressed a hand against the curls at the side of her head and pshawed. "You've already won the girl. You don't have to flatter me."

Caroline grinned, entertained by Mamie's obvious delight with Travis's compliment. "Okay then, we're all here. Ready to get going?"

Mamie's face crinkled into a frown. "In just a minute. I thought—"

"I'm here. I'm here. So sorry I'm late, Mamie." A thin, eighty-something-year-old man pushed his way in the door. "Caroline, my dear. Aren't you lovely?"

Caroline's heart leapt with joy at seeing her old friend. "Judge Hodges." She wrapped her arms around his neck. "I can't believe you're here."

"Are you kidding? Miss my goddaughter's wedding?" As he enfolded her in a loving embrace, he whispered, "Mamie was afraid she would forget the words or be too weak to do the whole ceremony. She asked me to come by as a backup."

Backup, my eye.

Patrick and Leslie greeted the long-time family friend with hugs and smiles. Neither appeared to be surprised to see him. The room now held two former judges and her Uncle Patrick, known by his congregation as Pastor Pat. Mamie was doing everything in her power to make this marriage stick.

She rolled her eyes upward. *Okay God. You're not helping*, she silently prayed.

After an introduction to Travis, she forced a cheery smile. "Well, seems like the gang's all here. I think we should get this show on the road."

Leslie and Patrick stepped to the left side of Mamie's bed. Leslie adjusted the head of the hospital bed to upright and helped Mamie scoot up into a sitting position. Judge Hodges moved to the head of the bed and stood next to Mamie. Travis took Caroline's hand and they moved to the right side of the bed. In her left hand, Caroline held a nosegay of white roses and baby's breath passed to her by Leslie. The bouquet shook in time with her hammering heart.

This was it. Showtime.

A wave of sadness swept through Caroline. Sadness that she had to go through with this ruse to appease her grandmother. Sadness that this might be the only time in her life she actually said these vows. But the deepest sadness was at the realization that very soon she would be losing the most important person in her life.

Part of her wished this was real. Not because she was in love with Travis, because she didn't know him well enough to have that degree of attachment. But she wished she loved a man that much, loved a man like Travis enough to pledge spending her life with him. She believed in these vows. Were they making a mockery of marriage by staging this fake one? Had she made a mistake?

Travis glanced at the people surrounding the bed. "Wait a minute."

Caroline startled. Her head snapped toward Travis. Her heart slammed painfully against her ribs. Was he having the same thoughts as she? Was he backing out at the last minute? "What's wrong?"

"I need a best man. Noah, would you come stand with us?"

Her heart swelled with unspeakable emotion. She was so touched that Travis thought to include her brother. Poor Noah's life was getting ready to undergo another drastic change. She hadn't considered how he might feel seeing his sister getting married and moving on with her life. Even if the marriage wasn't real, the impact on him could be the same.

Caroline rapidly blinked her eyes to prevent her tears from leaking out. She and Noah had never been close. There'd always been too much of an age difference and too many miles between them to develop much of a sibling relationship. At least she was doing the right thing by leaving him with Patrick and Leslie, allowing him to remain with school friends, even if Mamie hadn't been crazy about some of his friends.

"I guess so," Noah answered in a petulant voice. He rose from his chair and took a position beside Travis.

Considering the worn jeans, dirty sneakers and a T-shirt sporting the name of a hard-core metal band, then add in his shoulder-length hair, her brother wasn't exactly dressed for a wedding. Still, it was wonderfully nice of Travis to include him.

Travis handed the wedding bands to Noah. "Hold these for me, okay? I'll need them in a minute."

Noah shrugged and nodded before closing his fingers around the rings resting in his palm.

"Ready, my dear?" Mamie asked.

Caroline nodded.

"We are gathered here today to witness the wedding of my beloved Caroline to Travis Montgomery. Over my lifetime I have performed hundreds of wedding ceremonies, but none more important than today's." She paused to cough. Patrick handed his mother a glass of water. After a couple of sips, she continued. "I've prayed to live to see the day Caroline joins her life with the man she loves. Thank you, God, for allowing me to be here today." She coughed again. Her breathing became a little more labored. Caroline moved to help, but her grandmother waved her off. "I'll be all right. Just give me a minute."

"Mother, do I need to call a nurse?" Patrick asked.

She shook her head. "No. I can go on." She smiled at the bridal couple. "I'd give you the short vows, but I have some I use only for the special people I marry."

Travis leaned toward her. "I'm sure whatever vows you use will be perfect, Judge Bridges."

"Travis, take both of Caroline's hands and face her."

Caroline passed the roses back to Leslie and took both of Travis's hands. The shake of her hands had made its way up her arms. Muscles twitched and jerked with nervousness. Travis stood as straight and still as a post. He smiled and gave her fingers a light squeeze. Then he winked and Caroline's heart sighed.

Travis was a good man. She said a quick prayer that he find love again and live the remainder of his life in happiness.

"Repeat after me," Mamie said. "I, Travis Montgomery, take you, Caroline Bradley Graham, to be my lawfully wedded wife, my trusted friend, my faithful partner and my everlasting love from this day forward."

"I, Travis Lane Montgomery, take you, Caroline Bradley Graham, to be my lawfully wedded wife, my trusted friend, my faithful partner and my everlasting love from this day forward."

"In the presence of God, our family and friends."

Guilt about what she was doing tickled Caroline's nose. She nervously swiped her tongue across her dry lips since she couldn't possibly scratch her nose right now. She forced her eyes to focus on his face. His somber expression melted her fear. As the deep bass of his voice repeated each sentence of the wedding vows, shards of lust vibrated through her veins.

"I offer you my solemn vow to be your faithful partner in sickness and in health. In good times and in bad, and in joy as well as in sorrow."

Her heart jumped. Surely her ears were playing tricks on her. She could have sworn Travis had just said in bed instead of in bad.

Damn Texan accent.

"I promise to love you unconditionally. To support you in your goals. To honor and respect you."

If anyone ever found out about her staging this phony wedding and basically blackmailing Travis into it, Travis could be embarrassed socially and professionally, something she'd never want. She might become the laughing stock of Whispering Springs, but that didn't matter as much to her as protecting Travis's name and reputation. She vowed to do whatever necessary to protect his good name.

"To laugh with you and cry with you——" Travis flashed her a smile as he voiced her grandmother special vows. Her already trembling legs threatened to collapse under her, "—and to cherish you for as long as we both shall live."

Mamie pressed a tissue to her mouth for a long coughing spell. Caroline noticed the tissue had a small spattering of blood due to broken blood vessels from the violence of the cough. She leaned forward. "Mamie. We can stop if this is too much for you."

Mamie shook her head. "No. I've lived for this day. I want to go on."

Caroline stood and faced Travis. She still wasn't sure that she'd made the right decision to do this. Doing the wedding vows were using up every ounce of energy her grandmother had. But to stop now? *"I've lived for this day,"* kept reverberating through her mind. She wouldn't take this away from her grandmother. She stiffened her back...and her resolve to continue.

"Caroline," her grandmother rasped. "Repeat after me."

Caroline went through the same vows Travis had just recited. The sound of her voice repeating those words sounded foreign and dreamlike, as though she were in an amateur community production of a wedding play. But as she repeated after her grandmother, she felt every word in her heart, in her soul, deep in the nucleus of every cell in her body.

And she feared that could be a problem in the future.

"Can I have the rings?" Mamie's request jarred Caroline back to the hospital room. Noah placed the two gold bands on the Bible his grandmother held. "Patrick, would you bless these rings for me?" Mamie's voice was barely audible. Exhaustion pulled at the lines in her face.

"Of course, Mother."

After the blessing, Mamie said, "Travis. Take Caroline's ring and put it on her finger while repeating these words. With this ring, I thee wed."

Travis slid the cool metal down Caroline's overheated finger. "With this ring, I thee wed."

"Caroline, I need you to do the same."

She took the heavy gold band and pushed it onto Travis's ring finger. "With this ring, I thee wed."

Mamie coughed and blood tinged the tissue again. "With the power vested in me by the State of Arkansas, I pronounce you are husband and wife. What God has brought together, let no man divide. You can kiss your wife now, Travis."

Kiss her? Caroline had not given this part of the ceremony any thought. Bad planning on her part. What if he was a bad kisser? Worse yet, what if he wasn't?

Travis placed his hands on her shoulders and leaned forward. His hands were big, and hot and heavy. Erotic heat seared through her light jacket and silk blouse, burned right into her flesh. He lowered his face toward hers. Her nervous system was already over stimulated, but at the first brush of his soft lips against hers, her lungs seized. Her knees softened and threatened to fail altogether. She grabbed his waist for support, to hold her upright when her legs wanted to melt into the floor.

He angled his head to extend the kiss while he slid his arms around her shoulders, pulling her against his hardness. It was like a light was flipped on in every atom in her body. Jolts of energy rattled through her. Atomic fusion in action.

When he broke the kiss, she gasped in a breath. Her eyelids fluttered as though awaking from a deep sleep.

Okay, now she knew. This man could kiss. If she could bottle her reaction, the world energy crisis would be solved.

A harsh, ragged cough broke through Caroline's lust fog. She snapped her attention back to her grandmother. Leslie was holding Mamie's shoulders as she struggled to get her breath. Her face, already pale, seemed to have lost all trace of color except for the bluish tint to her lips.

Caroline stepped out of Travis's embrace. "Leslie, ring

for a nurse. Patrick, hand me the oxygen mask on the wall next to you."

After securing the mask around Mamie's mouth and nose, she reached over and turned the oxygen flow up to six liters. The door pushed open as she was pushing pillows behind Mamie's back.

"What do you need?" a nurse in blue scrubs asked.

"Get her doctor on the phone. I need a nasal cannula for her oxygen. Let's get an IV going too."

The nurse hesitated.

"Now," Caroline snapped.

The nurse left in a hurry.

With those few actions and words, Travis's pseudo-wife transformed from blushing bride to in-control doctor. Stepping back and out of the way, he bumped into Noah standing as still as a tombstone. His face bore a mask of despair and fear. His gaze was glued to the action around the bed. Travis put his hands on the boy's shoulders. "Your sister's got everything under control."

Noah's shoulders began to tremble. Travis put his arm around him. "Let's step outside until they get your grandmother settled. Okay?"

"No. I have to stay here. She might need me."

"Noah—"

"No. I'm not leaving." He jerked away from Travis and moved to the bottom of the bed.

Poor kid. There was no worse feeling than helplessness. Travis knew that feeling. He'd lived it. Pulling him away from Susan's side at the end had been almost impossible. Two-minute showers. Dinners eaten sitting at her side. Naps in uncomfortable chairs. His rational mind understood there was nothing he could do...not then and not now. Emotionally, he wanted to help...to do something, anything, to improve the situation. But like Noah, he had been unable to do much more than hold his late wife's hand.

The door swung open with a crash, admitting a heavy-set man with white hair. "I was doing my noon rounds when the nurse paged. Mamie, Mamie, Mamie. You causing trouble again today?" He kept a light, joking tone to his voice but his gaze moved rapidly to the oxygen mask then to the people at the side of the bed. "Dr. Graham. Good to see you. Care to fill me in?"

Caroline gave the man a tight smile. "Dr. Stewart. Mamie's having a little trouble catching her breath. I started oh-two at six liters. Her color's a little better but her coughing was quite explosive and harsh. I've asked that her IV be put back in and to get a nasal cannula to replace the mask."

"I agree." He looked at the nurse who'd followed him into the room. "Let's get this moving now."

"I'll be right back," she said and left.

"Probably be better if I got out of this fancy get-up before y'all begin sticking me with needles," Mamie said in a rough whisper. "And hand me that license, Travis. I need to sign it.

Caroline smiled. "Right you are. Out of your fancy clothes and into something more comfortable." She turned toward Travis. "Okay, guys, everybody out. Go to the cafeteria or outside or something. Don't come back for thirty minutes."

Travis placed his hand on Noah's shoulder. "You heard the lady. Let's split."

"But—"

"No buts," Patrick said. "We'll see you ladies in thirty."

Dr. Stewart followed the men into the hall.

"Shouldn't you be in there?" Noah asked. "You're her doctor. You should be doing something."

A sad smile creased the old man's face. A knowing sympathy reflected in the look he gave Noah. "Dr. Graham has it under control. They'll get your grandmother comfortable and you can see her later." Being almost the same height as Noah, he looked him straight in the eye. "But, Noah, we've had this discussion. Your grandmother's not going to get well this time. I've done everything I can for her, but sometimes things are out of a doctor's power."

Noah shoved the man. "No, damn it. She's not going to die. Don't say that. We'll find a better doctor than you."

"Noah—" Patrick said.

"No!" Noah turned and fled down the hall, slamming open the door to the exit stairs.

"Do we need to follow him?" Travis asked, admittedly a little alarmed by Noah's abrupt exit.

Patrick shook his head. "No. I know where he is. He just needs a little time." He turned his attention to Dr. Stewart. "I apologize for the boy. This is tough on him."

Dr. Stewart nodded. "No need to apologize. I understand. I wish there was something I could do, but you know your mother's smoking did serious damage to her lungs and her circulatory system." He shrugged. "I am sorry. There's just nothing more I can do but make her comfortable. She told me last week that she knows her end is near, and I think she's accepted that." He looked at Travis. "She mentioned that her granddaughter was getting married today. You must be the groom."

"I am. Travis Montgomery."

The two men shook hands.

"Well, good luck to you and your bride, Mr. Montgomery. It was a nice thing you did, moving up the wedding. I know how thrilled Mamie was."

Travis nodded, but before he could reply, the overhead hospital speaker blared Dr. Stewart's name. He sighed. "That's me. I'll check on our patient later."

"Coffee?" Patrick asked. He hitched his thumb over his shoulder. Travis saw the patient kitchen area behind the nurses' station. "C'mon. I can see the need in your eye."

"A rancher never turns down coffee."

Travis followed him to the kitchen and watched as Patrick poured two tall black coffees.

"You're taking this awfully well," Travis observed. "I mean, I would have expected you to be, well, I guess more upset."

Patrick sipped his coffee. "Mother has been sick for quite some time. I've watched her suffer and it's killing me. She might be only eighty-two, but she's got the heart and lungs of a ninety-year-old." He leaned against the wall. "I love my mother, but I'm tired of watching her suffer. She doesn't deserve that. She's an amazing woman who did wonderful acts of kindness, as a judge, as a mother and as a grandmother. I'll miss her more than words can express, but I don't want her to be in pain any longer." He looked at Travis. "Does that make sense?"

"Yeah, I understand."

Patrick glanced at him. "She's ready to die. She's tired of the struggle, and I don't blame her. She made all of her own funeral arrangements some time back. Told me she didn't want us to have to do it. She doesn't want a big to-do either. Graveside service only." He shrugged and looked away. "I didn't agree. She's been a legend in this town for years. There are a lot of people who will want to honor her by attending a funeral, but she was adamant on that. No funeral."

"I'm not sure if that's good or bad. Funerals are more for the living than the dead."

"I know, but she's my mother. This is her last request so I'll do as she wishes. She made me read her will too. That wasn't fun. But she's taken care of Noah and Caroline financially."

Travis knew he needed to say something about Caroline's financial future being secure with him as her husband, but he'd reached his lie quotient for the day. He said nothing instead.

The two men stood quietly drinking coffee for a couple of minutes.

"Well, I guess we should go find Noah," Patrick said.

"And that would be where?"

"The chapel."

The two men took the elevator to the first floor, and as Patrick had predicted, found Noah in the chapel. He didn't turn around to the noise of the door opening.

Patrick started toward the boy, but Travis held his arm. "I'll go. I'd like to talk to him."

"Fine. I'll wait outside."

Travis slipped on the pew beside Noah. "Hey."

"Hey." He hurriedly wiped his nose on the sleeve of his shirt. "How'd you know where I was?"

"Your uncle told me."

"Figures."

"Listen, I'm sorry about your grandmother. She seems like a great lady. I know you'll miss her."

Noah scoffed. "Bullshit! What do you know? Your parents are still alive, aren't they?"

Travis let Noah get away with cussing, but the kid was in some serious pain. "Yes, but—"

"Ha. What the fuck do you know then? You don't know what it's like. You've probably lived a perfect life. I bet you've got brothers and sisters too. Don't you?"

"Two brothers and a sister, but my life has been far from perfect."

Noah turned away. "You don't understand a fucking thing."

"That's enough with the cuss words. We're in a chapel. Got it?" His voice was stern and it apparently jarred Noah.

"Sorry. I'm just..." He gasped on sob. "You can't understand."

"I understand more than you can know. My wife died. She was everything to me. I was only twenty-six. She had breast cancer. We didn't know until it was too late."

Noah turned back to look at Travis. "That sucks."

Travis nodded. "Yeah, it did." He pressed his hands to his chest. "Losing Susan hurt so much I thought I would die from the pain. It felt like my heart would explode and rip me open from inside out. Some days I still miss her so much. It's like I look and expect to see her and don't. The loss will always be with you. You have to learn to live with it." He leaned against the pew cushion, stretched his arms along the back and stared at the cross under the spotlight. "Losing your grandmother's not fair, Noah. It sucks. It hurts. But do you think that your sister wouldn't try everything in her medical knowledge to heal your grandmother if she could? Do you realize how much she's in pain too?" He looked at Noah.

Noah crossed his arms. "It's not the same. Caroline's moved on. Grandma is all I've got."

"You're wrong. You've got family who care about you."

"Caroline doesn't."

Travis's brow furrowed. "Yes, she does. Why would you say that?"

"Then why didn't she ask me to come live with her instead of dumping me on Pat and Leslie?"

He put his hand on Noah's shoulder. "I'm sure she thought you would do better staying here where you have friends." He hoped he was right. This wasn't anything he and Caroline had ever discussed.

Noah didn't reply. Travis wasn't sure if the boy believed him or was too overwhelmed to talk anymore about the future.

"C'mon. Let's get back upstairs and check on your grandmother."

Seven

As Dr. Stewart had warned, Mamie Bridges's condition had not improved in the time the men had been gone from the room. If anything, Travis thought she looked worse, but his opinion could have been influenced by the plastic cannula in her nose and the IV tubing snaking up her arm. But at least the intense coughing had stopped. He moved across the room to where Caroline sat at her grandmother's bedside. Her hair was still twisted into a neat knot. Amazingly, the off-white suit still looked fresh. Stepping up behind Caroline's chair, he put both hands on her thin shoulders.

"How is she?" He was impressed with her calm, professional demeanor given he knew what she was going through.

Caroline turned to look over her shoulder at him. Her wrinkled brow and the dark shadows under her eyes reflected exhaustion and stress. "Resting. I took a glance at her medical records. Seems as bad as I thought she was, she was worse." She sighed. "I can't leave her right now."

Beneath his fingers, her shoulders were taut. Reflexively,

he gently massaged the knots he could feel drawing up her muscles. "Of course not. I wouldn't expect you to."

"Why don't you call for the limo? The driver can take you to the hotel for the night. At least you can get a good night's sleep."

"Don't be ridiculous. I'm not leaving you. I will call for the car so we can get our luggage. If we are going to be here all night, I'd rather be in something a little less formal."

The memory of the deep, bone-crushing pain of watching a loved one slip away hit him like a sledge hammer. Leslie was comforting a sobbing Noah, her arms around his shaking shoulders, her blouse absorbing his tears. At the same time, Patrick was rubbing his wife's back.

Who would hold Caroline when the time came? He feared no one if he weren't here. He couldn't leave her to face Mamie's death alone. She wore such a strong persona, he doubted the others would see through it to her shredded interior.

He'd always respected Caroline even if he hadn't known her that well. This short experience had shown him a whole new side to her. Professional doctor, sure, but more importantly, a loving woman suffering a loss no person should shoulder alone.

She covered his hands with hers. "Thank you. You don't have to stay, but I appreciate your doing so." She squeezed his fingers, which made his heart pinch. "I'd love to change clothes."

"Say no more."

Their driver must have parked in one of the hospital lots while waiting for them, because no more than five minutes passed before he was lifting their luggage from the limo's trunk. Travis handed money to the man, enough to cover their bill and a sizable tip.

"Thank you," he said. "I'm sorry about your wife's grandmother."

"Appreciate it," Travis replied.

Other than being able to retrieve her luggage, Travis felt useless until he walked back into Mamie's hospital room and a smile bloomed on Caroline's face. He straightened and returned her smile.

"Oh, thank you," she gushed. "I am so ready to get into more comfortable clothes." She stood and reached for her luggage. "My knight in shiny cowboy boots." She gave him a quick kiss and whispered, "For our audience."

"Of course," he said aloud and hugged her tight. "I'm sure we should stay here tonight." She opened her mouth to speak. "Now, don't say another word, wife. It's settled. Go change."

With her back to her family, she rolled her eyes and mouthed, "Thank you." She snatched her bag from his hand and hurried to the bathroom.

"Leslie and I feel bad about you both staying here on your wedding night," Patrick said." We'll stay. You two go on over to the hotel."

"Caroline would never rest away from Mamie tonight. I appreciate your concern, but as you said earlier, either you or Leslie have been here every night. You two go home and get some rest. Besides, I seriously doubt I could dislodge Caroline from here with rope and a winch." Travis grasped Patrick's shoulder. "Go home. I know you're both exhausted. We want to stay here. We'll see you in the morning. Okay?"

Caroline opened the bathroom door. "I heard all that and I agree. I'm not leaving Mamie tonight." She stepped out. "You too, Noah. Go home and get some sleep."

"I'm not leaving either," Noah growled. "And you can't make me."

Caroline went to where her brother sat in a corner chair. "Nobody is going to make you leave. If you want to sit here with us all night, of course you can." Then as if realizing that maybe she overstepped her bounds, her gaze snapped to Patrick. "I mean as long as it's okay with Patrick and Leslie."

Travis leaned over to Patrick. "Can I speak with you outside?"

Travis, Patrick and Leslie moved into the hall. "Let him stay. I think he and Caroline need this time together as brother and sister. If Mamie's condition worsens during the night, it'll be better if he's here. I've been through this. I know."

Leslie nodded. "I agree." She looked at her husband. "Let him stay. He needs to know everything is being done for your mother. He's young and impressionable. It'd be awful if he were to go through life wondering if something else could have been done. This way, he'll be sure your mother got the best of care. Okay?"

"Okay, but if Mother's condition does worsen, will you make sure I'm called?"

"Absolutely. Caroline has your number?"

"Yes," Leslie answered. "I'm going to go back and tell Caroline and Noah bye and get my purse."

"Thanks," Patrick said. "I hated to admit how exhausted I am. I need to get some sleep."

Travis clapped him on the back. "We'll call if anything changes. I swear."

When he went back into the hospital room, Noah stood beside Caroline. She was explaining about the oxygen, her grandmother's condition and the fluids in the IV bag. From what he could hear, she wasn't sugarcoating the situation.

As a fat tear rolled down Noah's face, Travis knew Noah got it...their grandmother was going to die, and it might be soon.

Sometime around midnight, Noah finally dropped off to sleep on the small pullout sofa. All the teenage angst and anger slipped from his face while he slept, leaving only an exhausted, scared child. Travis spread a blanket over him.

"Poor guy," he said.

Caroline looked over at Noah. "I know."

Travis pulled a chair up beside Caroline. "Why aren't you taking him with you? Why leave him here?"

She exhaled a long breath. "I just can't uproot him again. He needs the stability." Her voice dropped into a quiet whisper. "I know Mamie was having some trouble with him. I think being with Patrick and Leslie will be good. They'll make sure he gets to church and does his homework. By staying here he'll have his friends, be in a familiar place. I move too much, work long hours. I couldn't give him the supervision he needs right now."

"And your parents?"

"If you're asking if he could go to where they are, sure, but what fourteen-year-old boy wants to move to Rwanda with parents he hardly knows? Leslie said they've been in contact with Mom and Dad and they think this is the best solution right now." She glanced at her sleeping grandmother. "We'll all miss her so much. I wish you could have known her."

They watched Mamie's steady breathing for a couple of minutes. He remembered everything from Susan's final days. Watching her chest rise and fall. Watching her sleep. Wrapping her in blankets when she was cold. Wiping her face and neck with cool cloths when she was hot.

Right now, he wished there was something he could do

for Caroline. He wasn't family and really, other than recently, he hadn't had that much personal contact with her. He wasn't sure what, if anything, she needed.

He felt so impotent, so useless, which made his mind work overtime to find some way to help.

"Can I get you anything?" he asked. "Coffee? Tea? Something to eat."

She shook her head. "I'm fine."

"Why don't you take the recliner and get a little rest. I'll sit with your grandmother."

Again, she shook her head. "I'm fine," she repeated. "Why don't you take it? No sense letting it go to waste."

No way was he was going to take the recliner and leave her sitting up in a chair. He could wait her out because if her half-slit eyes were any indication, she was close to nodding off.

True to his prediction, Caroline laid her head at Mamie's side and fell asleep within thirty minutes. Once he was sure she was completely out, he picked her up to carry her to the recliner in the room.

She wrapped her arms around his neck then nuzzled her nose under his ear. Her perfume filled his senses. Her body heat soaked through his clothes. Inside, a flare sparked. She mumbled a couple of words, her hot breath blowing in his ear, sending sparks shuddering down his spine.

For Pete's sake...he was getting aroused. Bad idea. A minor attraction to Caroline he could handle. A major attraction would complicate everything.

With minds of their own, his arms pulled her tight against his chest. He dipped his nose into her hair. He allowed himself one sniff. Okay, two sniffs. That was it.

She wiggled a little, her curvy bottom rubbing against his forearm. He shut his eyes and stood statue still. He couldn't stop himself from resting his cheek on her soft hair. She felt so good in his arms.

Besides, walking across a room with an arm full of female and jeans tight with an erection would be hard for any man.

The distance between bed and recliner seemed to have grown by miles. With mixed emotions, he placed her carefully in the seat and pushed the recliner until she was supine. After tucking a blanket over her legs, he crossed the room and sat in Caroline's now vacant chair. Taking Mamie's hand, he whispered, "Judge Bridges. That's some granddaughter you raised." He swore he felt her fingers move.

He was jarred awake by the blaring of an alarm in his right ear. The last thing he remembered was getting a cup of coffee around three a.m. Apparently, he'd drifted off to sleep sometime later. He sprang from the chair, knocking it back into the wall.

Caroline pushed him away with a sharp, "Move."

"What's going on?" Noah asked, his scared expression still puffy with sleep.

Before anyone could answer, the door burst open and two scrub-clad women entered. Travis scanned the monitors, looking for the offending howler. Heart and respiration rates were slow and were slowing by the minute.

"Do something!" Noah shouted. "Don't let my nana die." He pushed his way over to Caroline. "Caroline. Do something. Why aren't they doing anything?"

One of the scrub-clad women had her stethoscope pressed to Mamie's chest. The other woman punched some buttons on the beeping machines, plunging the room into a loud silence.

Noah sniffed, blasting the quiet like a sonic boom.

Caroline moved to her brother's side and put her arm

around him. She glanced up at Travis. "Can you call Patrick and Leslie?" She held out her phone.

"Of course. Is there anything else I can do?"

She turned a sobbing Noah into her chest and shook her head. "No. We've done everything we can."

Mamie Bridges died at seven a.m., nineteen hours after marrying her granddaughter to the grandson of her brother's rival. She died a happy woman.

LATE FRIDAY AFTERNOON, Caroline climbed into the private plane Travis had leased to take them back to Dallas. She dropped onto one of the leather seats and snapped the low-riding seatbelt around her. Resting her head against the seatback, she thought about the last two days. Everything passed in a blur. Buying an appropriate outfit on Thursday for visitation and another for the graveside services on Friday. Maintaining a strong, supportive public face for Noah while losing hours of sleep at night grieving for her grandmother. She'd thought she'd been ready for Mamie's death. How wrong she'd been. She felt like there was a hole through her chest that could never be filled.

While her grandmother had requested a simple graveside service, a short family visitation had been held on Thursday night. Noah hadn't wanted to attend and the general consensus was he shouldn't have to. He and Travis had opted to go see some cutting horses Travis was interested in acquiring for his ranch. Once again, Travis had come through when Caroline had needed him. He might think he'd taken advantage of her trading his time for Singing Springs Ranch, but in the end, she knew she'd gotten much more than they'd agreed on.

On the way to the visitation, Caroline had asked that

Patrick and Leslie not mention Travis or the wedding, explaining that tonight should be about Mamie and her life, not about Caroline. They'd readily agreed so Caroline was able to simply focus her attention on the visitors without having to answer any embarrassing questions about a rushed wedding.

Friday morning broke out as a bright and sunny day. Rain would have better fit Caroline's mood. A dreary, cold rain. Exactly as she felt inside.

Noah had been inconsolable during the service, sitting alongside her sobbing. She'd tried to be strong for him, be supportive during his time of need, but she had nothing left in emotional reserves.

Travis had moved behind them, stood between their chairs, a hand placed at the junction of her shoulder and neck and a hand on Noah's shoulder. The gentle touch, the warmth of his palm on her neck, his scent were all seared into her memory. She'd wanted to turn into him, bury her face in his chest, let him carry her burden. But in the end, it'd been Noah who'd turned to Travis for support, and Travis had provided the shoulder her brother needed. And for that, she would always be in his debt.

"You okay?"

Caroline opened her eyes and looked into Travis's beautiful, crystal-blue eyes. Care and concern reflected in his grave expression. A slight frown wrinkled his brow as he leaned across the narrow aisle toward her. She wanted to rub her thumb along that crease, ease the worry from his face. Stroke her hand along his cheek, feel the scrub of the evening stubble in her palm. Instead, her hands remained clasped in her lap.

Travis was a temporary shelter in the hailstorm that was her life. She hadn't asked him to be more, and he hadn't offered more. If she allowed herself to fall in love with him—more than she already feared she was—leaving him in a few short months would be like a third death in too short a time frame.

"Thank you," she said on an exhale. "Those are such simple words that cannot begin to convey how I really feel. But they're all I've got. Thank you. I hope this week didn't stir up bad memories."

He gave her a gentle smile. "I'm glad I could be there for you and, no, no bad memories. Susan has been gone a long time."

"Do you still miss her? Love her?"

He shrugged. "I'll always love her. She was my first love. And, yes, I miss her. It's not as bad as it once was. Time does have a way of healing wounds, even deep ones."

She blew out a long breath. "The week certainly didn't turn out like I'd planned." She shook her head. "I knew Mamie's health had taken a turn for the worse, but I never expected her death to come so quickly." Unable to stop her eyes from filling with tears, large droplets rolled down her cheeks. She wiped at them with the back of her hand until Travis handed her the new handkerchief from his pocket. "Thanks," she said as she dabbed her eyes.

"Your grandmother died a very happy woman. You know that, right?" His smile got a little wider. "This crazy-assed plan worked just like you wanted. She saw you get married. She was happy. You gave her just what she wanted."

"Thanks to you," she said.

He shrugged. "Getting Singing Springs in exchange seems excessive. I would like to pay you what the ranch is worth."

She shook her head. "Absolutely not. We had a deal. Besides, don't you realize that I'm the one who got the bargain here? No, Singing Springs is yours." She sniffed then smiled. "I realize I only knew Uncle Angus for a short time, but I wouldn't be surprised if he didn't know that the ranch would somehow end up in your hands, and it has. Fair and square and to the letter of his request."

"So what are your plans now?"

"Go home. Get some rest and get back to the grindstone on Monday. I need to give Lydia some time off. She was so good to cover for me all week."

"And then?"

She frowned. "What do you mean?"

"Where to next?"

"Oh. Cut Bank, Montana. I'm supposed to be there by January fifteenth. I finish up with Whispering Springs Medical Clinic on January second, so that gives me a couple of weeks to move and get set up."

Suddenly, Montana in January didn't sound as appealing as it once had.

"That's kind of a narrow moving window, isn't it?"

"Not for me. I'm used to it. Been doing this long enough I've got moving down to a routine. Besides, I don't have that much stuff to move. Everything pretty much fits into my Honda or it doesn't go."

Like those African masks. No way would those fit into her car. Travis had shown an interest. Maybe she'd give them to him.

"Where all have you been?"

Caroline held up her charm bracelet, the action sending each charm swinging. "Every state on here is where I've been."

His eyes widened his surprise. "Wow. That's a lot of different places." He began fingering each state charm. "You never go to any state twice?"

"Sure I do." She appreciated his attempt to move the conversation away from this past week.

"But there aren't duplicate states."

"No. If I go back to a state, I usually get a charm that represents the state other than the state shape." She twisted the gold bracelet around. "For example, here is Georgia." She held out the charm in the shape of Georgia with her fingernail. "I've had contracts in Gainesville and Marietta." She dropped the Georgia charm and fingered a charm in the shape of a peach. "So I got a peach charm the next time."

"And if you go back to Georgia again?"

She laughed. "I probably won't, but if I do, maybe something from the movie *Gone with the Wind*. Anything that might symbolize Georgia. But I try to take contracts in different locations."

"Why?"

"Excuse me?"

"Why do you keep moving around? Why not your own practice, or why haven't you joined a practice?"

She shrugged. "I guess I just like to see new places."

"No Texas charm?"

"Not yet. I need to put that on my to-do list."

A tidal wave of exhaustion swept over her. "I'm so tired," she said with a sigh.

She reclined the back of her chair and shut her eyes. Right now, she didn't want to think about moving, or new places or new people. Not for the first time, she wondered if staying so long in Whispering Springs had been a good idea. She had grown some roots over the past eighteen months. Granted, they were shallow baby roots, but she felt the tug to stay fixed in the same spot.

And she could not let that happen.

As she drew in a breath, the tantalizing scent of Travis

Montgomery filled her senses. While he'd always had the power to make her knees weak, now that she'd spent so much time with him in a close environment, she knew his handsome face and muscular body only scratched the surface of his appeal. Inside, he had a caring heart. Her last thought as she dropped off to sleep was he had too much love inside to not share it with someone. Somewhere, there was a lucky woman just waiting for him to find her.

She jarred awake as the plane's tires touched the tarmac at Dallas's Love Field. She stretched her arms over her head then rotated her head from side-to-side to stretch her neck muscles.

"Feel better?"

She gave him a wan smile. "I needed that. How long was I out?"

"I have no idea. I decided to read a book after you nodded off. I made it one page before I dropped off too."

She nodded. "I doubt either of us got much sleep the last couple of nights."

"Speaking of which, as tired as you are, why don't I drive you home? I can send a couple of my men up tomorrow to pick up your car and get it back to you."

"Thanks, but no thanks. I'll be fine."

"I know you'll be fine but—"

"No," she interrupted. "Thank you, but really, there's no need for that."

"Caroline," he started, but she put her finger over his lips to stop him from saying more. She'd been dependent on him for the last few days, and while it'd been wonderful to let someone else shoulder her load, she had to get back to carrying her own baggage, no matter the weight.

"No," she repeated.

"Fine, but I'm going to at least follow you home so I know you made it."

She knew a hard-headed cowboy like Travis would keep pressing the issue, so she didn't fight it. Having spent most of a week with him, she'd discovered his propensity to protect. It'd been a long time since someone had put her first, and she found herself enjoying his attention...maybe a little too much. She had to let him go back to his life and get back to hers, but after he made sure she got home safely. Taking comfort in his concern for her, she nodded. "Okay."

Surprisingly, their two vehicles—his, a truck, and hers, an aged, small Honda—were parked very near each other in the long-term lot. They exchanged waves and climbed into their individual cars. Caroline shoved her ignition key in and turned. Nothing happened. She tried again, but there was no response from her engine. Something was dead.

Great. Just great. A perfect ending to a crappy week. She rested her forehead on the steering wheel as a tsunami-size wave of grief swamped her. Mamie was gone. A quiet wail escaped. Tears streamed down her cheeks. How would she ever make it without Mamie?

The rap on her window jarred her. The responding adrenaline rush shot her heart rate into double time. Hastily, she wiped her face and turned toward the window.

"Problem?" Travis asked.

"Car won't start."

He opened her door. "Let me take a look." He popped the car's hood and moved to the front of the 1995 Honda CRV.

Through the crack formed by the open hood, she could see him checking hoses and electrical connections. She should get out to show interest or support, but she felt like a stick of butter left in a hot car. She just couldn't force her body to move.

"Don't see anything disconnected," Travis said, leaning around the hood. "Try it again."

She did and got the same dead results.

He shrugged. "Sorry, darlin'. I'll drive you home. We can send a mechanic up tomorrow and check it out. How old is this thing?"

"I got it used in 2001."

He walked to the back hatch and opened it. After pulling her overnight bag out, he slammed it shut. "Might be time for a new one."

"I hope not."

"Come on. Let's get you home. You're as pale as the concrete under your tires."

She forced herself out of the car, which took every ounce of energy she had. Travis had already stowed her bag in the rear seat of his truck by the time she exited. He walked back and put his arm around her. She sighed and her shoulders sagged. She wrapped her arm around his waist for support. God, it felt good.

"When you get home, call Lydia. You have no business being on call this weekend. You're about to drop at my feet."

She looked up at him. "Maybe it's your devastating personality that's making me want to fall at your feet."

He laughed and pulled her tight against him. "You, Dr. Caroline Graham, are just full of surprises." He gave her a quick kiss.

They took the few steps to his truck together and he opened the passenger door. She climbed up and in.

As he slid into the driver's seat, he said, "I'm serious about Lydia. Either you call her or I will."

She arched an eyebrow. "And how would you know about my condition?"

He pulled out of the parking lot before answering. "I ran into you at the airport as I was returning from looking at some horses I am considering buying. Your car was dead and I gave you a ride home."

She shrugged. "Whatever. I'll call her."

"Do it now."

His overbearing tone stomped on her last nerve.

"Don't tell me what to do."

"Yes, ma'am."

She could have sworn the corner of his mouth twitched as though he was suppressing a smile. She snatched her purse from the back seat.

"I'm not calling Lydia because you told me to. I'm calling her so she has advance notice that I'm not quite ready to jump back in."

He nodded. "Got it," he said, followed by the twitch at the corner of his mouth.

Her conversation with Lydia was short. As soon as Lydia answered and Caroline began to explain she needed a little more time off, the pain from her loss came crashing back and she began to sob. Lydia insisted Caroline take as much time as she needed. As she pushed the button to end her call, a white handkerchief waved in front of her blurry vision.

"Thank you." She wiped her tears and blew her nose. "I'm thinking you'll want this laundered before I return it."

Travis turned his gaze on her and smiled. "See? I knew you were smart."

She stuffed the used cloth into her purse next to the one she'd used on the airplane and turned in the seat until she faced him. "Part of me is so sorry for dragging you into all the drama of Mamie's death. But a huge part of me is so thankful that you were there." She touched his arm. The muscles under her fingers tightened. "I'm not sure Noah would have made it without you. You made a big impression on him." She pulled her hand back to cover her mouth during a wide yawn. "I'm sorry."

"We've got over an hour before we get to your house. Why don't you get some sleep during the drive?"

"Are you sure you don't mind?"

"Not at all."

She leaned against the truck's door and tried to get comfortable by shifting and readjusting her position. Finally, Travis reached over and pulled her toward him.

"Scoot over here and lean on me. I'm probably softer than that door."

She did as he suggested, but boy was he wrong about being softer than the door. His shoulders and upper arms were thick slabs of chiseled muscles. Her last thought as she drifted off was whether the rest of him would be as chiseled.

TRAVIS HAD BEEN sure sitting by Caroline in church had been his worst mistake. He'd been wrong. Telling her to lean on him was. As he'd suggested, she'd rested her head on his shoulder, her left arm resting on his thigh. With each breath, warm air moved across his neck, heating more than just the flesh there. A vanilla scent wafted from her hair, and more than once he found himself taking a quick sniff. Her left hand rested just above his knee, close enough to his groin to have blood rushing to the area. His jean's crotch grew tighter with each mile. At one point, she sobbed in her sleep. He stroked her hair until she quieted.

Oh, Caroline. You are a complication I wasn't looking for in my life.

121

Eight

Her hand slid farther up his thigh, her fingers dangling right in front of his crotch. If she wiggled her fingers, she'd be stroking his cock, which seemed to like the idea as it stood up and paid attention. She sighed and nuzzled her nose against his neck. What blood had been servicing his brain dove south to his groin. As much as he hated to, he reached down and moved her hand to his knee. He suspected she would be mortified to wake up clutching his privates...not that he would mind a stroke or two from those long, slender fingers of hers.

"Caroline. We're home. You've got to wake up."

Her head snapped off his shoulder, just barely missing his chin.

"Oh my gosh. I must have fallen asleep." She yawned and rubbed the back of her neck. "Thanks for the ride home."

"I'll send someone out in the morning to take a look at your car."

"Appreciate it." She dug in her purse and came out with

a black garage opener. The double garage door began rolling up. "Pull in, okay?"

As soon as he turned off the truck, he slid from the seat and opened the back door to retrieve her bag. He'd expected to find her standing at her door ready to enter the house, so he was surprised when he turned and didn't see her.

"Caroline?"

He heard a sniff.

"Coming." The passenger door creaked open. Caroline's swollen eyes were visible even in the truck's dim overhead lighting. The keys in her hands jingled as she made her way across her garage. She unlocked the back door and turned off the alarm.

"Where do you want this?" he asked, indicating her bags with a tilt of his head.

"I'll take them." She reached for the bags.

"No, that's okay. Just tell me and I'll carry them back."

"Don't worry about it. Most of it has to go to the laundry anyway. Just leave everything here on the table."

He set the bags down.

"Travis?"

"Hmm?"

"Can you stay?"

Travis's heart skipped a beat then thudded violently against his chest. "Stay?"

She grabbed his arm. "Please. Just tonight." Tears glistened in her eyes. "I...I don't know how to explain it. I just don't want to be alone."

Using his free arm, he pulled her against him and pressed her face to his chest. "I'm so sorry. I know how you feel."

Hazy recollections of the days after Susan's death flashed in his mind. What he remembered most vividly was the black hollowness inside his chest, as though someone had cut out his heart. The pain of his loss had been so great his brain had shut off his ability to feel anything. He'd been numb. He'd needed human touch, but he hadn't realized that until years later. He'd instead reached for a bottle.

Hot tears soaked his shirt.

"I'm sorry," she said, her words vibrating into his chest. "I know that's a lot to ask and I've already asked for so much."

Placing two fingers under her chin, he lifted her face until their gazes met. "I'll stay," he said, then kissed her.

He'd meant for the kiss to be comforting. Unfortunately, he was less than comfortable afterward. He wanted more. He wanted to touch her, kiss her, take the pain away. But then what? They weren't really married and he needed to remember that. Getting involved with a woman who didn't want to be married to him and didn't want to live in Texas long-term—or live anywhere long-term as far as he could tell—was a dead-end road. He didn't need the heartache.

But he couldn't stop himself for going back for a second kiss. "I'm happy to stay. Really."

She smiled. "Thank you."

"Do you want to talk about your grandmother?"

She shook her head. "It's almost midnight. You have to be exhausted. Can we just go to bed?"

His cock twitched at the phrase go to bed. Suddenly he wasn't as tired as he'd been two minutes ago. And that dead-end road looked a lot more like an interstate.

CAROLINE TOOK his hand and led him down the hall. She rubbed her thumb along the calluses on his palm. Her mind was flooded with memories of the hugs and comforting rubs he'd given her over the past couple of days. At the funeral, she'd pressed her head to his hand resting on her shoulder as he'd nonverbally given her the emotional support she'd needed. He'd physically held her upright at the side of Mamie's casket when her legs had simply given away.

She'd been serious when she told him she needed him to stay. But she needed more. She needed to be touched, held, to feel alive. How does one ask for that? And even if she could find the words, what if he said not interested? She couldn't take the chance of rejection.

"The bathroom's that way," she said, pointing to an open door on the left. "If you don't mind, I need a quick shower."

"You do what you need to," he said. "I'm going to grab my bag out of the truck."

"Sure." She meant to let go of his arm, but her fingers refused to uncurl. They just kept clinging to him like ivy.

"Caroline. You're going to have to let go, unless your shower is big enough for the both of us." He chuckled. "I'm not leaving. I'll stay until you don't need me anymore."

He put his hand over hers holding his arm. Trapped between the heat of his rough palm and his thick muscular arm, she was sure her hand would melt. She knew her heart did. Reflexively, she leaned against his side.

"Darlin'? Are you okay?" Travis looked at her with such concern in his eyes.

"Make love to me," she said. "Make me feel alive...feel something."

He squeezed her hand. "If I thought that was what you really wanted, I'd have you on your back in one minute."

She released his arm and stepped away. "It's what I want.

It's what I need tonight, Travis. I need to be touched. Loved. Please."

He stroked his hand down her hair and sighed. "Trust me. I understand what's going on inside right now." He smiled, then grabbed her shoulders and turned her toward the master bathroom. "Go take your shower. I'll be here when you get out." He gave her a little shove. "Go. Shower."

She took a step then stopped and turned back to him. She walked back, cradled his face between the palms of her hands and kissed him. When their mouths met, a spark flashed, lighting a small fire in the darkness inside her soul. She angled her head to deepen the kiss. One swipe of her tongue on his bottom lip and he jerked her hard against him. He raked his fingers into her hair, pulling the strands taut as he positioned her to his liking. He slid his tongue between her lips and touched hers. He moved in and out of her mouth, mimicking the love making she'd asked for.

A moan vibrated her chest. Her moan? His? She wasn't sure. Her heart pounded so violently against her ribs she was sure he could feel it. She pressed her hips to the thick bulge in his jeans. He was as affected as much as she was.

As suddenly as it started, the kiss ended. Travis stepped back and pulled his hands from her hair.

"Don't start something we ain't gonna finish tonight," he said in a strained voice. "When I take you to bed, it'll be because you desire me, not because you want a warm body beside you."

"I know what I want. I want you...in my bed making love to me."

He slowly shook his head. A flash of something colored his expression. Indecision? Rejection? She wasn't sure, but it was there only for a second and then it was gone.

"No. Your emotions are a wreck. I don't want you to

hate me in the morning for taking advantage of you. So, no, that won't be happening tonight." He reached out to touch her face, but she jerked her head out of his reach.

"Damn you." She whipped toward the bathroom before he could see her embarrassment. "Leave. Just go. I don't need you. I don't need anybody." She slammed the bathroom door behind her.

Hot tears ran tracks down her face. She hadn't been with a man in a long time. Hell, she'd never asked a man to sleep with her, and the first time she does, he says no.

The shower steam fogged the mirror, finally blotting out the mortification on her face. She stepped in and let the steaming water flow over her. Hopefully, the shower jets would pound some sense into her head.

She was attracted to him and wanted sex. He wanted her ranch. If she pushed the issue, he'd probably have sex with her just to keep her happy so she didn't renege on their deal, legal paperwork notwithstanding.

But it didn't matter one way or the other. He'd be gone when she got out.

When the water finally turned cold, Caroline turned it off and reached for her towel. But even as she dried off, the embarrassment of begging Travis for sex inched back into her mind. This was worse than when Tommy Kline laughed when she'd invited him to the Sadie Hawkins Dance in eighth grade.

She sighed as she draped her damp towel over the towel rod and looked for her pajamas. The urge to beat her head against the wall was great. In her haste to get away from Travis, she'd walked into the bathroom with nothing but the clothes she wore. Her panties and pjs were still folded and tucked into her dresser drawers.

Damn it.

The light was off in the bedroom when she cracked open the door, as were all the other lights in her house. Just as she'd expected. He'd left, like everybody else in her life had.

She made her way across her bedroom and jerked open the top left drawer. "He's probably laughing at me right now," she muttered as she pulled on fresh underwear. She slammed the drawer shut and opened the next one down for a T-shirt. "I don't need him. I don't need anybody."

A bedside light clicked on. She screamed and pressed the extra-large T-shirt to her chest.

"Did you know you talk to yourself?"

She whirled toward her bed. Travis sat propped against the headboard. The bedside lamp threw an enticing play of shadow and light across taut flesh stretched tight over wide muscular shoulders, thick biceps and an impossible-to-believe six-pack. He looked like a fashion model posing for... well, to be honest, he could sell anything looking like that.

"Damn it, Travis. I'm naked."

He grinned, looking very much like a kid who'd gotten caught shaking presents under the Christmas tree. "Lucky for me my eyes had adjusted to the darkness."

She turned her back to him and pulled the nightshirt over her head before facing him again. "I thought you'd left."

"And I told you I wasn't leaving until you didn't need me." He pointed to both sides of the bed. "Wasn't sure if you slept on the right or the left, so I settled in the middle to wait."

"Travis..." A mental philosophical war raged inside Caroline. As much as she'd like to deny it, she did want him to stay. However, she needed him to want to stay, not just be doing a favor for her. But how could she tell the difference?

Truth be told, part of her would be crushed if he jumped out of bed right now and said, "Okay, then. See ya," and headed for the door. Her breath held as she waited for his next move.

He swung his legs over the side of the bed and stood. The lower half of his totally luscious body was hidden by a pair of tie pajama bottoms, not so dissimilar to what she wore in the operating room.

Her mental war continued as part of her—one very minuscule molecule—was relieved he wasn't clad just in his briefs. Most of her was disappointed. If Travis dressed solely in tie-pants was hot, heaven help her if he'd been standing there in his underwear, or better yet, wearing nothing at all.

Her heart, which had been slamming against her ribcage from being startled, now began hammering away due to the vision in front of her. Did he have any idea the effect he had on women? Was he totally clueless about how he looked? Did the poor man not own a mirror?

"Caroline. Come to bed. Nothing is going to happen but a good night's sleep, which we both need." He patted the mattress. "Left or right?"

Her sigh of surrender sounded more like a sigh of lust. She hoped he hadn't noticed. "Right."

"Good. I'm a left sleeper." He slipped back under the sheet. "Are you coming?"

I wish, she thought as she made her way around the bed and got in beside him.

"Now, here's what's gonna happen," Travis said as he put his arm around her shoulders and pulled her closer to him. "Nothing. Not a damn thing except sleep. If you need me, I'm here. Remember that."

They slid lower under the covers and put their heads on separate pillows. Caroline's head stayed on her pillow for a couple of minutes before Travis scooted closer. Then her head found comfort resting on his shoulder.

TRAVIS STRUGGLED to draw in a deep breath without waking Caroline. He'd awakened at his usual five in the morning and found Caroline's hot flesh pressed up to his. At some point during the night she'd tossed her leg over his crotch. He hesitated to disturb her out of fear she might accidently bash his stiff erection with her knee.

To add more discomfort to his situation, her nightshirt had worked its way up to her waist, exposing her satiny panties. Each time she moved in the least, the silky material polished the skin of his outer thigh. Now that he'd been awake for an hour, having his flesh buffed and shined by her hot silk-covered mons, any movement sent additional blood careening to his penis, which in turn made him more nervous that a sudden startle could maim him for life.

And his arm was dead from being under her head all night, but he wasn't complaining. He'd enjoyed the experience of sleeping with someone again. Enjoyed the comfort of not being alone. It'd been years since he'd woken up in bed with a woman. Recent sexual encounters—which were all he'd been able to emotionally manage since Susan's death —had been just attraction and sexual release. No emotional involvement. Definitely no sleepovers.

Caroline was different. Different than he'd believed her to be. Caring. Funny. And she needed him. It'd been a long time since anyone had really needed him.

Gently, he brushed her hair off her face. Dark lashes rested on her high cheekbones. Her nose was a perfect size for her diminutive face, but at this angle he could see it was a little pug on the end. For some reason that made him smile.

Her lips were slightly apart as a gentle snort escaped. Even with the petite snore, he yearned to run the tip of his tongue along her top lip, let it slide into the dip and then climb out to finish the trace to the far corner where he could continue his exploration on her lower lip.

The leg across his groin shifted and he positioned his free hand to protect the family jewels if necessary. She skimmed her calf down his thigh and across his knee before abruptly stopping. Her eyes flew open at the same time she tried to hurriedly move away.

"Stop, Caroline. You're okay."

As soon as he spoke, she stilled.

"Oh my God, Travis," she said, her hand pressed to her chest. "I forgot you were here." Under the covers she was trying to pull her nightshirt back down to her knees.

He grinned. "I think I like the fact my new wife isn't used to waking up with men in her bed."

She shoved her hair out of her face as she scooted up and over in bed. "What time is it?"

"A little after six." He yawned and scratched his morning beard.

"Thank you for staying. I slept better than I thought I would."

"First, I was happy to stay. Second, stop thanking me. It's getting old. But if you really want to show me some gratitude, you can either show me those satiny panties that rubbed on me all night or make me some coffee."

The blush on her cheeks deepened. Tugging her nightshirt down and holding the tail secure under her butt, she awkwardly climbed out of bed. "One pot of coffee coming up."

"Aw, shoot. I was afraid that would be your answer."

A blue silky robe hung on the back of a door he assumed

led to her closet. After pushing her arms down the sleeves, she spoke without looking at him. "You're a good guy, Travis. About last night..."

"Caroline."

She turned to face him.

"I meant what I said last night. You're a beautiful, desirable woman. No man in his right mind wouldn't want to make love to you. But I like you too much to have taken advantage of your emotional state last night. When we make love, it'll be because of good old lust and need." He grinned. "We okay this morning?"

A half-smile tweaked her lips. "We're okay. Coffee won't take long. I'll get some breakfast going. Anything in particular you'd like?"

"Besides seeing your panties? Man food. No yogurt. No health food."

"Forget the panties, bud. You didn't want to see them last night so you're not seeing them this morning. Bacon, eggs and biscuits are what you're getting." As she walked through the door she looked over her shoulder. "Hey, Travis."

When he looked toward her, she flipped her robe and nightshirt, exposing her cute silk-covered butt. "Changed my mind." Then she walked into the hall.

A wide grin split his face.

She was not what he expected.

BY THE TIME Travis finished his phone calls—first to a garage about Caroline's car and then to the Webster household—he had firm plans for the day, if he could convince Caroline to go along. He showered and made his way to the kitchen, bypassing the formal dining room that he noted was not set for a fancy breakfast. In the kitchen, Caroline had set breakfast on the small glass table in the nook formed by a bow window.

"Okay to eat in here?" she asked.

He inhaled and his stomach let out a loud growl that could be heard four blocks over.

"With the way that smells, I'd eat standing at the stove."

Laughing, she set the plate holding golden, buttery-looking biscuits on the table. She pointed to a cabinet. "Coffee mugs are there. Black, right? Can't remember you adding anything when we've had coffee at your parents' place."

Dramatically widening his eyes and dropping open his mouth, he gasped. "Darlin', I'm a Texas cowboy. We don't need no stinkin' milk and sugar," he said as he opened the cabinet door to retrieve a mug. He filled it to the rim and carried it over to the table.

She shook her head with a chuckle. "Silly me."

"If you're goin' to be a cowboy's gal, you gotta learn the rules."

After settling into a chair, she said, "Black coffee. Got it. What else?"

"Meat and potatoes. No sissy food."

She pretended to take notes on an imaginary notepad. "No sissy food. Right. Umm, exactly what would sissy food consist of?"

"You know, sissy stuff. Yogurt. Granola. Shrimp. Green stuff."

The corners of her mouth twitched. "Shrimp is sissy?"

He shoved a biscuit and sausage into his mouth and chewed. After swallowing and taking a sip of coffee, he continued. "Well, shrimp might be okay if it's grilled on a manly, outdoor grill. No shrimp stirred up with pasta."

She rested her elbow on the table and propped her chin in the palm of her hand. "Wow. I had no idea there were so many rules. What else should every good cowboy's gal know?"

"We don't wear shorts. Don't starch the work shirts. And, um..."He paused to make-up a few more rules. "Oh yeah, never ever set a cowboy's hat on its brim. Always set it upside down on its top." Except that rule wasn't made up. He was dead serious.

"Are you serious? About the hat?"

"Yup."

She gave him a thoughtful nod. "I didn't know that."

"Like I said, important stuff." He snagged another biscuit off the plate. "By the way, I called a buddy who has a garage. He's going to tow your car in today and have a look. Said it might be Monday before he can get to it."

She nodded. "Thanks." She sighed. "I hope I don't have to buy another one."

"You need a better car, Caroline. You can afford it, I'm sure."

"That's not the point. I've never been much of a car person, as long as what I have gets me where I need to go. Plus," she made a face, "I hate dealing with car salesmen."

"Fine. I'll let you know as soon as I've heard from Buddy. Now, since you're off today, I had an idea."

"Oh?"

"How much of Singing Springs have you seen?"

She shrugged. "Mostly the area immediate to the house."

"Great. Henree is making us a picnic lunch. I thought we could take a couple of the horses, ride over the property so you can really see it and then have lunch by the spring. Have you ever seen the spring the ranch is named for?"

CYNTHIA D'ALBA

When she shook her head, he continued. "You really need to. Nicest piece of land in this area."

She looked away from him as she drummed her fingernails on the table. Nervous? Of him? Of being alone with him?

Of course not. They'd been alone for days.

Then he had a thought that made his heart sputter. Was she afraid to see Singing Springs because she was having second thoughts about their deal? What would he say if that was the situation?

She stood and began collecting the dishes from the table. He reached out to wrap his fingers around her wrist and hold her still.

"What's wrong?"

Pulling out of his grasp she turned toward the kitchen counter. "Nothing."

"You are the worst liar," he chided. "Fess up. What's going on in that brain? Don't you want to see Angus's place?"

The dishes rattled when she set them firmly on the counter. "Can't we see Singing Springs by car?"

The legs of his chair scraped the floor as he pushed back and stood. "No, we can't. Riding the property is the best part. Webster is saddling a couple of horses for us. We'll be able to see a lot of the land by horseback."

Her knuckles were white from the death grip she had on the counter's edge. "I don't know. I've been away from the clinic. Maybe I should run by and see if there's anything on my desk that needs my attention."

When he put his hands on her shoulders to turn her around, he could feel her tension. "It's Saturday. No one is there today."

"But—"

"But nothing." When she turned, he hated what he saw. Her face was ashen. Her eyes wide with fear. The artery in her neck throbbed visibly. "Hey. What's going on? You look scared to death." He pulled her into a hug. "Whatever it is, tell me. Maybe I can help."

She mumbled something into his shoulder. He gently pushed her back until their gazes met.

"What?"

"I don't know how to ride a horse."

"Oh, Caroline." He smiled and pulled her back against him. "That's not a problem. You have jeans?"

She nodded.

"And some boots?"

She nodded again. "For some reason, your mom gave me a pair for my birthday."

"Then throw those on with a blouse, which is of course always optional, and I'll teach you. I've got the gentlest gelding. You'll love him. Name's Willard."

"But what if he starts running away with me? I won't know what to do."

Travis laughed. "Willard has been in my barn for years. He won't run away with you. Trust me." He hugged her then pushed her away. "Go get dressed."

By the time they got to his ranch, Caroline's jitters were close to full-blown panic. He pulled into his garage, turned off his truck and turned toward her.

"Caroline."

She jumped. When she turned to face him a cute pink blush was tinting her cheeks.

"I'm not going to force you to do this, you know."

She sighed. "I know. This is so silly. I'm thirty-two years old and I've never ridden a horse."

He draped his arm along the back of the bench seat.

"Honestly, there's nothing to be scared of. I'll be by your side all the time. Willard is gentle enough that I would let my nephew ride him. Trust me?"

Her nod came quickly. "Yes."

He stepped from the truck and hurried around to her side before she could change her mind. After opening her door, he extended his hand to help her climb down from his truck.

"C'mon. I'll make a cowgirl out of you yet. You'll never want to leave."

"Is that right?" she said with a laugh as she stepped to the ground.

"Yes, ma'am, it is."

He should have dropped her hand once she was standing safely on the concrete of his garage, but he didn't. He wasn't exactly sure why he didn't except that he liked how her hand felt in his. But that was okay. She wouldn't be in his life long. He might as well enjoy it while he could.

Nine

W hen Travis led her horse from the barn, Caroline stifled a relieved laugh and grinned. Willard was a gray-colored gelding who looked as though he hadn't missed a meal in years. His eyes sparkled as though he was glad to be out of the barn. As hard as it was not to back up, she held her ground as Travis led the horse up to her.

"Caroline," he said formally. "This is Willard. Willard, this is Caroline." He leaned in close as though to whisper a secret to the horse. "Don't tell anyone, but she's my temporary wife so you have to be nice to her. Understand?"

He pulled on the reins so the horse's head came down and back up as though nodding an agreement. Caroline chuckled.

"Hello, Willard," she said as she held out her hand for the horse to sniff. "Is that what I'm supposed to do? Let him smell me?"

"No. Step over here by his side and talk to him. You can stroke his neck or his face. He likes that." He handed her a wrapped peppermint. "Plus, he loves peppermint." He leaned to her as though imparting a secret. "Helps his breath too."

With a wide grin, she took the peppermint in the palm of her hand. She stepped to Willard's side and ran her palm along his neck. The muscles in his neck rippled.

"He's so soft," she said, enjoying the feeling of soft horse hair.

"Hey!" Travis said with a grin. "He's a boy horse. We aren't soft, right, boy?" He patted the horse on his neck. "We're manly men. Go ahead and hold out your hand with the treat."

Soft horse lips brushed her flesh as Willard sucked the mint from her hand and chewed. Her palm felt like she'd rubbed a clothing lint brush across it.

"Okay, enough messing around. Let's get saddled up."

"Umm..."

"Got you covered. I have a mounting block for Adam, Olivia's son." He pointed to a raised rounded platform that looked like a tree stump. When she reached the mounting block, she saw it was the base of a large tree.

"Step up," Travis said.

She did.

He led Willard over. "Put your left foot in the stirrup and swing your right leg over."

When she looked at him, she crossed her eyes and he laughed. Then she did what he said and found herself high off the ground on the back of a horse that suddenly looked a lot bigger and meaner than he had. Her heart slammed against her chest. She grabbed the knob on the saddle and held on with shaky hands.

She didn't want to look like such a wuss, but she felt like someone had rolled up a king-sized comforter and shoved it between her legs...not that Willard was soft like a plush comforter, but her legs were being shoved wide apart—wider apart than she'd spread her thighs in a very long time. The leather saddle creaked when she shifted trying to find the impossible soft place in the seat. How could a cowboy sit on something so hard for hours on end?

"Rocky!" Travis hollered over his shoulder. "Come over here and hold Dr. Graham's horse while I get Ransom." He looked back up at her and smiled. "Looking good up there, Doc."

Caroline tried to smile but her lips were stuck to her teeth. She licked her lips and tried again. Travis chuckled.

"Trust me, darlin'. I've never lost a date yet."

"First time for everything," she muttered, causing him to laugh again.

A young teenage boy hurried over and took the reins. Travis headed toward an even larger horse than the one she sat on. He stepped into a stirrup and slung himself on top of the enormous black horse. "Be right back," he said before turning his horse and riding back into the barn. In a minute, he was back carrying a straw cowboy hat. He walked the horse over to where she waited and slapped the yellow hat on her head.

"Olivia left this hat here last month. Sun's a little bright today. This should help keep it off your face."

"Thanks." She settled the hat firmly on her head. "Okay. Ready, I think."

"Hold the reins like this." He demonstrated how loosely he held them and the proper lacing of the leather strings.

She tried to emulate his actions but her fingers were shaking just too much. But she got the grip close enough that he nodded.

"Great. Let's go." Clicking his tongue, he gave Ransom a tap with his heel.

When Ransom moved, Willard followed. She clung to the saddle horn, so afraid she would fall off, embarrassing both of them. But she didn't fall. Her butt slid side-to-side in the leather seat with each of Willard's steps. Travis waited for them to catch up and then rode beside her as they headed out of the barn area and into an open field. He glanced over and smiled.

"You're doing great."

"I'm scared to death."

He chuckled. "So tell me about growing up in Arkansas."

The talking helped, as did the slow pace. Thinking about Arkansas and remembering the good details of her life kept her mind focused there and not on the fact she felt like she was on top of a moving mountain. When they reached the fence that separated Halo M from Singing Springs, she was surprised to find a well-maintained gate. Travis leaned over, opened it and then followed her through before relocking it.

"Your animals are looking good," he said with a point of his chin toward a pasture in the distance. "Hancock is doing a good job for you."

"Thank goodness," she said as they continued to walk the horses. "I was relieved when he agreed to continue helping with the livestock." She looked at him out of the corner of her eye. "What do you mean 'my livestock'? This place is yours, not mine."

He shook his head. "Go back and look at our deal. I took the ranch, but there's nothing in there about the stock."

"Travis! Are you kidding me? What am I going to do with....cows?"

He shrugged. "Don't know. You might need to make a deal with the new owner."

She laughed. "You're an ass." He grinned in response and she felt a sexual tug low in her gut. The man had no idea what one of his smiles could do to her.

"Tell me more about your next stop on your never-ending medical tour."

For the first time, thinking about moving on—moving away from Travis and Whispering Springs—brought a wave of uncertainty crashing over her. Usually, she was more than ready to move on when the time came. This time? Not so much.

"Headed to Montana." She explained about the pregnant doctor up there and how she would be filling in during the eight-week maternity leave. They talked about all her moves, the ones she'd liked, the ones she hadn't.

After about an hour, they turned the corner and came upon a babbling stream. Near the water's edge, under a tree, someone had spread a red blanket. Sitting in the middle of the spread was a large wicker picnic basket. To the side was a red and white cooler.

"Travis. Did you do this?"

He grinned. "Had one of the Webster kids run it over after we left. They'll come back and get everything when we leave." He swept his arm toward the setting. "I promised you a picnic."

He hopped from his horse as naturally as he walked. He tied the reins to a tree and came to where she and Willard stood.

"Need some help?"

"Please."

"Stand up in the stirrups, swing your right leg over and lower yourself to the ground."

She rolled her eyes. "You make it sound so easy."

"It is. Trust me. Besides..." He moved closer to her left foot. "I'll be here to help."

She stood, tried to lift her right leg, which refused to bend, throwing her off-balance. As she tilted backwards, a pair of large, strong hands circled her waist and lifted her down. Glad to be on solid ground, she opened her mouth to say so, but her knees took that moment to buckle. She grabbed at Travis's shoulders for support. He tightened his hands and pulled her to him. Her breasts flattened against his firm chest. Her breath caught as she looked up into his blue eyes.

If she kissed him right now, would he be shocked? Back away? Return the kiss?

A bead of sweat rolled down his throat. She ached to lick it, taste his saltiness, draw his flavor onto her tongue. Her tongue flattened against the roof of her mouth. Her mouth opened. But he didn't give her the chance to kiss or taste him.

Forearms thick with muscle and sinew wrapped around her legs, swept her up and carried her over to the soft blanket holding their lunch. He knelt, letting her legs slide onto the ground.

"I am so embarrassed." She dropped her head against his shoulder, not wanting to look into his eyes.

"Why? I'm the one who should have his ass kicked. I should have remembered what a first horseback ride can do to legs." Putting two fingers under her chin, he lifted her head until their gazes met. He shook his head, looking disgusted. "I'm sorry, Caroline. Feel free to call me a few choice names. Dunderhead. Idiot. Whatever."

She stared into his steel-blue eyes, her breathing coming in deep draws. For a minute, neither of them moved, and then she placed her hand on his face. "Here are my choice names for you. Wonderful. Thoughtful. Caring. Do those work?" She smiled, ready to move on. He didn't need to know any more about what she really thought about him. She dropped her hand from his face and made a point of looking around the picnic area. "This setting for lunch is perfect. I'm glad we rode over. I can't believe how much of Uncle Angus's ranch I've gotten to see today. It's beautiful. I can see why you wanted it."

He caught her hand and brought it to his mouth, leaving a kiss in the palm. For what seemed like eternity, they stared into each other's eyes, neither making the move to come closer nor to move away. His warm breath blew on her face. With each inhale, she breathed in his scent, a mixture of woodsy cologne, leather and something that was just Travis. She'd made up her mind to kiss him just as her stomach took that exact moment to rumble loudly. He smiled, leaned over and gave her a quick kiss.

"Sounds like you could use lunch."

She dropped her face into her hands and shook her head, laughing away her sexual frustration. Travis moved away far enough to get a hand on the basket handle and dragged it over.

"Let's see what goodies we have in here."

Strapped on the inside of the lid were two plates, knives and forks and two red-and-white plaid napkins.

"I'll get the food out," Caroline said. "See what we've got to drink."

Travis stood and retrieved the cooler. Looking inside he said, "Looks like ice tea, water and some Cokes." He grinned. "And I do believe there is a container of potato salad. You are going to love Henree's potato salad."

Caroline was pulling a container of hot biscuits out of

the basket to set alongside the fried-chicken strips. "This all smells heavenly." She drew in a deep breath. "And I'm starved."

They loaded their own plates, grabbed bottles of water and settled in to eat. For the first few bites, Caroline couldn't help but moan. Travis had been right. Henree was a wonderful cook.

"So, Travis," Caroline said, wiping her mouth with her napkin. "Tell me about growing up here. Your family seems so close."

He nodded and then washed the large bite of chicken and biscuit down with half the bottle of water. "We are. You know everybody except my brother, Cash, right? The one who's on the PBR tour?"

"Never got a chance to meet him. Is Cash his real name?"

"No. A nickname, and Mom hates it." He grinned. "Everybody thinks he got that name from all the rodeo winnings, but that's not it at all. When we were growing up, there wasn't a dare Cash wouldn't take, as long as there was money involved." He laughed. "He got pretty fast evading bulls, rolling unmanned tractors, you name it."

Travis continued on with his stories as Caroline set her empty plate off the blanket on the grass and lay on her side, her head propped in her hand. She watched his luscious lips move as he talked. Watched his Adam's apple slide up and down with each pull on his water. Enjoyed ogling the muscles in his arms as they bunched and flexed and show-cased their beauty with each movement. As she watched him talk and gesture and laugh, her insides tumbled like clothes in a dryer...jumbled and hot. He was pure raw male, and the female inside her roared her approval.

Above, birds sang and flew from tree to tree. The sun

painted muted stripes on the blanket and across Travis's lap. With each breath, she drew in both the earthy scent of the grass beneath them mixed with Travis's masculine aroma. The combination hit her like a powerful aphrodisiac. She licked her lips and tried to slow her runaway heart.

This wasn't real life, she cautioned. This was a temporary arrangement known only to her and him. He was being a class act, a real friend today. *Don't do anything that could put a roadblock on that friendship.*

Satisfied she'd talked herself down off the I-am-going-to-jump-him ledge, she drew in a deep breath and sighed in total contentment.

Travis set his plate inside the basket and then lowered himself onto his side, lying face-to-face with Caroline. The end of his lips lifted into a smile as he brushed a few wayward strands of hair off her face. The roughness of his fingers ignited the nerve endings in her skin, reviving all those emotions she'd just squashed. She pressed against his hand and allowed her eyes to drift shut. She wanted to experience his touch without any visual distractions. Wanted to lock this feeling into her memories.

His scent grew stronger seconds before his full lips touched hers. She angled her head, wanting to get as much lip-to-lip flesh touching as possible. He wrapped his hand around her head and held her as he plunged his tongue through her open lips. She gave him full access to her mouth, welcoming his tongue's touch in every nook and cranny. Powerful electrical surges flashed through her body. The area between her thighs grew hot and damp.

He pulled away and she opened her eyes. His steel-blue eyes were dark with desire. His breaths came in jagged pants. Reaching out, she put her hand behind his head and pulled him back to her for another kiss. This time she took control, probing and tasting, licking his tongue, his teeth...allowed her tongue to convey her message. She wanted him.

Apparently message received, Travis scooted across the blanket and lowered Caroline onto her back. He moved his hand to her waist and squeezed. The heat from his palm burned through her shirt as he slid it from her waist to the curve of her breast. He fondled her flesh as a shudder wracked her body. Caroline slid her tongue in and out of his mouth, trying to say without words what she wanted...needed.

She draped her leg over his hard-as-a-tree-trunk thigh and tried to press her aching center to his body...anywhere. But he took control, moving between her legs, pressing the hard erection behind his zipper against her center. She moved to press back, moaned deep in her throat.

He found the tail of her shirt, slipped his hand under and touched her skin, igniting flash fires with each stroke of his fingers. Surely she would burst into flames.

Then he was gone. Rolled away and onto his back.

Stunned and embarrassed at her own guttural reactions to his attentions, she stared up into the sky.

"Caroline..."

"Don't," she snapped. "Don't you dare apologize."

"Okay. I won't. But that wasn't what I was going to say."

She rolled onto her side and propped up her head. "What then?"

He turned his head to look at her and then turned away. "I was going to say I was too old for sex on hard ground." He looked at her and grinned. "I was going to suggest a soft bed instead."

She smiled. "Hmm. Sounds interesting."

"Ready to head home?"

"For a soft bed? You bet."

They made quick work of stashing everything either in the cooler or the basket. When it came time to remount, Caroline forced a smile. Travis laughed at her expression.

"Trust me. This ride will be as bad for me as for you."

She glanced down at the erection straining the zipper of his jeans. As she watched, the bulge got more pronounced.

"Stop looking at me," he said. "You're not helping."

He brought Willard over. She put her left foot in the stirrup and then felt both his hands covering her ass cheeks. He pushed and she found herself in the saddle.

Looking down at him, she smiled. "Well, getting on Willard like that was fun."

He gave her a cocky smirk. "That's what all the girls say."

She rolled her eyes but couldn't keep the grin off her face.

The ride back to Halo M was quicker than the ride away as Travis didn't need to kill any time, and frankly, he didn't want to either. He wanted Caroline Graham naked and in bed as fast as possible. And he hadn't been kidding about being too old for screwing outside. His knees weren't the best. They preferred a bed. His biggest fear now was that she'd change her mind before he could toss her on her back.

When they rode into the barnyard, Amy Webster, the oldest of the Websters' offspring was waiting.

"Have a good ride?" she asked, catching Willard's bridle.

"Good ride and good lunch. You have anything to do with the food?" Travis said as he swung from the saddle. He looped Ransom's reins over a rail.

Amy's face pinked. "Maybe."

"You want to take the Rhino and go pick up the leftovers?"

He'd hardly gotten the question finished before Amy took off at a run toward a large shed.

"I gather that whatever a Rhino is can be found in that shed?" Caroline asked, shading her eyes with her hand.

"It's a large all-terrain vehicle. It can carry a couple of people and has a holding tray on the back."

The shed doors flew open, and moments later, a green Rhino ATV roared out and across the field.

"So are you telling me that we could have taken a car-like thing rather than horses today?"

Travis walked over and began massaging her calf. "But then what excuse would I have to offer you a massage tonight?" Mentally, he crossed his fingers that she was still interested in massages, soft beds and sex. His heart raced as he waited for her response.

"In that case, as much as I love you, Willard," she said, leaning over the horse's neck, "I've got a better offer." She smiled down at Travis. "Help me down, please."

As before, she stood in the stirrup and this time was able to get her right leg swung over Willard's rump before tumbling into Travis's outstretched arms.

"You okay, Dr. Graham?"

Travis and Caroline's heads whipped toward the voice. John Webster stood just outside the barn, his hands on his hips, apparently watching Travis and Caroline's interaction.

"Fine, John. Just helping Caroline off. Did you know this was her first time to ride? She did great, I tell you, just great. Why, I bet we could make a first-rate rider out of her."

Why was he running on like he'd been caught by his parents with his hands down a girl's pants?

Webster cleared his throat. "Well, okay then. I'll take those horses from you. Rocky's here. Putting Ransom and Willard up for the night will give him something to do. Did

I hear you ask Amy to take the Rhino over to Fitzgerald's place?"

"Yep. You mind?"

"Naw. You're just spoiling her. You know she loves the fast machines."

"You can put me down now," Caroline whispered into his ear.

Chills hiked down each vertebrae of his back. Her breathy voice also got the attention of his penis, which began to come alive. He turned away from John. "Oh, right. Sorry." He lowered her legs to the ground but kept his hands at her waist until he was sure she would support herself. To his disappointment, she didn't need him to hold her up.

"I need to have a word with John. Can I meet you in the truck?"

"No problem," she said, and headed off, her walk a little wobbly.

"Tell Henree I might have a guest for a couple of days. Caroline...er, Dr. Graham's grandmother just passed away. Since she doesn't have any family here, I've been trying to give her some support...help her work through her emotions."

It felt like trying to explain to his dad why he needed to stay out all night after senior prom.

The foreman removed his cowboy hat, scratched his head and put it back on. "Now what you do with your time is your business, Travis. I'll just say I think Dr. Graham is a fine woman, and if you can help her right now then that's where you should be."

"Thanks." He turned to leave and then turned back. "And John, my family doesn't need to know anything about how I spend my time."

. . .

TRAVIS CLIMBED into his truck and glanced at Caroline, who was as far against the passenger door as she could be. He reached over and took her hand.

"Hey. We don't have to do anything. No pressure."

Her eyes were wide, her pupils dilated. Her breathing was loud and ragged. "Don't you want to sleep with me?"

He laughed. "Are you kidding? Look at me." He gestured to his crotch. His erection was straining against his zipper. "And why wouldn't I want you? God, you're beautiful. Funny. Smart. Sexy. Hell, Caroline. I've been wanting you for months."

The smile that crossed her lips lit her face like a thousand-watt bulb. "Seriously?"

"Let me show you how seriously."

He meant to take her to her house, but hells bells, that was a forty minute drive. His house was attached to his garage. He had a soft bed. He had condoms.

He jerked open the driver's door and pulled Caroline across the seat and out.

"Where are we going?" she said as he pulled her along into his home.

"I have a bed. It's closer."

Her reply was a grin and an increase in her pace.

She got a quick glimpse of a large stainless-steel kitchen that appeared spotless as he led her through. Then a comfortable living room, but the trip was too fast to discern much about it. Finally, they went through a door and down a short hall into a large room, the focal point being a raised four-poster bed. A fluffy blue comforter covered the mattress. She was surprised when he bypassed the bed and led her into a plush, granite master bathroom. He reached around a wall made of glass bricks and flipped on the shower.

"Are you suggesting I need a bath?" she asked with a wicked grin.

"Before I toss you into my bed, I need to wash Ransom off me," he said and stripped his shirt over his head. A set of developed pectoral muscles and a ribbed abdomen made her groan in pleasure. Light blond hair dusted his chest and down his abdomen, disappearing into the waistband of his jeans.

Her sex tingled with heat and need.

"You don't have to join me," he continued as he unfastened his belt and pulled it through the loops. "But you sure are welcome to." He lowered his zipper and shoved his jeans and underwear to the floor in one motion.

His penis rose from a bed of dark, curly hair and stretched up, resting on his abdomen. She licked her lips. She couldn't take her eyes off of him, which just made his cock grow thicker and longer.

"I'm feeling pretty dirty myself," she said with a raspy voice. Quickly, she toed off her boots and kicked them back into the bedroom. He reached over to help her and jerked her shirt over her head. He cupped her breasts before leaning over to run his tongue along the top of each cup.

"Perfect," he said. "I knew they'd be perfect."

He sucked on her breast through her bra and then bit her nipple. Her knees grew weak. Liquid heat dampened her panties. The tingle between her legs had grown to an aching throb. Then her bra was gone, replaced by his hot mouth, sucking, licking, nibbling, biting then licking again. She felt for her jeans button, popped it and quickly lowered her zipper. He slid a large, work-roughened hand into her panties and between her thighs. Then he slipped a thick finger into her wet folds.

"You're so wet," he said. "So wet. I can smell your arousal." He pulled his hands from her panties and licked his finger. He watched her, watched for her reaction.

Her breath caught for a moment as her insides turned to liquid. She reached out and took his penis in her hand. It was hard yet velvety soft. She stroked her thumb over the spongy head, collected his juices on her thumb, lifted it to her mouth and licked the salty fluid.

His growl was primal, animalistic. He roughly shoved her jeans and panties to the floor and then lifted her out of them and walked into the shower. Water poured down their bodies, making each touch, each stroke, slippery and more erotic.

He pushed her up against the wall and spread her legs with his knees. Sexual excitement strummed through her. He stroked large, work-toughened hands over the inside of her thighs and thick fingers up to her wet crease. He looked into her eyes, slipped a broad finger inside her. She moaned and arched toward him. He added another finger, moving both in and out, stretching her, getting her ready for him.

She stroked his cock in time with the movement of his fingers. He pulled his hips away and turned so that she couldn't touch him.

"Can't, darlin'. You're driving me over the edge just being here. I can't take your touch. It'll be over before it begins."

She bit his neck and then licked up his throat until she reached his mouth. "Next time, then," she said against his lips.

He moved his fingers at a fast pace and her hips gyrated in time. Then he pulled his fingers from her and dropped to his knees. He broadened her stance when he pushed his wide shoulders between her thighs. He flicked his tongue out, licked her from front to back and then traced a circle around her sensitive nub. Her legs wobbled and she grabbed his shoulders to stay upright. He licked again and again from her vaginal opening to her clitoris and back until she began to shake.

The muscles in her abdomen clenched and shook. The pressure building inside was almost painful in its intensity. He jabbed his tongue into her sex at the same time he pushed a finger into her ass. She cried out as she exploded into a million pieces. White lights flashed behind her closed eyelids. Wave after wave of electrical force like none she'd ever experienced continued to wrack her body until she could no longer stand unsupported. She slumped against the shower wall.

"Holy hell," she muttered.

When she opened her eyes, Travis wore a very self-satisfied smile. "Like that?" he asked.

She licked her lips and forced a shrug. "It was okay."

"I'll see if I can make it better than just okay."

Ten

Sunday morning, Caroline awoke in a strange bed with a naked man draped across her. Her heart slammed into panic mode until she remembered the preceding night and the rounds of sex. Damnation. The man had an incredible body and knew how to use it...and how to use hers too.

She stretched and muscles that hadn't been exercised in a while complained. She was sore...in such a good way.

Even though she knew last night didn't change anything, that they were still only friends, maybe she could claim some friends-with-benefits time.

A moan from the naked man in question made her laugh.

"Don't laugh," he said in a gravelly voice. "I'm too old to have sex that many times in one night."

"Please," she said. "No wonder Elsie Belle Lambert is after you."

He rolled over to face her. "Elsie Belle has never, and will never, be in my bed." He burrowed his head into his pillow. "Must be my sex-god reputation."

She couldn't restrain her hearty laugh. "Really? I can't believe I've been here for over eighteen months and nobody has ever mentioned your sex-god status."

"Closely guarded secret."

"I see. Well, does sleeping with a sex god get me breakfast?"

"Depends," he said, rising up on one elbow. "What are you cooking?"

After hitting him with a pillow, she climbed from the bed. Her thighs protested. First the horseback ride and then the Travis ride. It was more activity than they'd had in years, and they were letting her know it.

Heading back to the bathroom, she washed her face and found her clothes. Travis was still in bed when she got back to the bedroom, but he was sitting up against the headboard. Flesh, tanned from days of sun, pulled taut over firm, corded muscles formed from years of riding and hard labor. The sight of his chest—all naked and muscular and totally luscious—made her mouth water.

"Feeling better?" he asked, an expression of concern on his face.

"I am. Thank you. Yesterday was what I needed."

He patted the bed and she sat on the edge.

"I want you to stay here for a few days. Let the world go by without you."

"I wish I could, Travis, but I feel so guilty about leaving all the work to Lydia."

"But you'll be leaving soon anyway, right? You'll be leaving Lydia with the patient load then."

His words made her flinch. He was right, but that would be different. Her contract would be up. Her commitment fulfilled.

"I wish I could stay, Travis, but—"

"No buts. If you want to stay a few days, then do. If you feel you have to go back to work, then go. But come back here at night. Henree will leave us something wonderful to eat. You won't have to do anything at night but relax."

She wanted to snort. Relax? Around him? Mr. Sex God?

"As a friend, I want to be there for you right now. Stay, okay?"

As a friend. The words hurt, but at least she knew where they stood. She forced a smile she didn't feel. "Okay."

His face lit up with a grin she was sure had always made girls do what he wanted. "Great. I'll let Henree know I have a guest for a few days. They'll keep your presence to themselves. I promise."

She started from the room and stopped. "Damn."

"What?"

She turned. "My car. I need a phonebook. I'll have to rent one until I hear from your car guy."

"Maybe not." He got up from the bed, seemingly not at all concerned that he wore nothing but his skin...which did fit him quite well. And she should know. She was a doctor who'd spent the better part of the night exploring it up close.

She glanced away. Honestly. Was he so dense he had no idea what he did to her? Just looking at that body made her mouth water.

"I'll meet you in the kitchen," she said and made a dash down the hall before she unzipped the zipper she'd heard him close.

The heavenly aroma of coffee scented the air as Caroline hit the kitchen door. Apparently set on a timer, her morning choice of caffeine was hot and waiting. She pulled a couple of mugs down from the cabinet and was filling them when Travis entered.

"Here," he said, handing her a set of keys.

"What are those?"

"Keys."

She rolled her eyes. "Yes, I got that part. To what?"

He grinned. "Look, I've got a car I never drive. Take it until we know about yours."

"I don't know, Travis."

"Don't argue, and don't make more out of this than it is. Your car died. We're friends. I'm loaning you my old car until you get yours back." He made his way over the coffee. "No big deal."

Friend. There was that word again. Funny how much it hurt to hear that word this morning.

Screw it. She needed wheels.

"Thanks. I'll take care of it. What am I driving? Old truck?"

"2012 Porsche 911."

She handed him the keys back. "Uh-Uh. No."

He pressed the keys back into her hand. "It needs to be driven. You'd be doing me a favor. Really."

He closed his fingers around hers. The emotional jolt had her shaking. She pulled her hand away, taking the keys with her. "Insured?"

"Of course."

"Convertible?"

"Yes."

"Ever want it back?"

He grinned. Her knees softened. Her toes curled. Damn. The man was dangerous.

"Yes, I want it back."

"We'll see," she said. "I need to run. I'd like to get home in time to change and make it to church this morning."

"Hang on and I'll go with you."

She shook her head. "No. It's better if we don't start appearing in public as a couple. No need to feed the gossip trolls."

"You sure? It won't take me very long to get ready."

"I'm sure."

She stepped closer to him. "Thanks for being such a good friend." She snaked a hand behind his head and pulled him down for a kiss. "Later."

TRAVIS HEARD the roar of the Porsche's engine and he smiled. If only she could have seen her face when he'd told her about his car. There was no way she wasn't going to drive it.

A couple of hours later, he was standing in the Whispering Springs United Methodist Church when his black Porsche roared into the lot.

"Ain't that your car, bro?" Jason asked.

"Loaned it to Caroline. Hers died."

Jason's brows furrowed. "If I remember correctly—and I do—seems like you told me to take a hike when I asked to borrow it."

"You don't look good in a dress. Excuse me." Travis walked over to his car as Caroline was climbing out. "How'd she run for you?"

"You're kidding, right? I left a group of high school boys with their tongues hanging out when I passed them."

"Maybe it wasn't the car," he suggested.

She closed and locked the door. "Right." She snorted. "But I do love new-car smell."

Jason stood at the church door waiting. "Morning, Caroline. I was so sorry to hear about your grandmother."

"Thank you, Jason. I'm afraid I've left your fiancée shorthanded all week."

"She hasn't complained, but I know the office missed you."

"That is so sweet. Thank you for saying that."

"That's a fine looking car you're driving."

Travis glared at his brother, who noticeably ignored him.

"It's a loaner," she said.

Jason laughed. "Come on," he said, holding his arm out. "Let me escort you inside."

Caroline took Jason's arm. Travis gritted his teeth. His brother was so dead.

"Thanks, Jason," Caroline said as she slid into her usual church spot. Fitzgerald side, third row, directly across from the Montgomery family. "You and Travis go join your family."

Travis caught her eye and pointedly looked at the spot next to her. She subtly shook her. He turned and sat next to his mother. Caroline was probably right. After already sitting with her last week, there was no reason to give the rumor mill more grist.

"Good morning, Travis," Elsie Belle drawled in a deep Southern accent from the pew behind him. "You too, Jackie."

"Morning, Elsie," Jackie said over her shoulder without turning her head far. Travis knew his mother wasn't one of Elsie Belle's biggest fans.

"Good morning, Elsie," Travis said, trying to be polite without encouraging Elsie Belle.

"My family is going over to WSCC for lunch, Travis. We would love for you to join us."

Beside him, his mother snorted just loud enough for only him to hear.

"Thanks. I appreciate the offer. Unfortunately I already have plans." Which included not having lunch with Elsie Belle Lambert and her parents.

"Well, think about it," Elsie Belle whispered. "You can give me your answer after church."

Travis turned toward the front of the church. Hadn't he just given her an answer?

"Honey, if you need to miss the family Sunday meal, I'd understand," Jackie Montgomery said, a devious grin on her face.

"Shh. The service is starting," he whispered back.

He could feel his mother shaking with silent laughter.

It was all he could do to keep his mind on the service and not on the woman across the aisle. Once he was sure he felt her looking at him, but when he moved his gaze in that direction, she was staring straight ahead.

After the closing prayer, Jackie pushed past Travis. "Caroline."

Caroline turned and Jackie enfolded Caroline in her arms.

"I am so sorry about your grandmother. How horrible to lose family members so close together."

"Thank you. Mamie was ill for some time, and I think she was in a great deal of discomfort for the past couple of months. I'm glad she's no longer suffering, but I'll miss her so much." Her voice cracked.

"Come have lunch with us," Jackie said. "We'd love to have you."

Travis was waiting for Caroline's answer when a hand landed on his arm. "Travis? Lunch?"

He glanced down at the hand and then back at Elsie Belle. "No. I'm sorry. I've already made plans."

Her hand fell from his arm. She looked at his mother conversing with Caroline. An expression of ire flashed in her eyes.

"Fine." She whirled on her heel and marched out of the church.

"You need to do something about her, son," his dad said.

"What?" Travis said. "I've never encouraged her."

"Well, give it some thought." His dad slapped him on the back and moved on.

He drove straight to his parents' house, expecting Caroline to be there or to arrive behind him. She never came. When he asked, Jackie said Caroline had begged off, explaining she wanted to go to her office today and check the schedule for the week. As much as he wanted to blow off Caroline's absence, he couldn't. They'd been together nonstop for days and he missed her.

That evening, he wasn't sure whether she'd come back or not. They hadn't spoken all day, not that he hadn't picked up his telephone more than once to call only to set it back down. She knew she had an open invitation to come back. He wasn't going to beg.

At ten p.m., he heard the garage door grinding up. His heart leapt into his throat. Without looking at which magazine he'd grabbed, he snapped it open and began to read, inanely pleased that she'd come back.

"Travis?"

"In here," he called, still holding the magazine as camouflage.

"Hey," Caroline said, propping a small roller bag against the den wall. She draped a plastic-shrouded set of clothes on the back of a breakfast bar stool. The ever-present charm bracelet jangled with each movement.

"Hey, yourself."

"I hope you were serious about my coming back?"

He tossed the magazine on the table. "I was. I'm glad you did."

A tinge of pink colored her cheeks. "You were right."

"About what?"

"Being alone in my house. It never bothered me before, but it seemed like everywhere I looked, I saw something that made me think of my grandmother."

He nodded. "I remember. Sometimes it's the simplest thing that can set off a memory."

A tired, sad smile stretched across her mouth. "I went to make a cup of hot tea and I remembered when she and I would have tea parties. And once when I had a bad cold, she gave me tea with honey and a shot of bourbon to cut my cough. Just silly things like that."

He walked over and caught her face between his hands. "Not silly at all." He kissed her. Her lips were soft and plump and exactly the right size. When she leaned into the kiss, he enfolded her in his arms and took the kiss deeper, enjoying the tangle of their tongues. He soaked up her taste like a smoker's first drag on a cigarette. He pulled back to look into her eyes, now dark with desire. "I'm glad you're here."

"So am I."

He took her hand and led her back to his bedroom.

NERVOUS NAUSEA HAD FILLED Caroline's stomach when she'd pulled into Travis's garage. She'd mentally crossed her fingers that his invitation to come back for a few days was sincere. Now, as she held his callused hand and they made their way to his bedroom, a feeling of relieved bliss replaced the nervous nausea. Although, finding herself back in his bed produced a whole different kind of nervous energy.

The summer spread had been pulled back. The blue sheets from last night were gone. In their place, a fresh set of beige sheets covered the bed. On the right side, where she'd slept last night, a single red rose lay on the pillow. Her breath caught when she saw it.

"Oh," she said with a sigh. She looked at Travis, who seemed to be watching her with bated breath. "The rose. For me?"

He grinned. "Who else?"

He turned her to face him. Lifting his hand, he ran a finger along her cheek, the callused tip leaving excited nerve receptors in its wake. She leaned into his hand then turned to kiss the palm. Stepping closer until her breasts met the flat hardness of his chest, she slipped her hand behind his neck and pulled him down for a deep, soul-seeking kiss. When she parted her lips, he thrust his tongue into her mouth, starting a tangle with hers. Licking, nipping, kissing, he worked along her chin, down her neck and then back up to her ear.

"Come to bed with me," he whispered, his hot breath sending shivers down her spine. "I've thought of nothing else all day."

She reached for the top pearl-button snap on his shirt and pulled. *Snap.* Then she pulled again. *Snap.* Each snap raised her heart rate by five beats. By the time she reached the last snap, her hands were at his waist and her heart rate was soaring. She smoothed her hands over his hard pectoral muscles, enjoying the crinkle of his chest hair against the palms of her hands. She traced each muscle, each tendon of his upper torso until he was vibrating beneath her fingers with need. He jerked the tail of his shirt from his jeans, ripped it down his arms and tossed it into the corner.

He ran his gaze down her body and back to her face. "Looking at you right now is like looking at a wrapped present. I don't know whether to rip off all the wrapping and get right to the present or take my time, pulling off each ribbon and piece of tape until the prize is finally exposed."

The combination of his gritty words with the appreciative gleam in his eyes had her quivering with desire. She pulled her cotton top over her head and tossed it into a chair.

"Let me make the decision easy for you." She reached behind her back, unfastened her bra and let it skitter down her arms and float to the floor. After toeing off both shoes, she pushed the button on the waistband of her shorts through the buttonhole. Her fingers grasped the pull tab on her shorts' zipper. Slowly, she slid the zipper down.

"Aw, hell." Travis swept her into his arms and deposited her in the middle of his bed. With one swift move, he finished unzipping her shorts and had them off in a nanosecond. His jeans and briefs were hurriedly kicked into the corner to join his shirt. "Damn you're a tease," he said, joining her on the fresh sheets.

He pulled her into his arms. Hot, needy flesh met hot, needy flesh. He kissed her, his tongue doing long, complicated spirals inside her mouth.

Caroline rubbed her breasts through the coarse hair of his chest. Her nipples stood erect. She wanted to touch and rub against his body in every way possible.

He kissed and nibbled along her chin and down her neck. When his mouth latched on to her breast, she arched.

"More," she gasped out. "Suck harder."

He did, drawing more of her flesh into his mouth with strong suction. Her sex tingled and ached for relief. When he blew hot breath across her erect nipple, she squirmed with pent-up desire.

She cradled his head in her fingers as he licked and sucked her breasts. Involuntary guttural moans rattled in her throat. Technically, she hadn't been a virgin when they first made love, but she'd never had these feelings before, this overwhelming desire to touch and be touched everywhere. Travis had the ability to reach areas inside her no one ever had.

"God, Caro," he gasped as he kissed his way down her abdomen. "Your skin tastes like honey."

He wedged himself between her legs, spreading them wide with his hard body. Shoving his hands under her ass, he lifted her aroused sex to his mouth. He kissed her vulva, sucking gently on the inflamed tissues.

Caroline's legs quivered. She felt the muscle spasms of her vagina. She slammed her head into the pillow and knotted the sheet in her fingers.

With a flick of his tongue, he separated her folds, licking along each side, rimming the edge of her opening. She squirmed in his hands. Her insides whirled like a weather vane in a tornado. An intense, almost painful energy built inside her.

"Stop, Travis," she said with a low moan. "I can't take any more." She shifted her hips in his hands, trying to move away while simultaneously trying to move closer.

He wouldn't let her go. He dug his fingers into the flesh of her ass as he held her firmly against his mouth, using his tongue to torture her again and again, building the swirl of electricity inside. When he jabbed the tip of his tongue inside her, she screamed as wave after rippling wave coursed through her. There seemed to be no end to her climax. As the orgasmic jolts would begin to subside, Travis would use his tongue to ramp them up again. She grabbed whatever she could to hold on to...the sheets, the headboard, his hair. She pounded her head into the pillow. She lacked the ability to open her eyes or make a sound other than moans and cries. Finally, she found her voice.

"Please," she begged. "Mercy."

He lowered her hips to the bed and covered her with his body. "Caroline," he whispered in her ear. "Darlin', I need to be inside you."

"Oh, God, yes," she said with a plea. "Please."

She heard the rip of foil only seconds before she felt the head of his hard penis pressing at her opening. She spread her thighs wide. He pushed in, stretching tissue unused to such girth. Oh Lord, it felt so good. She moaned and pressed her hips down on his shaft until he was imbedded to the hilt.

A deep-chested groan rolled from him. "You feel so good," he said. "I hate to move."

She smiled, knowing he couldn't see it. She wrapped her legs around his waist and squeezed her thighs while tapping his butt with her heel. "Giddy-up," she said with a giggle.

He laughed and pulled slowly out of her. Her breath caught in her throat and held until he thrust back deep. He pulled out and thrust hard again.

"I'm trying to take it slow," he said with a gasp. "I just can't. You." He thrust into her. "Feel." He thrust again. "Perfect."

"Faster," she said. "Faster."

He did as she asked, moving in and out of her rapidly. The swirl of energy built again, each thrust pushing her higher until she came with a cry. He pushed inside one more time before he pressed firmly inside and held. The hard pulse of his orgasm rocked her.

Collapsing on top of her, he groaned. "Damn, woman. You're gonna give me a heart attack."

Caroline traced her fingers down his spine, enjoying the twitches of his firm muscles until she reached his butt. His hard, solid muscles barely indented when she squeezed.

"Yeah. I kind of liked it too," she said in a whisper. "I liked it a lot."

"Be right back," he said as he slid off her. He stopped suddenly. "Oh shit."

"What?" She sat up. Travis was staring at the broken remains of his condom.

He looked at her, his eyes wide. "Holy hell, Caroline. This hasn't ever happened before."

"No problem. Really. Don't worry about it. Give me a minute. I'll be right back and explain."

Caroline hopped from the bed and headed for the bathroom. By the time she returned, Travis had disposed of the faulty condom and was waiting for her in bed. She slipped under the sheet and moved across the mattress until their bodies touched.

"I am so sorry," he said.

She shook her head, a sad smile tugged at her lips. "Like I said, it isn't a problem." She lowered the sheet until the hem was just above her mons. "Surely you've noticed the scars here." She pointed to a number of faint lines criss-crossing her flesh. "I was in a bad car accident in high school." She pulled the sheet back up. "I probably shouldn't have lived. My boyfriend didn't." She paused as the easily recognizable survivor guilt rolled over her. She sighed and then continued. "I had quite a bit of abdominal trauma.

The surgeon who did my repairs took my right ovary out. She told me it'd been ruptured in the accident. There was damage to my uterus, but at my age she didn't want to remove it and the remaining ovary. She repaired everything the best she could, but I was advised that my chances of getting pregnant were like one in a million."

Travis wrapped his arms around her and pulled her tight. "That's awful, babe." He slid lower in the bed, taking Caroline with him. She rested her head on his chest.

"I think it was that doctor who stimulated my interest in medicine. Without her, I probably wouldn't be sitting here right now. Not having children is a small price to pay for living."

Travis toyed with the charms on Caroline's ever-present bracelet. "That sucks. Really, really sucks."

Caroline shrugged. "It is what it is. So anyway, this morning's broken condom is nothing to lose sleep over, at least as far as pregnancy is concerned. I promise." She looked up at him. "As far as sexually transmitted diseases go, you have nothing to worry about from me. One of the requirements of the company I work for is annual testing for most diseases I could transmit to a patient. HIV. Hepatitis. Herpes. MRSA. You name it and I've probably been tested for it." She glanced away. "And let's face it. I haven't been with a man in a couple of years, so yeah, I'm squeaky clean."

"It's been over ten years since I've had sex without a condom," Travis said. "Back when I was married to Susan. I haven't had all the testing you have, but I don't think you have anything to be worried about with me. I'm pretty careful. But I'm willing to be tested for anything if it would make you feel better."

She shook her head. "I don't think so. If anything happens, then we can deal with it."

They lay there in the quiet, Caroline listening to his heart's steady rhythm while he continued to finger her bracelet.

"No Texas?"

"Excuse me?" She raised her head to look at him.

"No Texas charm," he clarified.

Settling back down on his chest, she sighed. "Haven't found the right one yet. But I guess I need to get busy. I don't have much time left."

Not much time left. The words opened a canyon of regret. Regret that she was moving on. Regret that this thing with Travis was just friends with benefits. Regrets that she'd never have children—although that regret caught her by surprise. She'd thought she'd handled that one a long time ago, but here it was raising its ugly head.

Regret was a waste of time. Too bad she couldn't convince her mind of that.

Eleven

W hen Caroline awoke, she was alone in bed. She stretched her arms over her head. Tight muscles unused to her activities of late protested. After slipping on Travis's robe—the belt wrapped twice around her waist—she made her way to the kitchen. A white piece of paper was propped on the coffee maker.

Morning, darlin'.

Headed out at four. Didn't want to wake you. Have a nice day. See you tonight.

T

Caroline clutched the note to her chest and laughed at her silly response...like a fifth grader who'd just gotten her first note from a boy. Still, she couldn't throw it away. She shoved it in the robe's pocket and poured coffee. As she sipped, she glanced at the clock. Almost eleven. How decadent to sleep all day. She sort of liked it.

A muted beep had her searching for her cellphone. After finding it at the bottom of her purse, she scrolled for messages. A lunch invitation from KC Montgomery flashed from text messages. That sounded like a fun way to spend her last free day. She texted KC back to accept and then hurried to the shower.

After lunch, Caroline ran by her house to get clothes for Tuesday and to check her email. She had a couple of emails from Noah. They broke her heart. He was so lost without Mamie. She answered him back and promised to come see him soon, but her gut twisted at the thought of walking back into Mamie's house after she was gone. She wasn't sure she was ready to face that.

The office receptionist emailed Caroline's patient appointments and hospital round lists. Both lists were extensive, but she was ready to get back to work. Her real world—the one where she slept alone, ate alone and watched television alone—could wait a week or so.

Monday night, Travis surprised her with steaks off the grill and homemade ice cream. Somehow, the ice cream made it to the bedroom. As she licked the ice cream from the dips and valleys of Travis's chest and abdomen, she remembered how much she loved sweet and salty together. She was pretty sure she'd just found a new source for this favorite combination.

On Tuesday, the office staff greeted her return with hugs and sweet words of condolence. On her desk, she found a large floral arrangement. The card read, *"We are so sorry for your loss. We missed you. Your Staff."*

As she read the words, she had to sniff back the tears. She'd never been so in tune with an office staff. In fact, she'd never considered the people she worked with *her* staff. Instead, she had always thought of them as just *the* staff. To think that they considered her one of them... She smiled and tucked the card into her purse. It was definitely destined for her memory box, along with Travis's note from yesterday morning.

Travis called about noon, just to check on her, he said, which was nice. But what made her heart jump was when he ended the call with, "see you at home tonight."

When she got to Halo M ranch Tuesday evening, Travis was there waiting for her. Dinner was in the oven. The house was clean. She had no responsibilities other than what she wanted to do. And what she wanted to do was Travis...so she did.

Every morning she suggested she go back to her house. Every morning Travis talked her into staying another day... not that he had to work very hard at convincing her to stay.

By Friday, she knew she had to go home. Not because she felt like she was a burden, and not because she felt like she'd overstayed her visit. The fact she didn't want to go home clued her in that maybe it was time to go. She liked being with him a little too much. She liked having someone waiting for her when she got home.

But this wasn't her real life, and she had to continually remind herself of that. Travis never suggested she stay beyond her contract date in December. He never once hinted that he wanted more than the sexual relationship they were experiencing. They were playing with fire. She recognized that.

Finally, he must have too, because when she'd been at his house for a week and she said she really needed to go home, he didn't argue or protest. He simply said she should do what she needed to do and then helped her get her things loaded into his car, which she was still driving. Her car was dead, junkyard material. She hadn't gotten up the energy to car shop, but who would when they had a loaned Porsche to drive?

The next week rolled by filled with long hours of work broken up by lunches with Lydia or KC and evening phone conversations with Noah. He wasn't adjusting well to living with Patrick and Leslie. They didn't like his friends, which didn't surprise her much. Mamie hadn't liked the boys he'd run around with much either, more than once lamenting that they were a bad influence on Noah. Leslie had discovered Noah and his friends smoking behind the backyard fence and had forbid him from seeing them again. That hadn't gone over well.

Patrick and Leslie had decided that if Noah got a part-time job, he'd have less time to get in trouble. They'd put him to work in the church office of Patrick's parish. Noah had shown up exactly once. Threats, bribes, cajoling... nothing worked to stem what appeared to be an out-of-control downward spiral for her baby brother.

Caroline was at a loss what to do. Her parents were of little help, offering prayers and suggestions, but Caroline could envision Noah's eye rolls at anything their parents offered. Lord knew, she'd seen plenty of *those* looks from the teenagers in her practice who considered her, at thirty-two, old and out of touch. She prayed that time and a little more maturity would help Noah before he totally lost himself.

Travis called every night. They talked about their days and their plans for the next day, but he didn't ask her to come back to his house and she couldn't bring herself to mention it. While she loved listening to his voice over the phone, she would have rather heard it in person. Apparently, he was holding up his end of their friendship. She tried to keep her feelings in that friendship mode, which was getting damned near impossible.

The third week she was back in the office, she found Olivia Montgomery on her patient list. Pleased, she pulled the patient record from the door box. The nurse had taken vitals and weight, all within normal limits. No medical complaint was noted.

"Knock, knock," Caroline said as she opened the door.

Olivia was sitting in the room chair flipping through a magazine. As soon as she saw Caroline, her face lit with a bright smile. "Hey."

"Hey, yourself," Caroline replied. She stepped into the room and closed the door behind her. She set the patient record on the counter. "What's going on with you? Are you having a problem or is this just a regular visit?"

Olivia placed the magazine back into the basket next to her chair. "Well," she said, drawing out the word until it had three syllables. "I need a good doctor."

Caroline laughed and spread her arms. "Well, here I am. What can I do for you?"

"I took one of those pharmacy pregnancy tests last week and..." She grinned. "Jackpot."

Caroline crossed the room and hugged her. Caroline was thrilled as it was obvious that Olivia was beyond elated about this pregnancy. At the same time, Caroline felt a twinge of jealousy. Oh, not that she was the least bit interested in Mitch Landry. It was the obvious head-over-heels love glowing in Olivia's eyes that had Caroline wishing for things she ought not to wish for. Olivia was pregnant again with Mitch's baby, but unlike their first pregnancy, this time Mitch would be there for the entire show. This was a lucky couple to have found their way back to each other.

"Oh, Olivia. That's wonderful. I'll draw some blood today just to confirm your home results, but those tests are pretty accurate. Lydia told me you and Mitch had worked things out." She pumped her eyebrows. "Sounds like you did a little more than just work out your disagreements."

"I know," Olivia said. "I can't believe it."

"Have you told Mitch?"

"Last night. He was over the moon. It was all I could do to keep him from calling everyone."

Caroline sat on the rolling stool. "Do you have any idea of how far along you might be? When was your last menstrual period?"

"I know exactly when this baby was conceived. My last period was in April. I must have gotten pregnant in May while I was still at Mitch's place."

"Okay. That would make you about three months." She opened a drawer and removed a cardboard pregnancy delivery date wheel. "Now, let's see when this baby would be due. The first day of your last period was when?"

"April 18."

"So..." She twisted the wheel. "Looks like you'll have a new-year baby. Your due date would be about January 22."

Olivia hugged herself. "I am so excited.'

"Oh damn."

"What?"

"I'll have already left by then. You will have to promise to send me pictures." Caroline was surprised to hear herself request baby pictures. She'd never asked a patient to stay in touch or send updates.

Olivia sighed. "Of course I will, but are you sure you can't stay?"

Caroline shook her head. "I can't stay."

Olivia's bottom lip protruded in a pout.

"I'm happy to follow you until I leave, but I have to ask. Why did you ask to see me today instead of Lydia? After all, she's going to be your sister-in-law one day."

"Mitch and I thought it might be fun to have a dinner party for the family this Friday. Sort of a tell-everybody-at-once dinner. A big celebration. I wanted her to be surprised too."

Caroline nodded. "Okay. Makes sense. I'll just keep your chart in my office until you've spilled the beans." She leaned over and pulled a patient gown from the table. "I'll step out while you get undressed. Take a seat on the table and let me do an exam."

Olivia stood. "Works for me."

Olivia's physical exam revealed no surprises. A slightly enlarged uterus. Some breast tenderness. But overall, she was in excellent health.

"Well, I can't find a thing wrong with you," Caroline said with a smile. "How are we supposed to pay the bills if all our patients are healthy?"

Olivia laughed. "While I was changing clothes I realized that maybe you didn't realize that I meant for you to come for dinner on Friday too."

"Oh, no, Olivia. Thanks, but you said family and—"

"And the Montgomerys consider you family. Haven't you realized yet that once you're adopted by the Montgomery clan we don't let you go?" She smiled. "Please say you'll come, Olivia. Mitch and I really want you there."

When Caroline hesitated, Olivia added another, "Please."

"Are you sure?"

"Of course I'm sure. You have to be there."

Caroline nodded. "Okay. What time? And what can I bring?"

"About six. It's a little early, but Cash rides that night. The PBR is in Nashville and it's televised. I thought it'd be fun to have dessert and coffee while we watch him go for the points to get him into the finals in Las Vegas."

"Sounds like fun."

"And don't bring anything. This is our treat."

"I'll look forward to it."

After Olivia left, Caroline stashed her chart in the top drawer of her desk. As she was closing the drawer, Lydia tapped on her door.

"Hi. Got a minute?"

"Sure. What's up?"

"Did I see Olivia's name on your schedule today?"

"You did."

"She okay?"

Caroline waved her hand in a dismissive fashion. "It was nothing. A little poison ivy."

Lydia frowned. "I wonder why she asked to see you instead of me."

Caroline chuckled. "You're the big cheese here. I'm just the hired help, the low man on the totem pole. I'm sure she didn't want to take up one of your spots with something so minor."

Lydia shrugged. "I guess so." She looked hard at Caroline. "Are you sure that's all?"

"That's all," she replied, keeping her voice as neutral as possible. It was all she could do to keep from grinning. As a physician, Caroline didn't get to give good news that often. She loved when she could.

"Okay, as long as she's not upset with me about something."

"Nope. Nothing like that. I swear."

Lydia's cell phone chirped and she pulled it from her lab coat pocket. After reading the name on the display, her eyebrows rose. "Speak of the devil." She pushed the green answer button. "Olivia. What a nice surprise." She listened for a minute then said, "Friday? Sure. I don't think Jason and I have anything on our schedule. Oh? Well, if he said we were available for dinner then I'm sure we are. What time? Uh-huh. Uh-huh. What can I bring? Really? Well, okay then. We'll see you about six." She clicked off the phone. "That was Olivia."

Caroline smiled. "So I gathered."

"I guess I was being silly. She's having the family over for dinner Friday. Said you'd be there too."

Caroline nodded. "Yeah, she invited me this afternoon. She seemed so thrilled about being back with Mitch. I'm sure this is simply a celebration of that and maybe a way to show everybody their new house. Have you seen it?"

"Not yet. I've heard about it from Jason's mother but I've been dying to see it. You know their story, right?"

Caroline lifted one shoulder in a shrug. "Yes and no. I know about Adam and their long split. But what's the story with the new house?"

A dreamy expression flashed across Lydia's face. "It was so romantic. After Olivia came home from Mitch's house, she wouldn't see him or talk to him. Apparently, his ex-wife had been playing a few mind games with Olivia, the little bitch. His ex-wife, not Olivia," she said with a laugh. "Anyway, Mitch decided he couldn't live without Olivia and Adam, so as a surprise he bought this ranch with Jason's little brother, Cash. You've met Cash since you've been here, right?"

Caroline shook her head. "Nope. Everybody talks about him like he's a great guy, but really...any guy who rides bulls for a living makes me wonder about his sanity."

Lydia laughed again. "I know. I know. I am so glad Jason decided lawyering would be a better career move than the professional rodeo. I almost die every time we watch Cash ride. Whenever the rodeo is near here, Jason and I go, but I swear...sitting in those stands while someone I know and care about is being tossed around on the back of a wild bull drives me crazy. But watching it on television is even more stressful. It makes no sense, but what can I say?

"Anyway, Cash and Mitch have gone partners on raising bulls for the professional circuit. He did all this without talking to Olivia. He was desperate to have her back, or so he says. One Saturday, he shows up at her house, drags her out to this ranch and begs her to marry him." Another wistful expression passes across her face. "Isn't that the most romantic thing you've ever heard?"

Caroline nodded even though she thought she'd probably shoot a guy who thought it was romantic to buy a house without letting her have input.

To each his own.

"So," Lydia continued, "they've been in the house a couple of weeks and we've all been dying to see the place now that they've got everything settled." A broad smile stretched across her lips. "I am glad you're coming too. We are all sure going to miss you when you've gone."

Caroline felt a stab in her heart. Her breath caught in her throat. Swallowing back tears, she pulled the corners of her mouth up into what she suspected was a sad smile. "I'll miss all y'all too."

As general rule, Friday afternoons at the Whispering Springs Medical Clinic were kept open for completing medical charts, returning patient calls and emergencies. Lucky for them, the Friday afternoon of the dinner party was dead. No emergencies. No long-winded patient calls. At three, both Lydia and Caroline headed out leaving instructions with the staff to call if there were any problems. The day was beautiful, if a little hot. A bright sun and cerulean-blue sky met them as they walked out the back door of the clinic into the parking lot.

"What a gorgeous day," Caroline said. She drew in a deep breath and let it out. "Just wonderful. Nothing but minor problems all day. Is it not the most perfect Friday?"

Lydia stretched her arms over her head and twisted at her waist. "Yep. Perfect. Now let's get out of here before we get stuck talking to some old person about their latest hemorrhoid problem."

Caroline laughed. "You must have had Stephen Francis in today."

Lydia shook her head with a laugh. "How did you ever guess?"

"Hey. Question. Olivia said not to bring anything tonight."

"Right, so?"

"So, what are you taking?"

Lydia chuckled. "You know me too well. I thought a bottle wine, maybe some champagne to celebrate their new house. You?"

Caroline couldn't tell her that alcohol was out of Olivia's diet for the next few months, so she just nodded. "That sounds good. I think I'll run by that new nursery and check out their plants. Maybe a cactus or some other type of houseplant."

Lydia snorted. "A cactus. Yeah, that's the right plant for Olivia. She never remembers to water. See you later." She waved as she headed off for the small SUV she drove.

As Caroline's hand touched the Porsche car door, her phone began ringing. For half a second, she considered letting it go to voice mail. However, she was on-call so that wasn't really an option, but the day had been just too perfect to ruin it with a late-minute patient call. She sighed and looked at the screen. Her heart kicked her chest when she saw the name on the readout. She punched the green answer button and steadied her voice.

"Hey, you."

"Hey, yourself."

"How are you?" Her heart raced at the rumble of his voice. She hadn't talked to Travis in a few days as he'd been in Arkansas to ship some new mares to his ranch. She tilted the phone up away from her mouth and nose and prayed he wouldn't hear how rapid her breathing had become.

"Good, although I'll admit my bed's a little empty these days."

She drew in a sharp breath. "Travis—"

"No, that's okay. You made it clear that you wanted to go home. Anyway, I was calling about tonight."

"Tonight?" She felt her brows draw down into a frown. "What about it?"

"How do you want to play it?"

"Play what?"

"Us."

"What about us?" She opened the car door and slid into the driver's seat. "There is no us." Saying that made her heart ache. She had to keep reminding herself of that painful fact.

"I'm fully aware of that, Caroline." She heard him give a long exhale. "Sorry. Been a bear of a day. What I meant was that we might let my family know we're...friends."

"Friends." She repeated the word. Friends. Yep. That's what they were...friends. "Sure. Whatever, Travis. They know we're friends."

"My mom's pretty sensitive. She might pick up something's different in our...friendship."

Caroline blew out a loud sigh. "Good Lord, Travis. You're not that irresistible. I'm sure I'll be able to keep my hands off you." She said the words, but they were all lies. He was that irresistible. She would love to run her hands over his rock-hard chest. Feel his large fingers touching her. Enjoy the bliss of the neck and back massages he'd given her while lying on his soft sheets.

His responding chuckle sent chills skittering down her spine.

"Well, gee thanks. Good to know you find me so resistible." He chuckled again. "Okay. Next topic. Tomorrow night."

"Tomorrow night?" she asked as though she could forget the End of Summer dance at the WSCC. Like that day hadn't been circled on her calendar and in her mind.

What Caroline would never confess to him was that she'd headed into Dallas the previous weekend to pick up a dress designed to take his breath away and knock his socks off. Step one: Get the dress. Mission accomplished. Step two: Knock his socks off. She'd have to wait and see on that one.

"The dance. At the club." He chuckled. "Don't pretend you don't remember."

Playing it cool, she replied, "Oh right. The dance. Is that this weekend? It totally skipped my mind." Lying wasn't one of her strengths. She figured he could hear right through it.

"Yeah. Tomorrow. I know I sort of forced you into saying you'd go. We don't have to go if you don't want to. It wasn't like you had any say on whether or not to be my date for the dance, especially after Elsie Belle decided it was her place to tell everybody I was bringing you. But you don't have to. Really. I'll understand if you want to back out."

Was he trying to give her an out, a way to gracefully extricate herself from a date she'd never agreed to?

Or was he trying to give himself an out? Would he rather go with someone else?

After so much close time together, had he spent all the time he wanted with her and was now trying to distance himself back to where they'd been before the insane fake wedding and the fabulous sex? Sometimes the direct approach was the best, and she decided this was one of those times.

"Color me a tad confused, Travis. Are you asking if I want out of the date or are you trying to tell me that you want out of the date? If you don't want to go or if you don't want to take me, that's fine. Just say so. My mind-reading skills appear to be a little rusty."

"What? No, no. I don't think I'm making myself very clear." His chuckle sounded a little nervous. "It's sort of a tradition for the Montgomery clan to attend this dance each year as a family. The money raised is for a good cause and the family wants to show full public support. But to tell you the truth, I haven't gone the last few years."

"Too many single women hitting on you?"

He snorted. "Yeah, that's it. Anyway, Olivia told me you were coming to dinner tonight. With all the Montgomerys tonight and then again tomorrow night at the dance, I wanted to make sure you wouldn't be overdosed on all that Montgomery charm. That could be a real Montgomery overdose for some people."

To Caroline, the big family, all the members being together and supportive sounded downright wonderful. However, she was still a little confused on exactly how to respond. "So, are you saying that if I still want to go to the dance you'll take me?"

"Exactly."

Caroline dropped her head back on the car-seat headrest. What she really wanted to know was…did he really want to go with her or did he simply feel an obligation because of Elsie Belle's blabber mouth? She couldn't ask him of course, because he'd certainly assure her he wanted to take her and it had nothing to do with being painted into a corner by a jealous admirer. So it really was up to her. Did she want to go to a major country-club dance on the arm of the most handsome but least available bachelor in the county? Who was she kidding?

"Of course I want to go. I'm looking forward to it."

She heard him suck in a deep breath and let it out slowly. "Great. Me too."

"Great," she repeated and grimaced. They sounded like teenagers…all giddy that the other had agreed to a date.

"I guess I'll see you tonight then," he said.

"Absolutely."

As she was pulling her phone away from her ear to hang up, she heard him call her name. She pressed the phone back to her head and said, "What did you say?"

"I asked if you wanted me to drive you to Olivia and Mitch's place tonight."

She smiled. "Talk about going out of your way for someone." She chuckled. "Thanks for offering, but I'm on call tonight. Probably won't need to come back to town, but I'll need my own car just in case. Speaking of which, I swear I'm going to buy a new car soon and get your Porsche back to you. It's just…"

"Too fun to give up?"

She laughed. "Something like that."

"Okay then. I'll see you tonight. Oh, and, Caroline?"

"Yes?"

"Think about a stay-over at my place after the dance tomorrow night."

Her cheeks hurt from the wide grin on her face. "I'll think about it."

She clicked off her phone and dropped it into her purse.

Maybe she should call Leslie or Pat and check on Noah. It'd been a couple of days since she'd talked to him. Was it too much to hope things were going a little better? Probably.

She sighed. Damn. Today had been such a nice day so far, and she was in such a fabulous mood after talking to Travis and she was going to a good news celebration dinner. Call her selfish, but she didn't want to spoil her good mood by hearing about the latest trouble her brother had gotten himself into. She'd call tomorrow. She promised. Just let her have one day of peace and happiness. There was always tomorrow to face reality.

Twelve

❧

"Turn left."

Caroline followed the female metallic voice of the GPS and turned left, passed under an archway and drove down a curved paved driveway until she came to a grouping of trucks and cars parked in a circle drive in front of a white-columned two-story estate. White-wicker rockers on the porch moved in the early evening breeze. Hanging baskets overflowing with bright red and yellow flowers swayed as though playing tag with each other. A black and white dog raced from the back of the house followed by a dark-haired little boy. She smiled and opened her door.

"Hi, Adam."

The boy skid to a stop and stared at her. His head tilted to one side as though trying to remember if he knew her.

"I'm Dr. Graham, remember me? You came to see me when you fell and hurt your head while playing."

About a month before, Adam had been swinging on a weight bar in Olivia's gym after repeatedly being told not to. The hot gym had led to sweaty palms and to a crash to the floor and a big bump over his eye. There had been no real damage and just enough pain to convince him not to do that again.

He gave her a gap-tooth grin. "I remember."

"Looks like you lost something since I last saw you."

He stuck his tongue in the gap between his teeth. "My toof."

"I see that. Did the tooth fairy come?"

He nodded his head vigorously. "Yep. Gave me a dollar."

She smiled. The tooth fairy was paying more these days than when she was six. Inflation got them all. "Got big plans for all that money?"

He nodded again. "Gonna buy me a horse."

She laughed. "You sound like a man with a plan." The dog ran over to her. "Who's this?"

"Daisy."

When the dog heard her name, she began jumping and barking and running around Adam. In response, he started yelling and running so the dog would chase him. After a minute, the front door opened.

"Adam! What in the...oh, Caroline. I didn't know you'd arrived. I'm so glad you could make it." Olivia Montgomery stood in her doorway, a dishtowel thrown over her left shoulder.

"I love the welcoming committee."

Olivia laughed. "Yes, well, my committee is enthusiastic but noisy. Still driving Travis's car, I see."

Caroline grinned. "I know. My brain says it's time to buy a new car and give Travis his car back, but my wild side says 'no way, man. Let's keep it'."

"I think I agree with your wild child. Keep it until he makes you give it back. C'mon in." She turned toward the side of the house. "Adam. Take Daisy to the backyard to play please." She looked back at Caroline. "We're so far off the road I'm not worried about cars, but I feel better when I can see both of them from the kitchen window."

"Am I the last one here?"

"Still waiting on Travis. He called to say he was on the way."

The mention of Travis's name sent the tutu-attired hippos whirling in her stomach. No, sir. No butterflies for her. She had full-grown stomping hippos dancing around inside, accompanied by shaking hands on the outside.

She followed Olivia into a sunlit foyer. The sound of people talking and laughing filtered from a room off to the right. Olivia tilted her head in that direction. "Mitch's man cave."

Caroline grinned. "No kidding. Let me guess. It has a sixty-inch flat screen and overstuffed chairs."

"And you'd be wrong."

"What? How?"

"It has an eighty-inch flat screen. You'd be right about the overstuffed chairs."

Caroline laughed. "So what can I do to help you with dinner?"

"Follow me."

She followed Olivia toward the back of the house, the sound of female voices getting louder the nearer they got to the rear. They moved into a bright, stainless-steel kitchen with green and gray granite countertops. Lydia stood with Travis's mother, Jackie, and a woman Caroline didn't know.

Olivia took her arm and led her over to the unfamiliar woman. "Caroline, this is Mitch's mother Sylvia Landry. Sylvia, this is Dr. Caroline Graham. She's been here working with Lydia at the medical clinic for about a year and a half." She stuck her bottom lip out in a pout. "But she's leaving us at the end of the year. See if you can get any good blackmail material out of her so we can force her to stay."

Sylvia Landry held out her hand. "Nice to meet you, Dr. Graham. Olivia speaks so highly of you."

"Caroline, please," she said as she took the older woman's hand. "And I feel that way about Olivia." She leaned forward and said in a stage whisper, "But it's your grandson who's stolen my heart."

Sylvia's face lit up at the mention of her grandson. "Ain't he a little corker? You meet Daisy yet?"

"Oh, yes. It was quite the welcoming party out front."

"Yes, Daisy was a little surprise from his Nana Su-Su," Olivia said with a hip bump to Sylvia. "Good thing I'm so awesome to let her stay."

"Do you mean Sylvia or the dog?" Lydia asked with a wink.

All the women laughed.

Sylvia was obviously not put off at all by Olivia's comments and simply laughed with the rest of them. "Every little boy needs a dog."

"That's right," Jackie Montgomery said as she came over to give Caroline a quick peck on the cheek. "How are you? You look wonderful."

"Thank you. By the way, I meant to tell you that the flowers you sent for Mamie's service were lovely. It was so thoughtful of you."

"Of course, dear. You're like one of the family."

"See?" Olivia said over her shoulder. She'd stepped across the room to check whatever dish was in the oven. "That's what I told her, Mom."

"Can I do something to help?" Caroline asked, not wanting to think about those days in Arkansas. If she did, she'd remember the feel of Travis's lips on hers, the heat from his body when he'd held her while she wept, the roughness of his fingers when he'd stroked the tears from her cheeks.

Damn. Too late. Her heart sighed. She didn't need to get attached to people she'd be leaving soon.

"Oh, yes," Lydia said. She handed Caroline a wineglass with a golden-colored liquid. "You can help by drinking this wine before it goes bad."

Caroline laughed. "I'm here to help," she said and took a sip. Pinot grigio. Her favorite.

A dog barking followed by the sound of dog nails scratching on the hardwood floor announced the arrival of Adam and Daisy.

"Hey, Mom," Adam said. "Dad wants to know if you bought that spensive water for Uncle Travis?"

"You can go tell him yes," Olivia answered without turning around.

"Dad!" Adam yelled down the hall. "Mom says yes."

"Adam." Olivia turned, her hands on her hips. "We have guests. Plus, you know better than to yell in the house."

"Sorry," her son replied, not an ounce of sincerity in his voice. His gaze rolled to the plate of chocolate-chip cookies on the counter. "Can I have a cookie?"

"Don't you think it's a little too close to dinner for a cookie?"

In a motion that looked so much like his father, Adam looked at the inexpensive watch he'd gotten for his sixth birthday and sighed loudly. "It's ten minutes after six." Looking up at her, he added, "Dad says it's never the wrong time for a cookie or a beer."

Caroline stifled a laugh and watched Olivia pull the best stern face she could manage in the situation. The other women in the room suddenly found the need to take gulps of wine.

"Did he now?" Olivia said. "I'll be having a word with him."

Adam shrugged. "Anyway, Dad says Uncle Travis needs something to drink."

"Your poor Uncle Travis have broken legs that prevent him from coming for his own drink?"

Adam frowned. "No." His eyes rolled up and to the left as though in thought. "But Uncle Travis said he'd give me a dollar if I'd bring him a bottle of water."

Olivia looked at her mother, who returned the look with a one-shoulder shrug. "Don't look at me," Jackie said.

"You spoiled him rotten, Mom." She went over to the refrigerator, took out a bottle of sparkling water and handed it to her son. "Tell your dad it's time to eat."

"*Dad!*" Adam yelled as he charged down the hall. "Mom says come eat."

As soon as the boy cleared the room, all the women burst into laughter, Jackie Montgomery laughing the hardest. She looked at Sylvia and said, "Don't you love when they pay for their upbringing?"

Olivia rolled her eyes at the two cackling women.

"Okay, now what can we do to help?" Caroline asked.

Olivia pulled a large roast from the oven, followed by mashed potatoes, gravy, black-eyed peas, creamed corn and rolls. She cradled each dish with a heavy towel and passed it to one of the willing kitchen helpers. Heavenly aromas filled the air as each dish was withdrawn. "Will you take these to the serving sideboard? There should be hot-plate trivets already there. I thought each person could fill his own plate from there. It makes the table less crowded."

Caroline took the corn and peas and followed Lydia into

a large formal dining room set for ten adults and one child. Each adult place had been set with translucent bone china, sterling-silver flatware and crystal. Adam's spot sported a superhero plate with matching glass and small utensils. The sparkling chandelier over the table threw rainbow colors across the white tablecloth and onto the off-white china. An arch of burgundy candles stood at the ready to be lit.

"Your room is lovely," Caroline said to Olivia when she entered carrying the sliced roast.

"Thanks. I guess you've heard the story about this house?"

Caroline nodded. "I heard it was kind of a surprise."

Olivia snorted. "You could say that. But I can't imagine finding a house I love more than this one."

"Could it be the man and boy you share it with?" Caroline suggested.

"Could be. Help me get some drinks in here?"

"Sure."

When they came back with the pitchers of sweet tea, the men had found their way from the man cave to the dining room. Someone had lit the candle arch on the table.

"Grab a plate," Olivia said. "It's family-style serve yourself."

Caroline smiled. Family-style. When was the last time anyone she knew used fine china and sterling for a casual family dinner? On the other hand, why have nice things if you didn't share them with family and friends?

"Here you go." A plate bumped against Caroline's knuckles. She looked up into Travis's blue eyes. Her knees did their usual melting act whenever he was around. No matter what she had thought about him before this past month, she now knew beyond a shadow of a doubt he was one of the good guys.

"Thanks." She took the plate offered. "Everything smells so good."

"Mom always was a great cook. Olivia learned from her."

"Thanks, honey," Jackie Montgomery said and gave him a brush of her lips on his cheek.

"You were, Mom. Heck, still are."

Jackie beamed from Travis's compliments.

Plates full, the adults moved back to the table. Caroline found herself seated with Travis on her right and his father on her left and Sylvia Landry next to him. Mitch took the head of the table and his father snagged the corresponding chair at the other end. Across the table, Adam sat in an elevated chair between his father and mother. Next to Olivia was Lydia and then Jason.

Caroline allowed her gaze to move across the family faces, recognizing her small twinge of envy at not only their closeness but also their numbers. Becoming a doctor had required long hours of study and countless sacrifices, but she'd accepted long ago that a family and children would be one of those personal sacrifices for her professional career.

As soon as everyone was seated, Mitch stood and tapped his water glass.

"Olivia and I want to thank you all for coming tonight. We realize it was short notice but..." He reached over and took Olivia's hand. She stood and moved to stand beside him. "We have news we wanted to share with all of you at the same time." He looked at Olivia. "Right?"

She gave him a nod. "We do." She turned to the family and an ecstatic grin broke across both their faces. "We're pregnant."

Suddenly everybody was talking at once, congratulating the couple, asking when the baby was due, asking Adam what he thought about having a baby brother or sister. The noise level continued to rise until Travis stood. He tapped his glass with his knife, but no one paid him any mind. A red flush climbed from his neck to his face. He tapped again and again, but the congratulations continued. Finally, he stuck two fingers between his lips and produced a shockingly loud whistle. All heads turned to him.

"Let me get this straight," he said in a tone so quiet and calm it reminded Caroline of the weather right before a tornado. "You have gotten my sister, my unmarried sister, pregnant again? You lousy—"

Olivia answered his sharp whistle with one of her own. "You stop right there, Travis. I'm a grown woman. You have no right to pass judgment. I'm thrilled about this baby. Completely overjoyed."

"Now, Olivia," he started.

Mitch held up his hand like a football ref for a time-out. "Travis. Olivia has told the story a little out of order." He looked at Olivia. "Don't bait the bear. Behave."

Olivia's eyes twinkled as she linked arms with Mitch. "Oops. Maybe I should have mentioned this first. Mitch and I are getting married."

The hoopla of congratulations started up again. Travis dropped back into his chair. Caroline leaned over and whispered, "Why do I think you guys used to torture Olivia and her boyfriends when she was growing up? I think you just got served some revenge."

To her surprise, Travis laughed. "Yeah, I think you're right." He lifted his water glass. "Congratulations."

"So, honey," Jackie Montgomery said. "When is the big day? The wedding I mean."

Olivia and Mitch exchanged a quick look before she said, "We've been talking about that. We want to do it soon, but since both of us have been through the big church wedding, we think a small wedding with just family would be perfect. Then maybe a big celebration with all our family and friends."

"Sounds just like you two," Sylvia Landry said. "So do you have a particular date in mind?"

"We were hoping we could piggyback on Travis's annual barbeque. Most of our friends will be in town for that. It only makes sense to not make them come back just for our reception. What do you say, Travis?"

He shrugged. "As long as you two are paying, that works for me. But you do realize that the rodeo is in two weeks, right?"

"We know," Mitch said, then hugged Olivia. "That's what Olivia wants, and what she wants, I want." He grinned at Travis. "We'll pay for everything. The beef for the barbeque. The beer and wine. All the beans, cole slaw, bread plus the dessert, which will be cake."

Olivia crossed over to Travis and draped her arms around his neck. "Besides, your baby sister is kind of knocked up. It'd be better if we got married quickly."

Travis swatted her rear. "Mitch, I hope you know what you're getting into."

Olivia went back to Mitch and wrapped her arms around his waist. "Too late. He's mine now."

Mitch kissed her.

Adam, who'd been listening to the conversation, looked at his mother and said, "What's knocked up?"

The adults laughed. Olivia kissed his forehead. "I'll tell you later, but you'll like it. It involves cake."

"Goodie!"

The mood at the table was festive and the conversations lively. Caroline ate and laughed and tried to pretend she wasn't affected by Travis's closeness. The fact he'd pressed his thigh into hers hadn't gone unnoticed by her dancing hippos, who'd added tumbling to their routine. She hoped her face and overenthusiastic laughter at Travis's bad jokes didn't tip her hand.

So she'd developed feelings for him. Big deal. She'd live. She leaned close a couple of times just to store a memory of his scent...clean and masculine with a touch of sandalwood.

Olivia stood. "Why don't we have coffee and cake in the man cave so we can all watch Cash get those few points he needs to qualify for the Nationals in Las Vegas."

"But, Olivia. It's a man cave. Mitch told me no women allowed," Travis said.

Everybody laughed.

"Tough," Olivia said. "Tonight it's an eighty-inch-flat-screen-TV-viewing room. Or else no dessert."

"She plays rough," Mitch said in a stage whisper. "You better just agree."

Before everyone moved to Mitch's man cave, the door-bell began to chime. Olivia and Mitch exchanged quick glances.

"You expecting anyone else?" Mitch asked.

Olivia shook her head. "Nope. You?"

"No. I'll see who it is if you ladies will rustle up some coffee and dessert."

"We'll clear the dishes. C'mon, Jason. Give me a hand," Travis said, stacking his plate on top of Caroline's.

Mitch headed to the front door as the guys began collecting the dishes to carry back to the kitchen. Travis was shoving his chair under the table when Mitch returned with John Webster, Travis's foreman.

"John. Is something wrong at the ranch?" Concern

deepened the grooves bracketing Travis's mouth as his lips pulled tight.

"Sorry for bothering you folks, but, Travis, there's someone here who says he's your brother-in-law."

"Excuse me?" Travis's brow knitted into a frown.

Caroline stopped walking toward the kitchen and turned around. Her stomach fell to her knees. Surely not...

"Says he's her brother." Webster pointed toward Caroline with his chin. "Said you two got married three weeks ago. I told him he was mistaken, but he demanded that I bring him over here."

Noah pushed his way into the dining room. "Caroline," he said, a catch in his voice. "This man said I was lying. Tell him I'm not. Tell him."

"Noah." Caroline pressed her hands to her chest in shock. "What are you doing here?"

Noah's hands fisted. "Tell him," he insisted. "Tell him you and Travis got married. Tell him I'm not lying."

Caroline froze. How could she tell her brother that the whole wedding had been a staged scene for their grandmother? How could she tell him that she was the one who was lying? She risked a quick glance around the dining room. Everyone seemed frozen in spot watching the after-dinner show.

"Travis?" his mother said. "What's going on?"

"Son?" his father asked.

Caroline swallowed, almost choking on the boulder in her throat. "I'm sorry. This is all my fault."

Travis moved to her side and put his arm around her. "Now, honey. Don't go taking all the blame. I wanted to keep our marriage a secret for a while too." He plastered a big smile on his face. "Surprise. Caroline and I got married."

Thirteen

Travis pulled her snug against him. He was pretty sure she was getting ready to confess all. He didn't want her to say another word. When she opened her mouth to speak, he leaned over and kissed her. Her shoulders stiffened. Around them, a stunned silence filled the room.

He looked at his family. "Isn't anyone going to congratulate us?"

"Of course, honey," his mother said. "I think we're all thrilled for both of you. We're just a little..."

"Surprised?" Travis offered.

"Shocked," Jason said. "Where are your rings?"

"Well, personally I don't care where their rings are. I think it's wonderful," Olivia said, hurrying around the table. She pulled Caroline from Travis's arms and embraced her. "You are my favorite sister-in-law."

"Hey!" Lydia said. "What am I? Chopped liver?"

Olivia looked at her. "You haven't made an honest man of my brother yet. This one..." She pulled back to look at Caroline. "I am so happy, Caroline." She pulled Travis into a group embrace. "So happy for both of you. I can't believe you didn't tell us."

"Yes," Jason said with a suspicious glint in his eye. "Why haven't you mentioned this? Noah—it's Noah, right?"

Noah nodded.

"Noah says you two got married almost a month ago. Why keep it a secret?"

All the color had drained from Caroline's face. Her body shook like his old truck with no shocks. Travis feared she was either going to faint or blurt out the truth. They needed to talk...privately. They needed to get their story straight before going public. Her reputation was at stake.

"Noah, we—"

"We haven't worked out all the logistics," Travis interrupted her to say. "Like our rings." He pulled his wedding band from his front pocket and slipped it on. "We just weren't ready to go public."

Jason's gaze flicked from Travis to Caroline and back. "The logistics, like where to live? I mean, Caroline is still living in her house in town, right?"

Travis grabbed the lifeline tossed him by his brother. "Sometimes. We tried her staying at the ranch, but it was such a long drive to town every day. Caroline thought it'd be better if she stayed in town during the week when she's on-call for the emergency room."

Jackie Montgomery came over and pulled Caroline into a tight embrace. "I'm so happy. Thank goodness, you two finally got the hint. I mean, when I think of all the times I've thrown you together." She laughed and kissed Caroline's cheek. "I knew when I met you that you're exactly what Travis needs. I promise to be the most awesome mother-in-law. I'll never interfere in your lives or stick my nose where it doesn't belong."

"Can I have that in writing?" Mitch joked.

"Hush," his future mother-in-law said. "I'm not making you that promise."

Caroline laughed and Travis could see her shoulders relaxing as some of her tension let up.

"Not to change the subject," Travis said, "but what are you doing here, Noah? Do Patrick or Leslie know where you are?"

Noah assumed a defiant pose. "I'm not going back. I hate it there."

"Not my question," Travis said, his voice coated with steel. "Do your uncle and aunt know where you are?"

Caroline went to Noah and took his hand. "What happened?"

"I just hate it, Caroline. They've moved into Mamie's house like...like they own the place."

Caroline understood his loss...of home, of his grand-mother, of everything he knew. "That's what Mamie wanted, Noah," she told him in a quiet voice. She brushed his long hair off his face. "She wanted you to be able to stay where you'd been. She didn't want you to have to move."

"I don't care," he said, jerking his hand away from hers. "I hate them. I want to stay here. With you and Travis."

"Oh, Noah. I don't think that's such a good idea," Caroline said. Her house of cards was teetering. Soon it was going to fall and bury both Travis and her. She wasn't going to let Travis look bad because of her mess. "Travis and I—"

"We'll talk about it," Travis interrupted. He looked at his watch. "Cash will be riding soon, and I think Caroline and I have brought enough chaos to tonight's dinner. Maybe we should take Noah home and contact his uncle and aunt. They must be frantic since—" he glared at Noah, "—I'm sure they don't have a clue where he is."

"You don't have to go," Olivia said.

Travis hugged his sister then held out his hand to Mitch. "Congratulations, man. She's too good for you."

Mitch shrugged good-naturedly. "I know, but let's keep that between us. Maybe she'll never figure it out."

Caroline hugged Travis's parents. "Thank you for, well, for just being so great. I'm sorry we've thrown a kink into tonight's after-dinner plans to watch Cash ride."

Jackie kissed her cheek. "Are you kidding?" She grabbed Travis's arm and pulled him over for a kiss too. "I'm so happy for both of you." She gave Noah a squinted look. "I don't know you, son, but if you're going to be hanging around this family, you'd better learn right now that we don't like liars, cheats or dishonesty in any fashion. If you've run away from home, you'd best get on the phone to let those people know you're okay."

Caroline flinched at Jackie's words. All those words fit Caroline. A liar and a dishonest person. And maybe a cheat, if she counted cheating Olivia and Mitch out of all of the glory for tonight's announcement. If God had any mercy at all, He'd strike her dead right now. When He didn't, she decided leaving was the best option.

She and Travis said their goodbyes and headed for their cars. Once the front door had shut, she whirled on Noah.

"You are in so much trouble, mister. You have no idea."

Noah assumed his I'm-not-scared-of-you posture and sneered at her...until he found himself facing an irate Travis Montgomery.

"Let me tell you something, boy." His Southern accent became quite pronounced with his anger. "You don't have to love your sister, or even like her, but you will give her respect. You understand?"

Noah mumbled his answer.

"What'd you say?" Travis growled. "Speak up."

"Yes."

"Yes, what?"

"Yes, I understand."

"I'm sir to you. And you'll address Caroline with yes, ma'am. Got it?'

"Yeah."

"Excuse me?" Travis barked. "You deaf, son? If you have any hope of staying here, you'd better learn some manners and I mean now. Got it?"

"Yes, sir," Noah said through gritted teeth. "I got it."

"Great." He turned to Caroline who'd stood watching Travis whip her little brother into shape. "You okay?"

She nodded.

"Can you follow me to my house?"

She nodded again.

"Okay. I'll take Noah with me if that's okay with you."

She nodded a third time.

"Are you sure you're okay?"

Caroline blew out a long breath. "Am I going to wake up soon from this nightmare? I mean, this is a bad dream, right?"

Travis chuckled. "At least your sense of humor is intact." He brushed his lips against hers. "Follow me."

Caroline dragged herself to her loaner car and got in. Sense of humor? She didn't have a sense of humor. She was serious. This was the worst nightmare of her life.

She followed Travis's truck taillights as it rolled down the road about ten miles and turned onto a concrete drive she was well familiar with. She'd hoped to be back at his place soon but not exactly like this. Her legs and arms were shaking...from anger first and fear second.

Sure she'd be leaving Whispering Springs in only four

months and would never see these people again, so what everyone thought of her was of minor concern. Of major concern was leaving here with Travis's reputation intact. He'd stepped up and helped her when she needed it. Somehow she had to figure out how to make sure everyone knew she was the bad person in the marriage farce and Travis was the Good Samaritan.

Bright-red taillights flashed in front of her as Travis stopped in front of his old-fashioned farm house. Every time she'd been here, she'd parked in the garage, never in his circle drive. But each visit she'd taken a moment to appreciate the beauty of his place.

The large staircase that led up to a wrap-around porch supporting aged rockers. Potted green ferns hung from the porch eaves above the white railing. Dormer windows poked through the second-story roofline. This place was too big for one man. To her, it felt like the house cried out for a family.

As she turned her car, her headlights lit up a 1963 white Rolls-Royce Silver Cloud convertible.

"I'm going to kill him" she muttered as she slammed on her brakes. With a loud slam of her driver's door, she announced her anger. "Noah!" She marched over to where he and Travis stood. "Do not tell me that you drove Mamie's car down here." Her breathing was rapid and noisy as she blew hot, angry air toward her fourteen-year-old-unlicensed-driver brother.

Rather than taking his usual defensive stand, Noah slipped a little behind Travis as though he could protect him from his sister's wrath.

Travis's gaze whipped from Caroline to Noah cowering behind him. "What did you do?" he asked in a scary, calm voice.

"I saw Aunt Leslie sitting in the Silver Shadow, Caro.

It's not her car. Mamie gave it to you, not them. Leslie had no right. I think she was trying to figure out how to take the Shadow from you."

Caroline rubbed her hands over her face and tried to get control of her emotions. "So you what? Drove it down here?" She kicked a rock that had found its way onto Travis's drive. She walked away, kicked a tire on Travis's truck and marched back. "I don't know what is going on with you, Noah. You're fourteen. Do you have any idea how much trouble you'd have gotten in if the cops had stopped you? For all I know, Patrick or Leslie have reported this car stolen. That's grand theft auto. We're talking some serious jail time." She raked her fingers through her hair. "Damn it, Noah. What is going on with you?"

"Yeah, you don't know what's going on with me. You don't even care what's going on with me," he shouted. "You just go on with your life and never give me a thought."

"Okay, you two," Travis said in a composed voice. "Let's calm down. For tonight, let's call Patrick and Leslie and let them know where you and the car are. You can stay here tonight and we can talk about your future in the morning. Does that work for you, Caroline?"

She was grinding her teeth so hard her jaw was starting to ache. Of all the stupid—

"Caroline? You agree?"

She nodded, afraid that she'd begin shouting again if she tried to speak.

"You have clothes in the car?" Travis asked Noah, who responded with a nod. "Okay then, get them and let's go inside."

Noah set off for the Rolls like a demon was on his heels.

Caroline's shoulders sagged. "My God, Travis. Sorry doesn't begin to cover my feelings."

He moved over to where she stood and wrapped a comforting arm around her. "He's scared to death, honey. He thinks he's all grown up but he's just a kid. A lost, scared, desperate kid. I know you probably want to strangle him right now—"

"Ya think?"

With the full moon overhead, she could see his smile. "I'm sure Mom wanted to strangle me, or Jason, or Cash or maybe all of us at one time or the other. Let's take this one step at a time. We'll call Patrick and Leslie. Let them know he's okay and put him to bed. I suspect he's exhausted. Then you and I can talk."

"Travis. You are an incredible man," she said. "You don't deserve all the crap I've brought into your life."

He squeezed her shoulders. "To tell you the truth, life was getting a little boring until you came along. Now, don't worry. We'll get this straightened out."

Noah jogged toward them, the strap of a dark-green backpack flung across his arm. He handed the car keys to Caroline.

"I'm sorry you're mad at me, Caroline, but I'm not sorry to be here."

"We'll talk about this in the morning, Noah. Let's get that phone call done and then find you someplace for the night."

Travis swept his arm toward the stairs leading to the porch. "After you," he said to Noah.

Noah bounded up the stairs with Travis and Caroline following behind like sheep herders. He stopped at the front door and waited for Travis to open it. It wasn't locked. Caroline was thankful Noah had enough manners to not just open someone's door and walk in.

Travis flipped on a light. His boots thrummed on the

hardwood floor entry. Noah sneakers squeaked as he dragged his feet inside. Caroline tried to move quietly but her heels still tap-tap-tapped on the wood.

To the left was an archway leading into a formal living room. A little farther in the foyer was a staircase leading to the upper level. To her right was the archway into a formal dining room. Travis continued straight ahead, flipping on lights as he went through the entry into a large family room.

Large, overstuffed furniture in rust and brown tones filled the cavernous room. The hardwood continued into this room, but much of it was covered by a massive rug bearing the Halo M brand. Beside Travis's bedroom, this was her favorite room. They'd spent some nice evenings here watching television or talking during time together.

The kitchen was off to her right and the closed door to her left led to Travis's master suite. She glanced toward his bedroom and felt the moist heat as it built between her thighs.

Travis motioned to the furniture that had been arranged into a conversation pit. Noah flopped into one of the chairs and propped his head in the palm of his hand. Caroline sat on the sofa where Travis joined her.

"Unless spoken to, I want you to remain quiet while we speak to your uncle and aunt," Travis said to Noah. "Got it?"

"Got it."

"What?" Travis asked with an arched eyebrow.

"Yes, sir," Noah replied.

"Better." He turned to Caroline. "You want to use the house phone or your cell?"

"Cell is fine." She pulled her cell phone from her purse and pressed one key. She'd long ago programmed Mamie's house phone with a short-cut key.

The conversation was short. No, her aunt and uncle didn't know the car was missing. No, they didn't know Noah was missing. He was supposed to be staying at a friend's house. When they insisted they wanted to drive down and get him, Caroline asked them to hold on a minute.

"Can I borrow your office so I can speak privately?"

"Of course."

Travis led her through the closed door to the private office that was part of the master suite. "Do you want me to stay?"

She nodded. "Please."

He closed the door and sat on a leather sofa. She took a seat beside him.

"I'm back," she said to Patrick. "I don't want you to come get him yet. He's obviously upset. Maybe he should spend a little time with me."

"With you and your husband," Patrick said.

"Yes, right. That's what I meant."

"It's not right. You're a newlywed. You and Travis need this time alone."

Caroline had the phone on speaker so Travis could hear the conversation. At this point, he spoke up. "Patrick. Travis here. I understand your concerns, but trust me when I say that we are glad to have Noah stay with us. Caroline and I have the rest of our lives. Noah needs us now. I have to agree with Caroline. He should stay here for a while. Of course we'd stay in touch with you and Leslie and his parents. Keep you guys in the loop with how things are going. If he becomes too much for us to handle, then we can address that issue at that time."

"Travis, you're a good man. Thank you. And you too, Caroline."

"Oh yes. I'm a good man," Caroline joked.

Patrick chuckled. "You know what I mean."

"I do. Noah and I haven't ever spent much time together. I realized I don't really know my little brother that well. Maybe this is God's way of making that happen." She figured that might bring *Pastor Pat* around to agreeing with them.

"I hadn't thought of it like that. Maybe you're right. But the minute you want us to come for him, just call."

"Will do," Caroline said.

"Of course," Travis said.

"And, Caroline? I'm sorry about him taking the Rolls. I'm hoping it made it down there okay?"

"As far as I know. I'll look at it in the daylight tomorrow, but Noah hasn't mentioned anything."

"Okay then. It's settled," Travis said. "We'll keep Noah here for a while."

They hung up the phone and looked at each other.

"I don't know what to do with a teenage boy," Caroline confessed. "You know that. We talked about this."

"Not to worry," Travis said with authority. "I was one once. I know how they think, how they eat and how much they try to get away with." He smiled. "I think mucking out the stalls tomorrow will be a good place for Noah to start learning about ranch life, don't you?"

"Since I have no idea what mucking out the stalls means, I'll just trust you." She sighed and dropped her head into her hands. "I'm beginning to think you got ripped off."

He put one finger under her chin and lifted her head until their gazes met. "What are you talking about?"

"Singing Springs can't be worth what it's costing you."

He smiled. "Still a bargain. Besides, it got you here

again." He stood and held out his hand, which she took. He pulled her to her feet. "Now, let's go tell Noah."

They found him in the kitchen looking inside the refrigerator. He closed it with a guilty slam.

"Sorry. I was hungry."

"Have a seat," Travis said, pointing toward a set of barstools with his chin.

Noah climbed onto one. Caroline stood alongside Travis.

"Here's the deal," Caroline said. "Travis has agreed to let you stay here. Patrick and Leslie have also agreed."

A broad smile burst onto Noah's face. "Great."

"However," Caroline continued. "There are some rules."

"Sure. Sure. Whatever." Noah beamed. "Thanks, man," he said to Travis.

Travis scratched his chin. "Well, Noah, you've got to understand. I have a working ranch. I raise horses and train them. I have a crew of mostly men who work for me. Some of them have families. I have to keep this place profitable to keep it running and keep all those people employed. So here, everybody works. You remember John who brought you to my sister's house tonight? He's my foreman. Even his youngest kid, Norman, has a job. You know what I'm saying?"

Noah looked a little confused. "I'm not sure."

"I'm saying you can stay, but you don't get to hang around the house all day. You'll have jobs here that are your responsibility. Nobody else will do them for you. They can't. They have their own work to get done. And you have to go to school."

"I can't work and go to school."

"Why not?" Travis asked. "The rest of the kids here do."

Noah shook his head. "I can't. I'd have to be at school all day then homework at night."

Travis smiled, and Caroline had seen that smile before. She almost—almost—felt sorry for Noah. Travis was moving in for the kill.

"Well, you see, Noah. We have a private teacher here. Think of it as homeschooling. I am positive you'll have more than enough hours in the day to get everything done."

"But—"

"It's Travis's way or back to Arkansas. Take your pick," Caroline said.

Noah blew out a disgusted breath. "Fine. Whatever."

"And Noah?" Travis added. "All the men here will be addressed with yes, sir and no, sir. Got it?"

"Yes, sir," Noah said in a surly tone.

"Are you really hungry or were you nosing around?" Travis asked. "You are welcome to nose about the kitchen and the upstairs, but the master bedroom suite is completely off-limits. Understand?"

"Yes, sir," Noah said with a huff. "And I was really hungry. I was afraid to stop on the way down to eat."

That meant he'd been without food for at least eight hours, maybe more. For a teenage boy, that was a lifetime without food.

"What do you like to eat?" Travis asked. "I'm sure my housekeeper has left something."

"Anything," Noah said. "I'd eat a horse if you brought me one."

Travis lifted an eyebrow. "We raise them. We don't eat them."

Noah laughed, and it was the first time Caroline had seen his face with a playful expression. He was a handsome boy. He had their father's chin but their mother's eyes. She felt sorry for the girls in his future. He was going to be quite a looker, and she suspected, quite the heartbreaker.

Noah finished off two plates of spaghetti, six rolls and a full liter of Coke. As he wiped his mouth, he grinned. "That was awesome. Thanks. Do you have anything for dessert?"

"Dessert?" Caroline stuttered. "Are you kidding? Where are you going to put it? In your ear?"

Noah shrugged. "Just asking."

Travis picked up Noah's plate and fork. "This is the only time I'll be doing this for you," he explained. He pulled down the door of a dishwasher. "You finish, you put your dishes in here. Don't have to rinse them but you do you have to put them away."

Noah nodded. "Yes, sir."

"Great. There's some leftover pie in the refrigerator. You go get your backpack and we'll take the pie and a fork up to the guest room. You can eat it up there as long as you swear to bring the dirty dishes down with you in the morning."

"I will," Noah said with enthusiasm. "I promise."

"Don't you want to know what kind of pie it is?" Caroline asked.

"Doesn't matter," Noah replied. "Pie is pie."

Travis looked at Caroline and grinned. "Welcome to the world of teenage boys. We eat anything." He pulled a chocolate pie off a refrigerator shelf. "Let's go."

Noah hurried off to the family room for his bag. Travis followed then turned back. "C'mon, honey. I'm sure you'll want to see which room I put him in."

Upstairs there were three additional bedrooms. Two over the master suite that shared a bath and one bedroom on the far side of the house over the kitchen with its own full bath. Travis turned right at the top of the stairs and headed for the room farthest from the master suite.

He turned on the light revealing a room done in light-colored wood—oak or ash, Caroline guessed—with a queen-sized bed, two side tables, a dresser and a freestanding armoire. The doors to the armoire were shut. The room's multi-colored carpet was ideal for hiding the food stains she feared Noah would leave behind. The bed was covered with an old-fashioned patchwork quilt and four pillows. A comfortable reading chair sat next to the dormer window.

"This is lovely," Caroline said. "Did you do it?"

Travis laughed. "Are you kidding? My mother and John's wife, Henrietta, did all this. Don't get me wrong. I love what they did, but I'm a guy. What do I know about drapes and bedcovers?"

Noah tossed his bag into the chair and dropped on his back onto the middle of the bed. "Awww," he said. "Nice bed, bro-in-law."

Travis's eyebrows shot up but he apparently decided to let the remark slide. He set the pie and fork on the dresser and walked across the room and opened a door.

"In here's the bath. There should be towels, soap, whatever you need." He opened another door to reveal an empty closet. He swept his hand across the bare space. "Self-evident." He shut the closet door.

"You should be aware," he continued, "that there is a burglar alarm in the house. I set it at night. Every night," he emphasized. "If you open a window or an exterior door, an alarm will go off and the police are automatically called. You probably don't want to do that."

"Yes, sir," Noah said, his mouth already full of pie. "No alarms. No police. I got it."

"Caroline and I need to have a serious talk tonight. We'll be downstairs. I'd rather you stay up here unless there is an emergency."

"Okay," Noah said and then quickly amended it to, "Yes, sir."

"You have a cell phone?" Travis asked.

Noah brows pulled into a confused frown. "I do."

"Let me have it," Travis said with his hand outstretched.

"Why? It's my phone."

"My house," he stopped and started again. "Our house. Our rules. You haven't shown that you deserve the privilege of a cell phone. Hand it over. Once you've shown you can be trusted, you can have it back."

"Caroline," Noah whined. "Tell him that's not fair. It's my phone."

"Your phone?" Caroline repeated. "You pay for that phone? You have a job that pays for the monthly service?"

"What?" Noah asked.

"I didn't think so. Do what Travis says. Hand it over."

He glared at both of them before getting off the bed and heading over to his backpack. He pulled an Apple iPhone from a side pocket and handed it to Travis. "There," he said. "I hope you're both happy."

Travis slipped the phone into his front pants pocket. "We're getting there. Now, get some sleep. We start the day about five."

"Five what?" Noah said with wide eyes.

"Five in the morning."

"Are you fucking kidding me?"

"Hey!" Travis snapped at him. "Watch your language."

"Sorry," Noah said, but he didn't sound like he meant it.

Neither Caroline nor Travis decided to address it. It'd been a long day for all of them, and the night wasn't over for her and Travis yet. She moved to where Noah stood by the chair and hugged him. "I love you, Noah. I really do."

She thought she heard him sniff. "Yeah," he said. "Me too."

Travis came over and put his hand on Noah's shoulder. "I'll knock on your door in the morning. Now get some sleep."

Caroline shut the bedroom door and looked at Travis and grinned. "I can't believe you got his cell phone."

Travis returned her grin. "It was kind of a test…a how-bad-does-he-want-to-stay test. Apparently, he wants to stay pretty bad."

Caroline rubbed the tense muscles in her neck. "I guess so."

"Let's go talk," he said on a long sigh.

Fourteen

"**W**ell," Caroline said as they walked back downstairs. "Today has certainly been..."

"Eventful?" Travis suggested.

She gave a sad chuckle and then sighed. "Yeah, I guess that's one word for it." She stopped to look over her shoulder at him. "Can you believe he just showed up here?" Turning back, she continued down the stairs.

"I kind of feel for him. I mean, did you see the look on his face when your uncle and aunt said they would come get him? Pure panic."

"Want to head to the office to talk?"

"Sure."

They made sure the outer door leading to the rooms in the master suite was closed as well as the door to the study. Caroline collapsed onto the sofa, stretching her legs out in front of her.

"I wish I had a beer," she said.

"Sorry." He opened the mini-refrigerator. "I can offer Dr. Pepper, Coke or water."

"Water."

"Catch," he said and tossed her a plastic bottle.

She cracked off the top. "Thanks."

He popped the cap off a bottle of Dr. Pepper and took a long drink. Then he walked over and sat by her.

"What's your plan, Stan?" he said with a grin.

"Don't make jokes, Travis. This is serious." She raked her hand through her hair. "What are we going to do?"

He took another long draw of his soft drink. "Continue to be married is my suggestion."

His words made her heart flip even though she knew he didn't mean them the way they came out.

"But how?" She stood to pace, but he caught her waist and pulled her back down.

"I know you pace when you're nervous, but I'm too exhausted to watch you wear a rut in my rug tonight."

Bending her left leg onto the couch, she turned to face him. "This is getting out of control."

He shrugged. "Life happens. You have to play the cards you're given. We had a plan but now that's shot to hell. We'll have to adjust."

"What do you suggest?"

"We stay married." And then he added in a rush, "At least while you're still here. After that?" He shrugged again. "We make a new plan. That's how life works."

She stood. "Give me a minute to process. This isn't at all what I wanted." She walked away, her final words hanging in the air like a bad smell. She whirled back. "That last statement didn't come out right. What I meant is that I wasn't trying to trick or trap you into an unwanted public arrangement." Heat rose up her throat to her face. When he smiled at her obvious discomfort, relief flooded through her. "You know what I meant, right?"

He nodded. "But we're here now, so what we thought

we were doing or what we had planned is out the window." He patted the sofa cushion. "Sit."

Dropping heavily beside him, she sighed. "It's going to get out we're together. I saw the gleam in your mother's eyes. I'm leaving soon. Once I'm gone, I'll be a memory, but you'll be staying here. I don't want to do anything that would hurt your reputation in the community."

He laughed heartily. "Are you kidding? I couldn't care less about my reputation in the community, as you put it." He put his arm around her and pulled her close. "We're married in the eyes of my family. We'll stay that way until we decide to change things." He leaned over and kissed her. It was a soft, non-demanding kiss. A reassuring gesture one might give a skittish virgin, but she wasn't a virgin.

Wrapping her hand around the back of his neck, she pulled him down for an open-mouth kiss, slipping her tongue into his mouth, she hoped sending him a message that she missed their nights together. Message received, he changed the angle of his head and took the kiss deeper. He threaded his hands into her hair to hold her head steady for his plundering tongue. She pressed her free hand flat against his hard chest. Beneath her palm, his heart beat a fast, steady thrum. Hers was flying, a locomotive with no brakes. She walked her fingers up his chest until she reached his shoulders...broad and hard under her palm. His shirt was hot from his body heat. Her nose was filled with his scent. Sexy. Hot. Masculine. Raw sex magnetism.

She pulled back and stared at him. She flicked her tongue out to lick her lips. His gaze went to her mouth and then back to her eyes. His blue eyes were dark and flashing with lust.

She took a scary leap. "I've missed you over the past

couple of weeks. Missed your bed." Her heart kicked painfully at her ribs as she awaited his reply.

He traced his thumb across her lower lip. "I kept thinking you'd come back."

"I kept waiting for you to ask."

"Well, lucky for us your brother made the decision for both of us."

Like every time he touched her, the kiss shook her to the core. Trembling from the kiss's effect, she touched her fingertips to her lips.

"You pack a powerful punch, Mr. Montgomery," she said with a smile.

"We're supposed to be married," he said, his voice a gravelly rasp. "We have to be able to touch each other without one of us shrieking."

"Hmm," she said. "I might need a little more practice." She grinned at him.

"Right. Practice time. I'm pretty sure I can work that into my schedule if you can."

She laughed and kissed him again. "Let's get serious for a minute."

"I'm always serious when I'm talking about kissing and sex," he said, a twinkle in his eyes. "But okay. What do you want to talk about?"

"Living arrangements."

"What about them?"

"I really do need to stay in town on nights when I'm on call." She looked at him. "But it's not right that I dump my little brother on you and not be here. And taking Noah to my house in town doesn't make sense."

He rubbed the spot between his eyes with his thumb. "No, Noah should stay here. No doubt about that." He drew in a deep breath and let it out slowly. "As a newlywed couple, we have to live in the same house."

"I know. I know."

"Okay, here's what we'll do. When you're on call you'll stay in town. The other nights, you'll be here in the master suite. We'll work it out. I want to work it out." He brushed her hair away from her face. She couldn't help it. She melted at his touch. "Don't forget tomorrow night. We have to make an appearance at the dance, and I can assure you the news of our marriage will have spread by then."

She dropped her forehead to his chest. It was like hitting flesh-covered rock. "Can we skip?" She hoped he'd say no. After all, she had that killer dress.

"Nope. Family commitment."

Yes.

"Besides, you'd better get used to those for the next four months. The Montgomerys are nothing if not civic minded. The fall seems to be the worst for worthy-causes functions. Dances. Dinners. Silent auctions. You name it and we'll probably have to be there."

"I don't have the clothes for all those fancy occasions. I see some shopping in my future."

"Maybe, but we do have the most awesome car to drive."

She rolled her gaze up at him. "I swear. If you're staying fake married to me so you can drive the Rolls, I'll neuter you while you sleep."

He kissed her forehead. "I'll never confess to anything. It's getting late. Maybe we should get some sleep. I'm sure it's common for new brides to have dark rings under their eyes but—"

She stepped on his toe. "I don't have dark circles under my eyes...do I?"

He laughed. "No." He gave her a soft kiss on the mouth. "Want to go to bed?"

Oh God, yes.

"It is getting late, and since you've already mentioned I'm getting dark circles—"

She screeched as he swept her up into his arms. "Honey, you better learn you don't argue with a man who can pick you up."

He grinned as he carried her to the master bedroom. He dropped her in the middle of his king-sized poster bed.

"Oh, no," she said, letting her head fall on a pillow.

"What's wrong?"

"Now everybody will know we're sleeping together."

He laughed. "I think they might have figured that out anyway, what with the way you eat me up with your eyes."

She threw a pillow at him. "Stop it. I do not."

He caught the pillow and tossed it back with a deep chuckle. "Come on, raccoon eyes, you need some sleep."

"Sadly, you're right. I have to get up in..." She rolled over to look at the clock. "Oh crap. I've got to be at the hospital in a few hours. I've got rounds in the morning." She started to get undressed and stopped. "Do you have a T-shirt I could borrow?"

He opened a dresser drawer and tossed an extra-large tall shirt. "That do?"

"Perfect." She slipped her feet over the edge of the bed, kicked off her shoes and slid off the bed. "I'm heading to the bathroom for a quick shower."

He pulled his shirt over his head and tossed it into a chair in the corner. "Fine."

She turned around to say something, but all the words in her head melted when she got a good look at Travis's upper naked body. Thick, muscular upper arms that shifted and bulged when he moved to unbuckle his belt. Pale, coarse hair covered his rock-hard chest, running down his flat abdomen until it disappeared into his slacks. The area between her thighs grew warm. Good God. What a perfect male body...or at least what she could see at the moment. Lucky for her, she knew the rest of it was just as delicious.

He looked up with a lifted eyebrow. "See what I mean? If you don't stop looking at me like that, neither of us will get any sleep tonight."

"What?" she was able to rasp out. She grabbed her water bottle and took a long swallow.

Damn if he wasn't right. Just looking at him kicked her libido into overdrive. Those tutu-attired hippos weren't just twirling in her stomach right now. They were doing flips and cartwheels and flying ninja kicks to her gut. And the idiot man knew exactly the impact he was having on her.

He took a couple of steps toward her. "Darlin'?"

She snatched the T-shirt up against her body. "Shower," she said and raced from the bedroom, his knowing laugh following her.

She was surprised that Travis wasn't in the bed when she came out from the bath. After flipping off the light, she slipped in his bed, her body practically cooing with pleasure. In a couple of minutes, the light in the hall flashed off and the mattress dipped as Travis got into the bed. She rolled toward him and he wrapped her in his thick arms before kissing her.

"Go to sleep," he said in a whisper. "This will all work out. I promise."

His breathing quickly became regular. She envied his ability to drop off to sleep so easily.

. . .

HER CELL PHONE vibrated on the wooden bedside table. Caroline threw out her arm to grab it only to realize she wasn't near the edge of the bed. As consciousness began to sweep the sleep fog from her brain, she realized she was draped over a firm, hot male body. Her head rested on his chest. Her legs were braided through his like a rag rug.

Her phone vibrated again. Reluctantly, she disengaged her legs from his, trying to move slowly so to not wake him up. As she was congratulating herself, he wrapped his arm around her waist and pulled her against him. He pressed his face into her neck and nuzzled. He moaned a couple of words and his death grip around her lessened.

Slowly, she lifted his arm and slid across the bed and then gently placed his arm back on the mattress. Very sly.

She stood, letting his enormous shirt fall around her knees.

"You know I'm awake," he said.

She jumped and then slammed her hand over her heart. "Don't do that. You scared me to death." She remembered their sleeping position and wondered if he'd been aware of how she'd plastered herself to him probably all night.

"How long have you been awake?"

"Long enough to know your legs were all twisted up with mine and that you used my chest as your pillow."

Thank goodness for the dark, she thought as the warmth of an embarrassed flush climbed up her neck. Apparently, she had no restraint when it came to Travis, whether she was awake or asleep.

The lamp on Travis's side of the bed lit up the room.

"Eek," she said, pressing her hands over her eyes. "Warn me before you turn on a light."

The sheets rustled. Peeking through the slit of one eye, she saw he'd sat up and was now leaning against the headboard. He scratched his chest. Her fingers itched to do the same.

The sheet covering the lower half of his body reminded her of a carnival tent...spiked high in the center and draping off at the side. She wished she had time to explore his tent pole.

She opened both eyes. "Sorry. I didn't mean to wake you."

"I need to get up any way," he said as he threw back the top covers, got out of bed and headed for the closet.

Caroline couldn't take her gaze off the squeezing and releasing of his butt muscles as he walked. She fisted her fingers, leaving small half-moon marks in the palms of her hand.

"Why are you standing there?" he asked, coming out of the closet buttoning up a pair of jeans.

"It's not fair, you know."

"What's that?" Travis zipped his jeans carefully to avoid damage to his hardening Johnson.

"I have bedhead and bad breath at five a.m. and you, well, you make me want to brush my teeth and climb back in the bed."

"Oh, darlin'. You are so wrong." He dropped the fresh shirt he'd just pulled from the closet. Unzipping his jeans, he said, "I love bedhead and bad breath." He shoved his jeans and briefs to the floor and moved across the room to where she still stood beside the bed.

When he'd awakened and found her draped over him like a saddle on a horse, his cock hadn't just twitched but grown uncomfortably hard. Instead of moving her or waking her, he lay there and enjoyed the feeling of having a woman pressed next to him in his bed. It'd been a long time since a woman had been in his bed. He'd thought he didn't miss it, but he'd been wrong.

Putting both hands on her shoulders, he pushed her backwards. She landed on the mattress with a bounce and a giggle. He made quick work of removing her T-shirt and panties.

"Shh," she said, laughing as he nibbled on her neck. "My brother might hear us."

"Please. He thinks we're married. Plus, teenagers keep vampire hours. He's not awake." Travis pressed his rock-hard shaft into her hip. "I, on the other hand, am awake."

"Yes," she said with a hip thrust against his throbbing cock. "I can see that all of you is awake."

She pulled his head down for a deep kiss, mixing their morning breaths, tangling her tongue with his. Wrapping his lips around her tongue, he sucked it. She moaned with pleasure.

Using lips, teeth and his tongue, Travis nibbled and licked his way down her neck, pausing to dip the tip of his tongue into the hollow at the base of her throat before continuing on until his lips circled her nipple. He drew her nipple and a large portion of her breast into his mouth and sucked it hard.

"Oh damn, that feels good," she said with a groan and wrapped her legs around his calves. "More, please."

"So polite," he said, blowing cool air over her rigid nipple. He moved his attentions to her other breast while slipping a hand down her abdomen. He stroked her short, curly hair before gliding between her legs. She was warm and wet and ready for him. When he plunged a finger in, her hips arched off the bed. She groaned.

"Another one," she demanded, and he smiled against her breast.

After kissing her nipple one last time, he moved back to her mouth, giving her an open mouth, deep tongue kiss. At the same time, he pushed three fingers into her. He felt the air intake of her gasp.

"Like that?" he said in a whisper against her lips. He slid his fingers in and out, driving them hard against her clit. Instead of a verbal response, she moved her hips in time with his movements. She was close. He felt the muscles in her abdomen twitching and contracting. Her vaginal walls were beginning to tighten around his fingers when he pulled them free, leaving her hanging on the edge.

"Wait," she demanded. "Don't stop."

He positioned the tip of his cock at her opening. "Together," he said, his lips brushing hers. He drove hard into her. It'd been years since he'd felt the hot flesh of a woman's passage without the barrier of a condom. Holy hell. He'd forgotten the sensation, the sheer eroticism of the act.

Twisting her legs around his waist, she arched upward to meet his thrusts. She ran the tip of her tongue around the rim of his ear as her quiet pants and gasps sent electrical jolts from his head to his toes. He wouldn't last long, not with Caroline. She drove him to his edge much too fast for his liking.

"I'm almost there," she whispered into his ear, followed by a puff of hot breath as she moaned. "Harder. Harder."

He pounded in and out, jerking the bed beneath her. He felt the tightening of her walls around him, milking him, dragging him to his peak. As she came, she buried her mouth into his shoulder, sinking the edges of her teeth into his skin.

He answered in a rush, pouring himself deep inside, no longer worried about the consequences of no condom.

It was unfair that sex rejuvenated a woman but left a man in a coma. Travis lay on his back, his arm draped across his forehead. So unfair.

Caroline slipped from the bed and headed for the bath. "I'm going to take a quick shower."

Waving an arm in the air, he said, "You know where everything is. I'm just going to lie here and find some energy to move."

She was laughing as the door shut. He was still in the same position when she came out dressed in what she'd worn last night.

"Get up, lazy," she said. "I'm going to go make some coffee before I head into Whispering Springs. Okay?"

"Darlin', not only is it okay, but I'll worship you all day if you make enough for me."

She gave a short snort of laughter. "I doubt it will be that good."

By the time he'd finished brushing his teeth and shaving, the aroma of freshly brewed coffee filled the air. On the mornings that Henree didn't leave the coffee maker set on a timer, he never made a pot just for him and usually snagged a cup from the crew supply. But crew coffee never tasted as good as fresh brewed at home. Having Caroline in his kitchen with a fresh pot of coffee before he left for work was definitely the ideal way to start his day.

In the kitchen, he found Caroline sitting on a bar stool, a cup of coffee in one hand and her phone in the other.

"A call already this morning?" He took a mug from the cabinet.

"No. I was scrolling through my emails to see if there were any that needed my attention."

"And?"

She clicked the phone off. "And, no, nothing's there

unless you need Viagra from Mexico."

"Nope. First, don't need it. Second, I'm a good American. I like to buy my drugs off the dealer down the street." He took a sip of the coffee. It was very hot and very strong, exactly like he liked it.

She laughed. "I hope you don't mind, but I found a travel mug in the cabinet to take with me."

Travis leaned against the counter and crossed one booted ankle over the other. "You're welcome to anything in this house. Make yourself at home. Seriously."

"Thanks." She stood. "I've got to scoot. Good luck with Noah today."

"Yeah, I guess I need to be getting him up soon. Do you have any idea when you'll be back?"

She shrugged. "Not really. Probably early. What time do we need to leave for the dance?"

"We're all meeting at Mom and Dad's about seven-thirty and going together from there."

"Shouldn't be a problem. I'll be back here long before then."

"Okay." He snagged her arm as she passed and pulled her in for a kiss. "Have a good day."

She licked her upper lip and smiled. "Later."

After the front door closed, the house was still and quiet, but he figured that wouldn't last for long. He finished his first cup of coffee and headed upstairs.

He knocked on Noah's door. When there was no reply, he knocked again. The third time he knocked and opened the door, letting the light from the hall into the dark room.

"Shake a leg, boy. We've got work to do."

Noah groaned and pulled the covers over his head. "Go away."

Travis flipped on the room's overhead light. "I'll see you

downstairs in fifteen minutes. What kind of shoes did you bring?"

From under the covers came the muffled reply. "Sandals and tennis shoes."

Travis shook his head. Mucking out the stalls would be nasty work. The kid needed better shoes. "You got some jeans with you?"

"Yes."

"You'll need to wear those today for working. I'll see if I can round up some better shoes."

The reply was another muffled groan. Travis smiled. He remembered his dad waking him and his brothers up at ungodly hours to work. Their responses had been very similar to Noah's.

"Get up. I'll see you downstairs in fifteen minutes. Ten would be better."

Noah threw the covers back and stood, a wide yawn stretching his mouth.

"You drink coffee?"

Noah frowned. "I'm fourteen."

"We'll find something for you for breakfast." Travis turned to leave and then said over his shoulder, "Glad to have you here, Noah."

The teenager grinned and began pawing through his backpack.

Travis headed back to the kitchen. If Noah was going to be with them for a while—and it looked that way—he was going to need more clothes. There couldn't be that much in the backpack. He thought about calling Patrick or Leslie and asking them to send his stuff, but he decided that as touchy as Noah was about his uncle and aunt, he might resent their going through his personal belongings. Later today he'd check with his mom. She probably still had a pair of old boots lying around Noah could use. Probably no old jeans, but that could be easily taken care of.

For today, John Webster might have something. He rang up the Webster household.

"Morning, Travis. You're calling early," John Webster said when he answered. "Something wrong at your place?"

"Remember the kid from last night?"

"You mean your brother-in-law?"

"Yeah. That's the one. He's going to be here for a while. I want you to put him to work."

"Okay. What did you have in mind?"

"Today, mucking out the stalls. Can you get Amy and Rocky to show him the ropes?"

"Sure. No problem. My kids will love having someone else to help with their chores."

"One other thing. Noah only has sandals and tennis shoes. You have some rubber boots you can loan him?"

"What size?"

Noah had come into the kitchen during the conversation. Travis looked at him. "What size shoes?"

"Nine and a half."

"Nine and a half or ten."

"I've got something that'll work. Got some leather gloves he can use too."

"Great. Thanks, John. Tell Amy and Rocky I appreciate their showing Noah what to do today."

He hung up and turned to Noah. "Okay. You're all set for today. You're going to be mucking out the stalls with a couple of John's kids. Amy and Rocky."

Noah frowned. "I don't know how to muck out a stall." He scratched his head. "I don't even know what mucking a stall means."

Travis chuckled. "Don't worry. You're going to love it."

Fifteen

The boots were a little big, but as long as Noah left his sneakers on they stayed firmly on his feet. The gloves pulled on easily...snug, but perfect for what Travis had assigned to Noah.

"I'm not going to be with you today," Travis explained while Noah shoved his feet in to the knee-high rubber boots John Webster had provided. "I've got some training to do with a new horse that just came in, so you'll be on your own working with John's kids. Amy and Rocky know the ropes, so don't hesitate to ask either of them what to do."

Noah looked around, his uncertainty and unease with the new situation evident in every word, every movement. "It smells like horse shit in here."

"Yeah, I know."

"Can't you do anything about that?"

Travis stifled a smile. "Yup. The staff will be tackling that this morning. Oh, here come Amy and Rocky."

A pretty blonde teenage girl wearing jeans, a Texas Longhorns T-shirt and rubber boots was making her way toward where Travis and Noah stood. A dark-haired teenage boy dressed in pretty much the same fashion followed.

"Morning, Amy. This is Noah Graham. Noah, this is Amy Webster and her brother, Rocky. They'll be showing you the ropes today." He looked at Noah. "You'll be working with Amy and Rocky today."

"Morning," the girl said. "Thanks for the help, Mr. Montgomery."

"Hi." Noah's voice was soft, exposing his nervousness.

"Hi, Noah.," Amy gave him a bright smile. "We'll be glad to have the help, right, Rock?

"You know it. Good to meet you, Noah," Rocky said with an upward lift of his chin.

"I'll check on you later." Travis gave Noah's hair a quick tussle as he walked past.

As he was walking out of the barn he heard Amy say, "You ever mucked a stall before? It's gross."

Travis smiled and went to find Dustin, the cowboy assigned with cutting horse training today.

About noon, Travis climbed off the most stubborn horse he'd ever tried to train. The gleam in the horse's eyes said he thought he'd won. Travis ran his hand down the horse's nose. "You haven't won, you sonofabitch. I'll be back for more."

The horse tossed his head as though to say, "We'll see."

He left the horse in the corral and headed for the barn. As he neared, he heard laughter, a couple of shrieks and then more howls. He looked in. The first thing he noticed was the improvement in the smell. The teenagers had made significant progress on the stalls. The second thing he noticed was the big cow eyes Noah was making at Amy. Well, well, well. Noah and Amy. Interesting, like storing gasoline with a blow torch. It was possible that nothing would happen between them, but if it did...ka-boom.

"How's it going, guys?" he shouted as he walked in.

"Hi, Mr. Montgomery," Amy and Rocky said.

"Hey, Travis." Noah wrinkled his nose at Travis. "You didn't tell me my job was shoveling shit."

Amy and Rocky burst out laughing.

"You said it smelled like horse shit in here and that I ought to do something about it. I told you the staff would take care of it. Welcome to the staff," Travis said. "Everything going okay?"

"Yes, sir." Noah turned his infatuated gaze toward Amy. "I think we're done, right, Amy?"

Travis hid his smile. If Amy told Noah to do it all over again, he believed the boy probably would.

"We're done. Dad told us to brush down the horses before we brought them back in. We were just getting ready to start. Okay if Noah helps us with that too?"

Noah gave him a pleading look to not make him leave.

"Sure. Noah, you ever been around horses?"

"No, sir."

"Tell you what, why don't we take your sister on a trail ride tomorrow?" He looked at Amy and Rocky. "You guys are invited along."

Rocky's head dropped. "Can't. Still grounded."

Travis nodded. "Right. The spooked stallion. Amy?"

"Yes, sir. Thank you."

Travis turned to leave. "I'll let y'all get back to it." He looked in a couple of stalls as he exited. "Nice work everybody," he tossed over his shoulder.

At about three, he headed back by the barn to check on Noah. He wasn't there. Neither were Amy or Rocky.

"Webster," he hollered.

"In the tack room."

"How did the day go?" he asked when he found his foreman.

"Good. Noah is a hard worker."

Travis smiled. "He's trying to convince me to let him stay. Any problems?"

"None at all."

"Where are the kids?"

"They got done an hour or so ago. I told them they could go to the pond to swim. I hope that's okay with you."

"Sure. No problem, but I'm surprised you let Rocky go since last I heard he was grounded."

John grinned. "I made him take Marshall and Norman with him."

Travis laughed. "I hated having to take my little brothers with me. I think that punishment might be worse than the grounding or even the stall mucking."

John shrugged. "It'll teach him a lesson."

Travis leaned on the door frame. "You know, I think Noah's got a little crush on Amy."

John scowled. "She's too young for boyfriends."

"And you were what age when you fell in love the first time?"

He waved off Travis's question. "Bah. I was advanced for my age."

Travis laughed. "I thought Caroline and I would take Noah to the dance tonight. I wondered about asking Amy if she wanted to go with us. I think it would be easier for Noah if he had a friend there."

John thought about it for a minute before slowly nodding his head. "That'd be nice of you. If she wants to go, it's fine with me."

Travis straightened. "Good deal. I'm heading down to

the pond then home for the day. Call me if you need anything."

The pond was a fountain of many good memories for Travis. The spring-fed pool was on the backend of his parents' land. The Montgomery kids had spent many summer afternoons swinging on the rope and dropping into the cold spring water. In a way, it was nice to see the next generation carrying on the tradition.

He made it to the pond in time to see Noah running and then swinging wide over the water before dropping in. Noah had let out a loud Tarzan yell with the swing, which made Travis grin. Amy was sitting on the small pier that jutted out into the lake, her younger brothers sitting with her watching as Rocky did his run and Tarzan yell.

"Hey, gang," Travis called and walked down to the pier.

"Hi, Mr. Montgomery," the Webster children yelled.

"Hi, Travis." Noah's face flashed with concern. "Am I in trouble?"

Travis lifted an eyebrow. "Why would you be in trouble?"

Noah climbed out of the water and shrugged. "I don't know. Mr. Webster said it was okay for me to come."

"As long as your work is done, it's perfectly fine. I'd rather you..." he pointed to the rest of the children, "...make that none of you swim alone here. It's too dangerous. But it's fine that you're here." He looked at Noah. "I'm heading to the house. Your sister should be home soon. We have to go to a dressy affair tonight and you're coming along."

"But..."

"No buts. Caroline is bringing home some clothes for you to try on for tonight. You'll have fun. It's a dance."

His eyes widened in what appeared to be adolescent fear. Travis remembered the days when the thought of a dance would produce a blinding horror. For Noah to not know anyone would make his dread even worse. But leaving him at home alone wasn't an option. Noah hadn't gained Travis's trust yet.

He mentally crossed his fingers he was getting ready to do the right thing.

"I was wondering if maybe Amy would like to come along with us tonight." He looked at Amy. "You're more than welcome to ride to the country club with us. You know so many of the kids that'll be there. Maybe you could introduce Noah around."

If Noah's eyes got any wider, Travis worried the orbs would pop out of their sockets.

Amy's gaze darted to Noah and back to Travis. She licked her lips nervously. "I would love to. I'd have to ask my parents first."

Travis nodded. "Talked to your dad a little while ago. Said if you wanted to go with us it was fine with him."

Out of the corner of his eye, he saw Noah cross his fingers. He bit back a smile.

Amy's face lit with a broad grin. "Really? I'd love to..." Her voice dropped along with her smile. "If Noah wants me to."

Noah's fingers uncrossed and he made a fist, like he was going to shove it in the air in success. "I...um...I...yeah. That'd be great."

Her smile returned. "Cool." She looked at Travis. "What time do you want me at your house, Mr. Montgomery?"

Travis smiled. "We'll pick you up. Say about seven or so."

She leapt to her feet and grabbed the hands of her younger brothers. "We have to go," she said as she dragged them off the pier. "Come on, Rocky. We've got to go home."

"Geesh, Amy. You've got hours to get ready," Rocky complained. He opened his mouth to say more but the glare from his sister shut him down. "I can't believe I have to go home so early," he groused as he followed her up the hill.

"You too, Noah. Let's go. I thought we'd give the Rolls a quick wash before tonight."

Travis was in a rush to get home. He was sure Caroline had gotten back with new clothes for Noah, but that wasn't why he hurried. They'd talked by phone at least four times today. Between calls, he'd been surprised to find himself thinking about her, wondering what she was doing, where she was, what time she'd get home.

As they reached the house, Noah looked at him. "Thanks."

"Okay. For what?"

"Asking Amy to come tonight."

Travis smiled. "She's very pretty, don't you think?"

A pink tinge colored Noah's cheeks. "Yeah."

Travis laughed. "Hey, I was your age once. I remember what it was like."

"Well, thanks."

"Happy to help."

Caroline's car was parked in front of his house when he and Noah arrived.

"Listen up. Your sister is a little nervous about the clothes she bought for you. Realize that she's never had to do that before, and I think she's worried you won't like them. I'm sure she did a fine job, but whatever she bought, you be sure to thank her. Got it?"

"Yes, sir."

Amazingly, for a woman who'd never bought clothes for

a teenage boy, Caroline had done quite well. Jeans that fit. Rubber boots for mucking. Leather gloves. Work shirts. Underwear and socks. And a suit for tonight.

The suit was a dark-grey pinstripe. She'd bought a couple of different shirts to go with it. One lighter gray and one white. A couple of ties. A new belt and a pair of dress shoes.

At six-forty-five, Noah came down the stairs wearing the suit, grey shirt and a red tie. "Wow, Caroline. Thanks. This is totally cool."

Travis noticed her shoulders relax at Noah's words.

"I'm so glad you like it," she said. "You look quite snazzy."

"You do too."

Caroline grinned. "Thanks."

Travis didn't know the first thing about women's dresses but as a red-blooded male, he knew what he liked, and the emerald-green dress Caroline wore was a libido stimulant. Cut low in the front, he liked how the material—which looked sort of soft and silky—flared out when she walked or turned, giving the appearance she was floating a couple of inches above the floor. The tips of his fingers itched to trace the folds in the material from the narrow straps over her shoulders down to where the material crisscrossed over her fleshy breasts. Strands of pearls pulled the material up under her breasts with the rest of the dress hanging in long folds down to the floor. The back was cut much lower than the front, meaning he could tell—and so could every man at tonight's dance—that she wore no bra. On her left hand, the diamonds in the wedding-ring set sparkled as she held the skirt of the dress out and turned in a circle.

Even with the rings, he would be fighting the other men off all night.

"Excuse me," Travis said with a growl. He held out his arms. "A little appreciation, and not from you, Noah."

"Dude." Noah held up both hands. "I don't have an opinion of guy attire."

Caroline walked over to where Travis stood. She walked around him a couple of times and then nodded. "Yes, yes. You'll do," she said with a mischievous grin.

"Why, I ought to...to...mess up your hair," Travis replied.

Caroline backed away, her hands up to protect her updo. "Now, Travis. Let's not do anything that would make us late."

He studied her dress and grinned. He could think of a few things that would make them late, and none of his ideas had anything to do with her hair.

Noah gagged. "You two are disgusting."

Travis wrapped his arm around Noah's neck and gave him a noogie with his knuckles. "What did you say?"

Noah struggled to get free but he was laughing too hard.

"Okay, you two," Caroline said, laughing. "Break it up. We need to go."

Travis let Noah go. Noah immediately began trying to smooth his ruffled hair.

Travis held out his hand to Caroline. Caroline stared at it.

"What?" she asked.

"The keys to the Rolls."

She blew out a short breath. "No way, bucko."

"Caroline..." Travis was surprised by her response. Hell. He'd been looking forward to driving that car all day.

"I've got to warn you, bro," Noah said. "She don't let nobody drive the Shadow."

"Doesn't let anyone," Caroline corrected. "She doesn't let anyone drive the Shadow."

"Right," Noah said. "That's what I said."

"But, honey—"

"Waste of breath, Travis. Ain't gonna happen," Caroline said. She kissed his cheek. "Enjoy being a kept man tonight, *honey*, because you are not driving my car."

Travis scowled. "I ought to make us take my truck."

Noah laughed.

Caroline waltzed past him, leaving a trail of floral scent in her wake. He had to smile at the swing of her hips and the pep in her step.

Looking back over the past month, he'd come to see her in a totally different light. She wasn't the quiet, soft-spoken practice partner of his future sister-in-law. She was a strong, determined, intelligent woman who, when she loved, gave her whole heart. And sexy? Yeah, she had a sex appeal that rocked his world.

He found he liked the surprise that was Caroline Graham—or for a while at least, Caroline Graham Montgomery, although he wasn't sure how much he should. She would be gone in four short months.

On second thought, anything could happen in four short months, something that could change her departure date, maybe forever. He needed to give some thought to that. Caroline pulled the Rolls out of the garage and got out. She glanced at Noah. "This is my first chance to see my baby since you drove her down." She walked around, studied a couple of areas and then smiled. "Looks like no harm done, but, Noah, I better not ever catch you taking my car—or any car—without prior permission."

He nodded. "Yes, ma'am."

"She's been washed," she said, referring to the car.

"Yes, ma'am. Travis and me did it."

"Travis and I," she corrected.

Noah nodded. "Right."

Travis tried to make it around the back of the car and into the driver's seat before Caroline saw him, but she was a little too sharp. Her head snapped toward him edging alongside the car and gave him a wicked glare.

"Where do you think you're going?"

Travis laughed and threw his hands in the air. "Caught me."

Caroline shook her head. "Okay, fine. You can drive... this one time."

Travis knew the grin that plastered itself across his mouth probably made him look like a six-year-old on Christmas morning instead of a mature thirty-six-year-old man. He didn't care. He grabbed Caroline, dipped her back and kissed her hard. He meant for the kiss to be playful, but the minute his lips touched hers, a fire ignited in his gut, shooting flames through his system.

It'd been a long time since a woman had affected him like that. Sure, he'd been aroused by lovely women and had had lovers since his wife died, but he hadn't felt that heart pang in years.

He stood her back upright and grinned. "I like to drive."

"Well," she said with a pat on her hair to make sure it was still up, "if I'd known I'd get that kind of response, I might have agreed sooner."

Travis held out his arm. She took it and he walked her around to the passenger side. Since the Rolls was a two-door convertible, she stepped back and let Noah climb into the back before she got in. Travis shut her door and jogged around to the driver's door.

"Ready?" he asked as he started the vintage automobile. "Let's go pick up Amy."

After he pulled the car into the Websters' drive, Travis shut off the engine and got out of the car. He pulled the driver's seat back forward. "Get out, Noah and go to the door for her."

Noah shrugged. "Just blow the horn. She'll come out."

Travis heard Caroline stifle a laugh with a cough. "No. Real men do not blow the horn for ladies. You go to the door and get her."

Noah scooted out. "Yes, sir."

They didn't have to wait long. Amy answered the door to Noah's knock. She was dressed in a short red dress that hit a couple of inches above her knees. The satiny skirt was covered with some type of net overlay. A pair of red high-heel shoes put her at almost Noah's height.

Great. He'd be fighting men away from Caroline and the teenage boys away from Amy.

Travis smiled. "Good evening, Amy. You look lovely."

A red flush rode up her neck to her cheeks. "Thank you, Mr. Montgomery." She slipped past him and into the back seat, followed closely by Noah.

Travis got back in and turned toward the rear seat. "Tell you what, Amy. You're going to be with a quite a few Mr. Montgomerys. For tonight, call me Travis."

Her blush deepened. "Okay, Mr. Montgomery."

Caroline looked at him and winked. "Well, Mr. Montgomery. What do you say? Let's get this show on the road."

The rest of the family had already assembled at his parents' house by the time Travis and his crew arrived. He parked the Rolls behind Jason's Lexus and turned to the teenagers in the rear seat.

"We're going into my parents' house for drinks. We'll

only be here a short while then we'll go with the family to the country club." He laughed at the look on Noah's face. "And, no, you can't have a drink."

Noah grinned and snapped his fingers. "Dude."

As they exited the car, the front door opened. Olivia and Lydia stepped out.

"Oh my God!" Olivia shrieked then hurried down the front steps. "How beautiful."

"Why, thank you," Travis said and straightened his tie. "I knew I was looking good but..."

"Not you, idiot," his sister said. She lovingly stroked along the hood of the car. "Where did you get this?"

"Special delivery from Arkansas," Caroline said with a nod of her head toward Noah. "Seems my little brother used it for transportation down here."

"It's yours?" Olivia asked. When Caroline smiled and nodded, Olivia looked at her brother. "Man, bro, you married up."

Travis laughed and cupped Caroline's elbow in the palm of his hand. "I know, sis. I know."

Olivia walked to Noah. "I'm Olivia, Travis's sister."

Noah nodded. "Yes, ma'am. I remember you from last night."

She looked at Amy. "Amy. You look lovely."

"Thank you." The teenager blushed again.

"Travis, y'all come on in the house. It's hot out there," Jackie Montgomery said from the door.

"Yes, ma'am," he said. "Let's go, gang."

His parents greeted Caroline with warm hugs. They really liked her. He hated knowing how disappointed they were going to be in four months, but he didn't know if he could do anything about that. He couldn't keep her away from them. They'd practically adopted her when she came to town, had included her in all the family activities. Not because his parents thought they had to but because they sincerely liked her.

He understood. He had come to like her too...a lot.

"What can I get you to drink?" Travis asked as he led Caroline into the family room. He stepped behind the bar to scan the supplies he had on hand.

"Something non-alcoholic, I think. I've rushed around all day and I'm hot. What do you suggest?"

"Trust me?" He smiled.

"Of course," she said with a shrug.

"Got you covered then." He motioned to Noah and Amy standing uncomfortably in the hall. "Hey, Noah. Amy. Y'all come here. I'll make you something to drink."

The teens hurried over to the bar and slipped onto stools.

Travis chuckled at their expressions. "What do you want? Cokes? Sparkling water?"

Noah slammed his fist on the bar. "I'll have a beer, bartender."

Amy and Caroline laughed.

"Not gonna happen. Got a second choice?"

Noah grinned. "A Coke I guess."

"I'm making something special for Caroline. You two want to trust me to make you something different?"

The teens exchanged glances. "Sure," Noah replied.

Travis pulled out cranberry, pineapple and lemon juice from the under the counter refrigerator. After filling a shaker with ice, he poured the juices in and shook. He pulled three highball glasses off the wall shelf behind him. He strained the mixture into each glass then filled the glass to the top with club soda.

"There you go. A Flamingo for each of you." He slid the glasses across the bar.

Caroline was the first one to try his concoction. "Oh my. That is wonderful." She licked her upper lip. "You will have to teach me how to make this. It's my new favorite drink."

He grinned, ridiculously pleased with Caroline's comment. Then it dawned on him he'd be teaching her to make this drink so she could replicate it after she left. The acid in his stomach bubbled, making him a tad nauseous. He forced the expression on his face to remain pleasant.

"Sure." He looked at the teens. "What do you think?"

"Awesome," said Amy.

"Dude," Noah said, and exchanged a high-five with Travis.

Jackie Montgomery put her arms around Noah and Amy. "Why don't you two come join the family? I've known Amy her whole life, but I'd like to get to know this guy better," she said with a smile directed toward Noah.

"Yes, ma'am," Amy said and slipped off the stool.

Noah followed her actions.

Jackie led them across the room to the seating area where the rest of the family was gathered. "Now, we need to talk about what you're going to call me," she said to Noah.

Caroline shook her head. "Your mom is something else."

Travis poured a club soda over ice and added a slice of lime. "I know. A force to be reckoned with for sure."

"Shouldn't we go over there too?"

Travis gave a short snort. "She's giving the newlyweds some private time, I'm thinking."

Caroline leaned forward. "Travis, I don't feel right about this."

He leaned toward her to whisper. "We're in too deep

now. What would your brother think if we began telling everyone we lied? Great role models, both of us."

"I know, I know," she whispered back. "I really thought we could keep this whole marriage thing quiet, just between us. Now?" She sighed.

"I have an idea. Come on," He came around the bar and took her hand to lead her over to where his family was seated. "Okay, family," he said in a tone that demanded attention. "Caroline and I want to talk to you about this marriage situation."

He hoped he was doing the right thing, whatever the right thing was.

Sixteen

～≪～

Caroline's knees quaked under her long gown. Panic wrapped itself around her chest like a boa constrictor squeezing so tight she could barely draw a breath. Travis tightened his work-hardened hand around her fingers as he whispered, "Trust me."

His whispered words should have calmed her. Instead, his hot breath sent an army of goose bumps down her arms.

The group quieted. Travis put his arm around her. His clean, woodsy cologne tickled her nose. Man, he smelled so good. She wanted to bury her face in his neck. At least that way she wouldn't have to face his family right now.

"Caroline and I are just getting used to being married. I hope y'all understand when I say that we wanted to keep this quiet as we figure out all the changes in our lives." He looked at Noah. "Now, I'm not sorry to have Noah here with us, so don't go blaming him for spilling the beans. We don't. But we'd rather not make a big deal out of this, right, honey?"

"Right." She saw exactly where he was going with this. Keep the damage contained within the immediate Montgomery clan. "So we'd appreciate it if you didn't do anything, like a party or some big announcement. We'd like to keep the news within the family circle for now."

She removed the wedding ring and placed it inside her purse. He slipped his ring off and tucked it in his front pants pocket.

"Exactly," Travis said with a nod. "Think y'all could do that?"

The group looked around at each other before Jackie Montgomery spoke up. "You're kidding, right? Do you remember where you live, son? Who you are? If you believe for one minute the news that you've married won't spread through the Whispering Springs grapevine like a wildfire in dry grass, then you're pulling your own leg." She shook her head and began to laugh. "Oh my. You two almost had me going for a minute." She elbowed her husband. "Can you imagine? I thought they were serious for a minute there." Her laughter got the others chuckling along.

Lane Montgomery joined in his wife's amusement and his loud booming laughter filled the room. "Right, son. It'll be just among us Montgomerys."

"I don't think your idea worked," Caroline whispered in Travis's ear. "Nice try though."

Olivia stood. "Thanks guys for the best laugh I've had in a while." She pulled Mitch off the sofa. "We need to get moving or we're going to be later than is socially acceptable."

The rest of the party stood and began collecting personal items to leave.

"Oh my God," Olivia said in a loud voice. "I have the best idea. Why don't all the females ride with Caroline? We can talk girl stuff during the drive. You guys can meet us there. Travis, you ride with Mitch. Okay?"

"Wonderful idea," Lydia said. "Can I drive her car?"

Travis shook his head. "No way, sis. I know exactly what's going on in your little pea brain. You want to arrive in her Rolls at the country club. Nope." He pointed his finger at her like a pistol. "Not gonna happen. I'm driving to the club."

Caroline snatched the keys from his hand. "I'll drive," she said and headed for the door.

"Aw, darlin'. Wait a minute," Travis said as he rushed behind her. "We had a deal."

She could hear the rest of the family laughing. She stopped short. *Family.* Suddenly she didn't feel so alone in the world anymore.

TRAVIS INSISTED on parking the antique Rolls far from the other cars. He'd finally talked Caroline into letting him drive, and he hadn't wanted to chance any other car dinging it, or at least that's what he said when he dropped her at the front door.

She was standing at the stairs leading into the club when a green Range Rover pulled into the lot and parked. A tall, attractive blond man exited from the driver's side and hurried around to open the passenger door. Elsie Belle Lambert slipped from the large SUV, her azure dress shining under the full moon. After securing her hold on her date's arm, she led him directly over to Caroline.

"Hello, Dr. Graham," Elsie Belle said. While her voice was Southern sweet, the sharpness could have sliced Caroline's jugular vein.

"Good evening, Elsie Belle." She looked at the man at Elsie Belle's left. She'd have sworn she saw a twinkle in his eyes. "I don't believe we've met. I'm Caroline Graham."

"Drake Gentry," the man said. "I know your date well. And I've heard wonderful things about you. I believe you've seen my mother in your office. Mary Gentry?"

"Of course. I adore Mary. I know you are close with the Montgomery clan. I'm surprised we haven't met before now. Travis should be here any minute. He's parking the car."

Elsie Belle looked around. "Where is that old truck of his? I don't see it. Or is he driving that new Porsche? I heard it's been seen around town lately."

Caroline exchanged glances with Elsie Belle's date. He seemed more amused by Elsie Belle's preoccupation with Travis's location than jealous.

"Oh, we're not in his truck." She caught a glimpse of Travis walking down the parking lot. "Here he comes. Travis," she said with a wave. "I'm over here."

Travis picked up his pace as soon as he caught sight of her and he hurried to her side. Once there, he put his arm around her shoulders. "Sorry. Couldn't find the right place to park," he said as a way of explanation. He held out his hand. "Hey, stranger. I wasn't expecting to see you here tonight. I thought all those co-eds at SMU would have you tied down with urgent questions about dinosaurs."

Drake chuckled as he shook Travis's hand. "Not yet. Still early in the semester. I believe you know my date, Elsie Belle?"

"Of course." Travis nodded to her. "Nice to see you, Elsie Belle. Beautiful dress."

"Why, thank you, Travis," Elsie Belle cooed and stroked her hand along the front of the long skirt. "You are looking mighty fine in that suit tonight."

Unfortunately for Elsie Belle, her Southern drawl woke the sleeping green-eyed monster inside Caroline. She snuggled closer to Travis then straightened his tie. "I agree, sugar," Caroline responded, channeling her inner Scarlet O'Hara. "Good enough to eat."

Travis laughed. "Good to see you both," he said in dismissal of Elsie Belle. "We'd better head in. The rest of the family's already inside."

Caroline lifted the hem of her dress as they made their way up the stairs to the club's ballroom. Travis's hand at her back warmed her way beyond simple body temperature. First that dazzling kiss at the car earlier tonight and then his subtle contact at her back left her breathless and hungry for more of his touch, even if she knew that was probably a bad idea.

Behind her, she'd have sworn she felt the sharp points of daggers slicing into her back.

"So," she whispered to Travis. "Is there a knife jutting from my back?"

"I'm not sure," he whispered back. "I'm afraid to look."

She chuckled. "She really had you on her radar, didn't she?"

He shrugged. "I guess."

"I'm guessing she had plans to be the next Mrs. Travis Montgomery."

"Maybe, but trust me. I haven't been out with her in months."

She gave him a gentle nudge with her elbow. "How many other women am I going to have to fight off tonight?"

He looked at her with a wide grin. "Well, sugar," he said in a dead-on imitation of Elsie Belle's overdrawn Southern drawl. "I guess that remains to be seen."

She was still laughing as they walked into the ornate ballroom. A large hardwood dance floor, packed with women in long gowns and men in suits, bisected the room. A stage at one end held a live band, currently playing an up-tempo country song about hometown girls and their loving ways. Large round tables had been set up on the other three sides of the dance area. Across the room in the most advantageous location for seeing and being seen were the designated Montgomery tables.

"I remember when all the Montgomerys could get around one or two tables," Travis said as he led her around a couple moving to the music. "Now, with our family and Uncle Clint's family, we have to have four. Have you met that side of the family?"

She shook her head. "Other than KC, no. They have a ranch around here too?"

"They do. A small one that my cousins, Darren and Reno, are trying to get going, if they don't kill each other first. My uncle and aunt have a large cattle operation in Florida."

Being that much of the beef produced in the US came out of Florida, Caroline wasn't surprised to hear that the Montgomery family would have a toehold there.

"Are they here tonight?"

"Yup, and I can't wait for you to meet them."

As Travis had predicted, the Montgomery clan had commandeered four tables, and looking at how packed in everyone was, Caroline suspected they'd need at least five next year. Then she realized she'd never know. She wouldn't be here. An odd sense of loss settled low in her gut.

"There they are," Lane Montgomery announced in a loud voice. "Where you two been? Necking in the parking lot?"

Raucous laughter followed. Caroline was sure the heat to her face was more embarrassment than a response to the room temperature.

"Leave them alone, Lane," his wife chastised.

"Hey, you two." KC Montgomery hugged Caroline from behind. "I'm hearing interesting rumors."

Caroline turned to KC with a grin. Her stomach did a backflip at the knowledge that their *marriage* had already leaked out. "I swear, this family cannot keep a secret."

"Why would we want to keep something like you having an antique Rolls Royce a secret?"

Caroline stifled a giggle of relief. "I worry about car thieves driving off in my car, sort of like my date did tonight." She reached out and pulled Travis over to where she and KC stood. "I think you know my date."

KC pulled an exaggerated shocked look. "I really thought you could do better than this," she said to Caroline in mock sympathy. "Next time you need a date, call me. I'm sure I can find someone much more handsome."

Not likely, Caroline thought as she laughed. "Well, it was last minute."

Travis grinned at the women and Caroline's heart dropped to her knees. She felt like she'd just walked off a Tilt-A-Whirl...off-balance, shook-up and a tad nauseous.

"Hey, Cuz." He gave KC a hug. "Your ugly brothers here too, or have they killed each other yet?"

"Here. Can't say much for their dates, however." KC leaned in and Caroline and Travis mimicked her position. "Darren's date is a stripper from Dallas, and Reno's is a gal who's way too old to still be rocking the Goth look. Now don't say anything to my parents. They think the girls go to school in Austin."

Caroline bit her lip to keep from laughing. Travis didn't bother to hide his amusement, responding to KC's descriptions with a loud, guttural laugh.

"Come on, hon," he said taking Caroline's arm. "I've got to meet these two ladies."

They followed KC back to a table to where a younger version of Travis's father sat. Beside him was an attractive dark-haired woman. Caroline assumed these were Travis's uncle and aunt. Two young men stood as soon as Caroline stopped at the table.

"Caroline. These are my parents, Clint and Nadine. Over there—" KC indicated the standing men with a tilt of her head, "—are my brothers, Darren and Reno, and their dates, Candi, with an I, and Angel. Family, this is Dr. Caroline Graham."

"Nice to meet you all," Caroline said.

Travis greeted his uncle and cousins with handshakes while engulfing his aunt in a bear hug.

"It's been too long since I've seen you," he said to his uncle and aunt. "Everything okay in Florida? I'm hoping you'll still be here for the barbeque and ranch rodeo."

"Everything is going great," his uncle replied. "And we'll be there at the rodeo. Those two—" he pointed with his chin toward his sons, "—have entered the D&R cowboys this year." Clint Montgomery grinned. "Gotta go root for their ranch."

Travis nodded. "Great. Oh, and you'll want to make sure you're there on Friday night. Olivia and Mitch Landry are tying the knot...finally."

"I know," Nadine interjected. "I talked to Jackie today. She is so excited."

Travis took Caroline's hand, interrupting her conversation with KC's brothers. "If you'll excuse me, I have to get my date on the dance floor before she finds someone else to dance with."

"Nice to meet all of you," Caroline said with a wave. "Get me on the dance floor?" she whispered.

"If we don't move on, we'll be there talking to them for hours. I know my uncle. He'll talk ranching until my ears fall off my head."

"Got it. So are we really headed to dance?"

"Sure." He swung her around and caught her with a hand at her waist.

She put both hands on his strong shoulders. No padding needed in his jacket. All man and all muscle. And for tonight—and the next four months—he was all hers. A dangerous trill raced through her. She slipped her hands up and around his neck. As though of a mind of their own, her fingers stroked the back of his neck. Up and down and then around in a circle.

He hissed out a long breath. He tightened his hands at her waist. Jerking her snug against him, he whispered, "You are the sexiest woman in this entire room. And if you don't stay close, everybody else will know exactly the effect you are having on me."

The hard evidence of his arousal pressed firmly into her stomach. His chest vibrated against hers as he hummed along with the song. She found herself perversely pleased by how comfortable she felt in his arms.

But on the other hand, maybe she needed to get a hold on her feelings. They had no future beyond this fall. She had to keep telling herself that.

As the song came to its closing note, Travis hugged her before ending the dance with a deep dip. She laughed with delight. Travis grinned and then brushed her mouth with a quick kiss.

. . .

CAROLINE TOUCHED up her lipstick in the ladies' lounge. Her cheeks were rosy red with a flush. Whether that was from the Texas heat or from being kissed by Travis was unclear.

She pressed her hand against her chest. Her heart pounded and raced beneath her palm. Travis was sex with legs. How in the world would she be able to sleep in the same bed with him night after night for the next four months without attacking the poor man?

She pulled the wedding ring set from her purse and pushed it on her left hand. Holding that hand up in the mirror, she studied the rings. They looked good on her finger. Perfect shape and size.

No. Stop that. She shouldn't be thinking anything like that. This was a business deal, pure and simple. She had to remember that. *Don't make this more than it is.*

The bathroom door opened to admit a couple of women Caroline didn't know. She dropped her hand down to her side and took one last swipe with her lipstick.

After replacing her lipstick in her purse and securing a couple of stray strands of hair—what was Travis thinking dipping her on the dance floor like that—she walked back to the country-club lobby. Through a pair of glass double doors, she could see Travis standing on the balcony that overlooked the eighteenth green. Standing next to him in a sparkling dress that matched his sapphire eyes was Elsie Belle Lambert. She was clutching Travis's arm as her mouth ran non-stop. Travis shook his head and removed her hand from his forearm. When he started to walk away, she stopped him with another arm clutch.

"Looks like my date is trying to convince your date to swap partners."

Caroline looked over her shoulders into Drake Gentry's grinning face, amusement sparkling in his eyes.

"Aren't you upset?" she asked.

"Of course not. Elsie Belle only asked me to come with her because she thought it would make Travis jealous. I could have told her it wouldn't work but..." He shrugged. "I didn't have a date and she wouldn't have believed me anyway."

"She asked you out?"

"Sure. I've known Elsie for years. She told me her date had to cancel tonight and she needed someone to take her. Since my love life is currently in the toilet, I figured why not." Drake hitched a thumb toward the couple. "Do you want me to go out there and break that up?"

"No. Travis is a big boy. He can handle her."

They watched the balcony action for a couple of more minutes.

"So why's your love life in the tank?" Caroline asked.

"Thought I'd found the one, you know? But she dumped me like I had fleas."

"Do I know this woman who obviously has such poor taste in men that she would let a prize like you get away?"

Drake laughed. "I'm sure you do, but I'm a gentleman. I don't kiss and tell. Ah, looks like the talk is over. Oh dear. She looks pissed. You might want to step behind me for protection. I'm thinking he might have mentioned that set of rings on your hand."

Reflexively, she put her right hand over her left. "You know about the rings?"

"I know about the wedding."

"How?"

"Travis told me. Of course, that was only after I

mentioned I'd heard about the new doctor and was thinking about getting to know her better."

Caroline laughed softly. "I would love to have heard that conversation."

"It went something like this. 'Hey, Travis. What do you know about Dr. Graham? I've been giving some thought to asking her out. What do you think?'"

"And what did he say?"

"He said something like, 'I think I'd mind. That's my wife you're wanting to date'."

One of the glass doors flew open as Elsie Belle stormed back into the lobby. She saw Caroline and Drake standing together and marched over.

"I hear congratulations are in order," she said with a forced smile. "Can I see the rings?"

She jerked Caroline's hand up for inspection before Caroline had time to respond.

"Lovely," she said and dropped Caroline's hand as though it were contaminated with poison ivy. "Come on, Drake. I need a drink." She stomped away before Drake answered.

Travis moved in to take the spot where Elsie Belle had been standing. "Still trying to pick up my wife, Gentry?"

Drake chuckled. "You're a lucky SOB. Caroline's a keeper." He leaned over and brushed a light kiss on Caroline's cheek.

"Drake! Are you coming?" Elsie Belle yelled across the lobby.

He responded with a wave and a chuckle. "You two have a nice evening. I've got to go rescue a damsel in distress. Let's get together for dinner soon." He walked back toward the ballroom. "I'm coming, Elsie Belle."

"So," Caroline said. "You told Elsie Belle we got married,

didn't you? You do realize it'll be all over the ballroom in an hour."

"Don't be ridiculous," he said taking her hand. "Fifteen minutes, tops."

They were both wrong.

Travis took her arm and led her back into the ballroom and toward the Montgomery tables.

"You want to dance or sit down?"

Caroline twisted sideways to get through the crowded dance floor. "Let's grab a seat for now."

When they reached the set of tables, most of the chairs were empty. KC pushed a chair out.

"Sit," she commanded. "Keep me company while I drink myself under the table."

Travis held the chair for Caroline as she sat. "Be right back," he said. "Gonna grab us something cold to drink."

As soon as he was gone, Caroline turned to KC "What's going on with you? What's with the drinking yourself under that table nonsense?"

"Pay me no attention." Her gaze flickered toward Drake and Elsie Belle as they danced by. She drained her wine glass. "Bastard."

Caroline followed KC's gaze. "Drake Gentry? That's who's got you drowning your sorrows tonight?"

"Absolutely not," KC answered. "Why would I care if he's here with the biggest social skank in the county? Damn. I should have had Travis get me another drink." She turned her back to the dance floor. Her gaze dropped onto Caroline's hands. Her eyes opened wide as she grabbed Caroline's left hand. "I thought this was a secret I was sworn to carry to my grave. What the hell are you doing wearing these?"

Caroline blew out a long breath. "It's a long story."

Travis set a couple of waters on the table and a fresh white wine for KC "You looked like you needed it."

"What I need is a pair of boots to kick your asses. Why is she wearing those rings in public?"

"We got married. Haven't you heard?"

Before KC could answer, a loud tapping came from the microphone on the stage.

"Can I have everybody's attention?" A very Southern, very drunk female voice slurred through the speakers. "I have news."

"Oh shit," Travis muttered as he ran his fingers through his hair.

Caroline looked up at the stage and groaned. A wave of nausea rolled through her gut. She didn't have a good feeling about this.

KC grinned and leaned back in her chair. "Finally. This year's ball was getting a little dull. Leave it up to Elsie Belle Lambert to liven things up."

"I said," Elsie Belle hollered into the mic. "Listen up. I want to tell you all something."

Drake jumped on the stage and tried to pull Elsie Belle away from the microphone, but she wasn't leaving. She jerked her arm away, spilling her wine on his jacket.

"Oh, good Lord," Jackie Montgomery said as she and Lane sat down. "That girl has had way too much to drink. Let's hope she doesn't decide to sing again this year."

"Cats in heat sound better," Lane said in agreement.

The crowd turned toward the developing show on the stage.

Elsie Belle lifted her wine glass high in the air. "I want to make an announcement. Lift your glasses to the newlywed couple. Travis Montgomery and Caroline Graham."

There was a moment of silence and then a mumbling rumbled through the group.

"Y'all stand up," Elsie Belle demanded.

Drake tried again to lead her off stage, but she wouldn't leave the microphone.

"To Travis and his new bride, right?" The red wine in her glass sloshed over the rim. "Let's all drink." She drank the rest of her wine and then put the stemmed crystal on the stage and stomped on it. "I'm not Jewish," she said with an intoxicated giggle, "but I've always wanted to do that." She stumbled back. Drake caught her before she fell and led her off the stage.

"Well, leave it to Elsie Belle to make a scene," Jackie said.

People were beginning to come by the table to congratulate Travis and Caroline. Caroline's cheeks were quivering from holding her smile. Travis seemed to be taking it all in stride, laughing and slapping backs, taking all the wishes of good luck and a long marriage with a grin.

The band began to tune up, ready to start the next set. The lead singer stepped up to the microphone, avoiding the broken glass.

"I'm not sure we can top the intermission show, but we'll try."

Laughs and chuckles rolled through the crowd.

"Travis," the man said. "It's been a while since we've had the pleasure of hearing you sing. Why don't you come up and do a song for us?"

Caroline's head whipped toward him. She knew he could sing, but she had no idea that others knew too.

There were some whistles and words of encouragement shouted toward him. Even through his tan, the flush to his cheeks was apparent.

"Do you mind?" he asked Caroline.

"Gosh, no. I'd love to hear you."

As he headed toward the stage, Jackie leaned over. "It's been years since he sang in public. He'll only sing when he's happy. I think I have you to thank." She squeezed Caroline's hand.

After a brief consultation with the band members, Travis strapped a guitar around his neck. Caroline noticed the crowd moving toward the stage, not to dance but to listen.

"Well, as Buddy said, it's been a while since I've done this. I might be a little rusty, so y'all bear with me."

He strummed the guitar strings. Caroline's heart jumped and raced, nervous for him, wanting him to do well.

"Here's one by Chris Young I think you'll all know. It's called 'Getting Her Home'." He moved his fingers on the strings and music poured out. He leaned forward and his deep bass voice carried the melody across the room. Chills ran up and down her arms. She wrapped them around her waist to hold herself steady in her chair. She'd thought his voice sexy before, but now? Each note was a sensual touch.

When he got to the line in the song about a black dress hitting the floor, he looked at Caroline and exchanged the word black for green.

A rush of heat ran north and south through her body. Her face was hot while the area between the thighs swelled with warmth and need.

The crowd obviously got his little joke as smiles and chuckles and quite a few elbow jabs moved through the room. If Caroline hadn't been so enthralled by his singing, she might have hidden her face, but she couldn't take her eyes off him.

The room broke into loud applause as he strummed the

last cord. He shook his head at calls for more, handing the borrowed guitar back to its owner.

"Thank you very much," he said and leapt from the stage.

More than a couple of minutes passed before he made it back to the table. Somewhere between the stage and table, he'd picked up Noah and Amy, both of whom couldn't stop talking about Elsie Belle's drunken rant and Travis's song.

"Travis," Noah said. "That was awesome."

"Yes, Mr. Montgomery. It was." Amy was apparently still struggling with calling him Travis.

"Thanks, gang. What do you say we head for home?"

"It's early," Noah complained. "Do we have to go?"

Caroline and Travis exchanged glances, silently acknowledging that Noah had clicked with Amy and the teens of the area.

"Tell you what," Travis said. "Let's put the top down on the Rolls and ride over to Tilly's for a late dessert."

Tilly's was the area's teen hangout, famous for burgers and ice-cream sundaes. In short, *the* place to be seen, especially in a cool car.

Amy's eyes went wide. "Seriously?" She looked at Noah. "That'd be so wicked."

"Really?" When she nodded, Noah shrugged. "Let's go."

"Let's go tell the gang. We'll meet you at the front door, okay?" Amy grabbed Noah's hand and dragged him back across the room to where the younger crowd was hanging out.

"Leaving?" Jackie asked, a twinkle in her eye. "Do you want us to take Noah and Amy home?"

"Thanks, Mom, but we've got it."

Caroline pushed her chair back and stood. "I'm ready."

Jackie and Lane stood when she did. "It was an, um, interesting night."

Jackie laughed and pulled Caroline into an embrace. "That's one way to look at it." She passed Caroline off to Lane for a hug as she reached for Travis. "Y'all be careful getting home."

"Mom," he said with a shake of his head. "I'm not sixteen."

Jackie kissed his cheek. "You're still my baby."

Travis reached for Caroline's hand. "We'll talk to you later."

"Bye," Caroline said over her shoulder as Travis led her away.

Too many people to count wanted to congratulate them and wish them well as they crossed the room to leave.

"Now what?" she asked.

"I don't know about you, but I can't wait to see your green dress hit the floor."

She laughed, but her insides melted at his words. Yes. These next four months were going to be hell. How could she leave here with her emotions intact? Men could have great sex without emotional ties. Women struggled with that.

She'd just have to be more like a man.

Friends with benefits, she mentally chanted. *Friends with benefits.*

The ride to Tilly's with the top down on the Shadow wrecked her updo hairstyle. A quick glance in the mirror confirmed it, making the style appear more rat's nest than a fancy creation, but the thick, rich, creamy milkshake made her dishabille worth it. Besides, she wasn't sure she was ready to head back to Travis's place. Somehow having sex and sleeping with him in secret was fun and exciting and seemed just a tad bit naughty. Now that everyone believed them to be married, and thus sleeping together as part of the marital relationship, she felt an immense sense of pressure, as though things had changed drastically without warning. Was wife sex different from date sex?

Logically, she realized none of her thoughts made sense, but inside she was on an emotional rollercoaster.

After depositing Amy safely at home, they drove back to Halo M ranch with Noah talking non-stop about the other teens he'd met at the dance. How cool Sam was. How Robin and Steve's dancing made everybody laugh. How Nita's date was a dud and she kept trying to ditch him. With each comment, Caroline would laugh or shake her head or give some response to give the indication she was listening, but she wasn't. She couldn't think of anything but Travis's bed and how different everything would be tonight.

Travis eased the Rolls into the garage and shut down the engine.

"You'd better get some sleep," he said over his shoulder to Noah. "Five a.m. will come early."

"Tomorrow is Sunday," Noah said in a protest.

"I know, but ranch work is seven days a week." He opened his door and exited the car. After hurrying around the hood, he helped Caroline out her door and shoved the seatback forward to give Noah room to get out. "See you in the morning," he said to Noah.

"This sucks," Noah said, a snarl working up on his lips.

Travis shrugged. "Sure does. Remember, you have the option to go home. Pat and Leslie would be more than happy to come get you."

"See you in the morning," Noah said as he stomped across the garage and into the house. The door banged shut behind him.

Caroline shook her head. "I am really worried about him, Travis. It's not much longer until I leave and he'll have to go back to Arkansas. Maybe letting him stay was not the right decision. I mean, it might make it harder on him later."

They began walking toward the door, Travis's hand resting at the small of her back. She loved the feel of his broad hand there, warming that spot...as well as the rest of her, if she wanted to be honest.

"There's nothing wrong with him that hard work and maturity won't cure. He's a teenage boy. We were all surly and rude at that age. Trust me." The hand on her back slipped around to her waist and he pulled her close. He nuzzled her neck and pressed kisses to that sensitive area behind her ear. "Walking through the garage door," he sang in a deep voice. "Waitin' for your green dress to hit the floor."

Chills wracked her body. She shivered. Maybe wife sex wouldn't be so bad.

An hour later, a sweaty, sated Caroline lay on her back, her breath and heart racing. Oh man, wife sex turned out to be toe-curling, hair-on-fire orgasmic.

Seventeen

ven though Noah had been on good behavior since his arrival, Caroline wasn't fooled. There was no way he could turn from troubled teen into choir boy overnight. Plus, she hadn't quite forgiven him for driving the old Rolls down from Arkansas.

Leaving Travis to deal with Noah and his possible antics every day wasn't fair. Travis hadn't signed on for teenage wrangling with their fake wedding vows. Noah was her responsibility, and that meant she had to make the long drive to Whispering Springs Medical Clinic every morning and back to Halo M ranch every night. To make her hospital rounds before seeing patients in her office required her leaving the ranch by five a.m. and not getting back until seven or later every evening.

And then there was the nightly sex. It wasn't as though Travis was forcing her to have sex. Heck, it was the sex that had her driving over the speed limit every night to get back. But as the first week of playing wife to Travis, guardian to her brother and doctor for her patients drew to a close, she found herself becoming overly exhausted and cranky.

Compounding her irritability—and adding to an already guilty conscious—were the cards and gifts that found their way to her office, her house and Halo M, all wishing her and Travis years of marital bliss. A couple of male patients—and one female—admitted they'd wanted to ask her out and were now bemoaning their lost opportunity. She made sure to keep an accurate record of the gifts and the givers, fully intending to return each gift with a note of gratitude.

True to her prediction, Noah couldn't keep up the good conduct beyond the first ten days. After a weekend of being on call and staying in town, Caroline arrived back at Halo M late Monday night. After pulling into the garage, she sat in the Porsche trying to collect enough energy to pull herself out of the car. Finally, she convinced her legs to move, albeit slowly. When she opened the back door and walked in, heated voices echoed down the hall.

"I am so disappointed in you," Travis said. "One warning wasn't enough."

"Dude," Noah said in a lazy voice. "Chill. It was just a cigarette. Caroline doesn't need to know."

Caroline's heart dropped. She forced herself to quietly close the door—when what she really wanted to do was slam it in frustration—and headed for the voices.

"What's going on?" she asked, walking into the den.

Noah was slouched on the sofa. Travis was sitting on the coffee table directly in front of her brother, who—at this exact moment—she wanted to string up by his heels.

Noah straightened when he saw her. "Hey, Caroline." He gave her a broad smile, as though he hadn't a care in the world.

"Somebody want to tell me what's going on?" she

repeated with a pointed stare at Travis, who responded with a hitched thumb toward Noah.

"Seems Noah thinks it's cool to smoke. John caught him a day or so ago but let it slide with a warning. Today, I found him with all five of John's kids behind the hay barn trying to teach Rocky how to blow smoke rings." He frowned. "Two lit cigarettes in the hands of minors plus the dry grass compounded by the hay-barn location adds up to a huge fire risk. And you know how fast a fire can sweep across the dry fields, not to mention the potential for harm to the cowboys who have to fight that fire or the animals that could be injured."

Caroline propped both hands on her hips. "I see." She targeted her glare at Noah. "And what do you have to say?"

He shrugged and slumped on the sofa. "What's the big deal? I was careful."

"Sit up," Travis snapped. "Show your sister respect."

Noah glared at Travis but straightened.

"The big deal is, outside the risks to the ranch and the animals, smoking will kill you. It smells bad. It rots your lungs. And it'll take years off your life. I hate to say this, but I bet Mamie would still be with us if she hadn't been a smoker all those years." She walked over and sat beside him on the couch. "She didn't know better when she started smoking. Today, we do. It's not cool no matter what you might read or see on television." She put her arm around him. "I love you, Noah. I want years and years with you. Someday, you'll get married and have kids, and I want you to be there with them for years and years. What you do today matters. Do you understand?"

Noah's shoulder sagged. "Yes, but Travis's punishment is stupid."

Caroline looked at Travis still sitting on the coffee table. "Stupid? What horrible punishment did you dream up?"

A twitch at the corner of his mouth made her believe he was fighting a smile. Good. He obviously came up with something suitable.

"He's making me clean the barn stalls all by myself for an entire week," Noah said. "None of the Webster kids can help and that's not fair. Rocky was smoking too."

She nodded. "I see. All by yourself, huh?"

"Right." Noah's voice held a tone of victory, as though he'd made his point that the punishment did not fit the crime.

She pulled Noah to her and hugged him. "Well, if it were up to me, you'd be mucking the stalls solo for a month and washing every horse in the barn until their hair gleamed. Plus, you'd have no television, cell phone or internet for at least a couple of weeks. So you'd better take what Travis offered."

Noah pulled away. "You're kidding."

"I'm not," she said with a slow shake of her head. "I'd do anything to make you live longer and healthier, whether you liked it or not...well, short of serving liver every night."

He grimaced at the mention of liver.

"Here's the deal. What Travis says goes. Period. No argument. No whining."

Noah released a long-suffering sigh. "Fine."

"You have homework?" she asked.

"Yes."

"Then get at it. One of us will call you when dinner is on the table."

Noah stood and left, his pace slow and dragged out.

The minute he was out of hearing range, Caroline

sighed. "I am so sorry, Travis. I know you didn't agree to parent a headstrong teenage boy."

Travis dropped onto the sofa beside her. "We both knew it was only a matter of time before he messed up. To be honest, I think he was surprised neither of us suggested he go back to Arkansas."

"You think he's testing us?"

Travis draped his arm behind her on the back of the sofa. "Maybe. Who knows. The poor kid's world has been torn apart. I kind of feel for him."

She leaned against his shoulder. "Still, this is asking a lot."

"Let me just say that you were great with him."

His words lightened her mood. Her heart leapt at his praise. "Really?"

"Really. You would have been a wonderful mother. I think it sucks that the doctor couldn't do more for you years ago to give you a chance to have a baby."

"Thanks. It means a lot to have you say that."

"Funny how things work out. You thought you'd never be a mother, and I gave up on having children when Susan died, and yet here we are. Parenting a teenage boy."

"And doing a damn fine job," she said with a joyless laugh. She stood. "I need to go wash the day off me. What's for dinner?"

"Henree left a salad in the refrigerator and a chicken casserole that needs to go in the oven for forty-five minutes. Why don't you go get your shower and I'll put the casserole in the oven."

"Sounds wonderful. Thanks." She took a couple of steps toward the master suite and turned back. "I hope you're wrong about having children. When I'm gone and all this is behind you, I hope you find a woman who can give you the children you deserve. You would be a wonderful father."

She hurried from the room so he wouldn't see the tears filling her eyes. He did deserve that and so much more. Just another reason she needed to keep her feelings in check and never let him know. When she finished her contract and moved on, she'd pray for the right woman to come into his life.

She stripped off her clothes and stepped into Travis's luxurious master bathroom. Without a doubt, come January in Montana, she would miss his huge shower with its multiple showerheads. When she leaned around the glass wall to turn on the water, a large, rough, warm hand caressed her left butt cheek.

Smiling, she looked over her shoulder into Travis's crystal-blue eyes. "Aren't you supposed to be putting the casserole in the oven?"

"I did," he said, wrapping an arm around her nude waist and pulling her against his fully clothed body.

The erotic sensation of her naked flesh against his rough jeans and cotton shirt made her knees weak and quaking. Her sex grew warm and swollen with desire.

"But I got lonely all by myself in the kitchen," he continued. "Then I remembered seeing a spot on your neck that needed some attention, so here I am."

"A spot on my neck?"

"Yeah. Right here." He pressed his lips against the skin beneath her right ear and nibbled at the skin. "And maybe here too," he said, his lips tickling as they moved against her skin.

She arched her neck to the side to give him better access as he nibbled his way down to where her neck joined her shoulder.

"Hmm. Maybe there's a spot a little lower that was covered by my blouse."

His lips moved into a smile against her shoulder. "I think that what you need is a good overall body inspection... in the shower." He released his hold on her, stepped back and stripped out of his clothes with efficient moves.

Within seconds, her eyes feasted on his taut skin, the ripple of his abdomen, the jut of his erect penis from his groin. She smiled and licked her lips. "Yeah. I think you're right. A full body inspection is just what I need."

His responding grin was just wicked enough to send her heart on a jog and her insides melting. Grabbing her hand, he walked around the glass brick shower wall and pulled her into the shower behind him. Hot water from the multiple jet streams sluiced down her back. She sighed, enjoying the heat at her back and the luscious sight of Travis's nude body in front of her.

As she ran the palm of her hand down his body, her arousal soared as she traced the peaks and valleys of his firm muscles. His erection grew longer and thicker as her hand neared. She gently dragged a fingernail down the engorged vein protruding along the side. He hissed and captured her hand.

"Easy," he said.

She grinned. "Trust me. I'm a doctor," she said as she wrapped her fingers around his swollen cock. The girth was wide enough that the tips of her fingers didn't come close to touching. She slid her hold down his penis and back up before rubbing her thumb across the head.

Travis pulled her against him. Her stiff nipples raked through his coarse chest hair. He palmed one breast, massaged it and lowered his head to take her erect nipple between his lips. He licked the shower water off the end and sucked hard on her flesh, pulling a large portion of her breast into his mouth. Her sex tingled, demanding relief. She tried to squeeze her legs together but he jammed a thigh between them and pressed hard against her clit. She ground against his thick, muscular thigh trying, and failing, to find release.

"I'm trying to go slow," he gasped. "But I'm failing. Maybe next time, okay?"

She dropped her head back and laughed softly. "I'm dying here. Slow is overrated sometimes."

He glided his big hands down her thighs and then around to cup the backs of her legs. His biceps bulged as he lifted her off the tiled shower floor. Turning, he braced her against the wet wall. She wrapped her legs around his waist and adjusted herself until her sex was poised over the head of his straining penis. When he didn't immediately enter, she dug her heels into his ass.

"Move it, cowboy," she said with a smirk.

His mouth spread into a wicked grin. With a hard thrust, he drove deep. She gasped at the sudden intrusion and stretching of her vaginal walls. He pulled back slowly, allowing her to feel each inch of him leaving before thrusting again. The slow withdrawals were killing her, driving her wild, pumping her arousal to a new zenith. The hard pounding of each plunge pushed her against the tile, pushed her response up another degree.

The building tension was almost intolerable. She bit his shoulder, ran her tongue across the mark she'd left and up his neck. She showered kisses behind his ears, over his cheeks, across his lips. Finally, the pressure was too much and it erupted. She cried out his name and shook in his arms. Two hard thrusts and he ground himself against her as he filled her with hot ejaculate.

His breaths came in pants. Dropping his head against her shoulder, he blew hot air down her chest. He stayed that way for a couple of minutes before lifting his head to stare into her eyes. Their gazes held.

Tell me you love me, Caroline thought. *Tell me you want me in your life Ask me to stay.*

"I love..." he gasped out.

Her breath caught as she waited.

"...being with you," he continued in a breathy voice. He kissed her and lowered her legs to the floor. "We better get a rush on. I'm sure dinner must be done by now."

Caroline forced a smile to her face that she didn't feel. "I'm sure you're right." She gave him a shove toward the shower exit. "Give me five minutes alone."

"I know. I know," he said with a laugh. "You have girl stuff to do." He gave her another quick kiss and stepped out.

She could see enough through the glass bricks to know when he'd left the bath. As soon as the door shut behind him, she let the build-up of tears flow.

He'd never know that she'd fallen in love with him. She'd make sure of that.

Eighteen

Over the next couple of weeks, the ranch was a flurry of activity in preparation for the upcoming ranch rodeo. Caroline remembered the rodeo from the previous fall but she hadn't realized the amount of work that went into getting Halo M ready to host.

Barns and outbuildings were given fresh coats of red paint and fences painted white. Grazing cattle and horses not involved in this year's event were moved to outlying fields for the event duration. But foremost attention was given the outside arena.

The existing dirt was tilled then compacted. A mixture of dirt, sand and stone dust was delivered and worked into the arena's base. As Travis explained over dinner one evening, the idea of the ranch rodeo was to not only recognize the working cowboys in the area, but also to showcase the cutting horses Halo M had bred and trained and were now ready for sale. Since he wanted his horses to show well, the arena base was given special attention to allow for tight maneuvers without fear of the horse losing his footing in the dirt. Plus, a good thick base might help prevent injuries to the competing teams.

As exhausted as Caroline felt each evening, Travis and Noah looked even worse. Close to seven each night, they would meet Caroline for dinner outside on the patio, their clothes too filthy to sit inside. Afterwards, Noah headed upstairs for homework and Travis headed back out to handle more details with the rodeo.

But the nights...oh, the nights were filled with steamy sex followed by sleep in Travis's arms. It was all she could do to not verbalize her growing emotion for him. She said what she could with touches and kisses.

Whatever Travis was feeling for her remained a mystery. He held her, kissed her, made love to her, but he never said the words she longed to hear.

Mornings were met with blurry eyes and tired smiles. Nonetheless, the vision of a naked Travis stepping from the shower, or his tight ass as he slid a pair of jeans over it still made her heart race and her palms sweat. She doubted she would ever tire of looking at him or wanting him with the heat of a bubbling volcano.

Her medical-services contract with Whispering Springs Medical Clinic would end in three short months. She needed to start making plans for packing up the house, transferring patient care to Lydia, talking with her parents about long-term arrangements for Noah, even buying her own car. Somehow, she couldn't bring herself to do any of these. Her clothes kept moving from her town house to the ranch until very little remained in town but token items. When she was required to stay overnight in town because of medical call or patient responsibilities, she had to pack a bag and bring it with her. Dust covered most surfaces in her house.

And yet Travis took her gradual move into his place without comment, pro or con.

The week of the ranch rodeo finally arrived. Having had many years of the pre-rodeo hullabaloo, Henrietta Webster scheduled a daylong educational field trip to the Dallas Historical Society for Wednesday. All the ranch children gathered at the Webster home for an overnight stay on Tuesday to allow for an early start the next day.

Official events didn't begin until Thursday evening, but Travis had warned Caroline to expect some teams to come early in the week. He hadn't been mistaken. Tuesday evening, Caroline and Travis sat down to the first meal they'd had alone since Noah's unexpected arrival. The meal was simple—spaghetti, yeast bread and salad—but Caroline had been looking forward to the alone time. She'd just taken the first bite of salad when the doorbell chimed.

"You have got to be kidding," she said.

Travis wiped his mouth with a napkin and stood. "Nope. I'll bet it's Reno and Darren. And I'll also bet they left my uncle and aunt running the D&R so they could come early and stake out a prime location for their camp." The bell chimed again. "Coming," Travis hollered as he started for the front door.

Caroline remained at the table, unsure what she should do. Turned out she didn't need to do anything. Travis was back momentarily with Reno and Darren at his heels.

"Hello, guys," Caroline said. "We were just sitting down to dinner. Would you like to join us?"

"Hell, er, heck no," Reno said. "We've got to get our camp staked out quick. I saw a couple of other cowboys with their RVs headed this way."

"Evening, Dr. Graham," Darren said.

"Caroline, please."

He nodded.

"So, Travis, want to head out with us to show us exactly where you want our rigs? Got to unload the horses too."

Travis nodded. "Might as well. If you're right about the other teams right behind you, I need to be out there to make sure the guys from Lonesome Trail don't get into another fight with the guys from Riggs & Riggs." He looked at Caroline. "Sorry, but..."

She stood. "I understand. Go. Take care of the arriving teams. I'll put your food in the warmer and you can eat it when you get back."

His face lit with a smile. "Thanks. I knew you'd understand." He turned to his cousins. "Let's go." He'd taken a couple of steps before he turned around and headed back to Caroline. "It'll probably be late when I get back."

"No problem. I've got some medical journals I need to read, and I can promise they'll put me to sleep."

He leaned in to give her a kiss. "Later." He headed back to his cousins waiting in foyer. "Okay. Let's go."

She didn't know when he finally came to bed. When her alarm went off at five a.m., Travis was stepping from the bathroom, drops of water clinging to his chest. Man, how she wanted to lick each and every one of those. Sadly, she didn't have time, and apparently he was all business today, quickly dressing and heading downstairs after a quick kiss.

"What's on your agenda today?" she asked as she poured a cup of coffee.

"I had some problems last night with parking some of the large rigs in the fields." He shook his head. "When I started this rodeo ten years ago, most of the cowboys slept in tents or the back of their trucks. Now they're hauling in forty-five-foot motorhomes, fancy fifth-wheels and decked out trailers."

"The cowboys have these vehicles? I can't believe any of them can afford those."

"Point taken. No, it's the owners, and maybe I might have exaggerated a tad, but it's still going to be a tight fit. Plus, there was a little brawl between a couple of the ranch hands."

"The two you mentioned last night?"

"Nope. Two new ones." He rubbed the back of his neck. "I have already got a headache and the day's just starting."

The house phone rang.

"Now what?" he muttered. "Hello? No. No. Yes. No. Are you kidding, Olivia? When do you plan to do this?"

As his conversation with his sister continued, Caroline could see the muscles in his neck and face tightening. For the first time, she noticed the stress lines etching the corners of his mouth. His lips pulled into a tight line across his teeth.

"Fine," he said with a long exhale. "Fine."

When he hung up, he looked at Caroline. "Olivia has decided that there are going to be so many people at her wedding that she needs to use the arena so everybody can see, which would be fine, but she needs to—and I quote—practice riding a horse in while wearing a wedding dress."

Caroline snorted. "I am so glad her friend, Emily, is standing with her as maid of honor. I can't imagine anything worse than me trying to ride, or should I say stay on a horse, in front of people while trying to get that horse to a specific spot and make him stay. Thank goodness Lydia is in the wedding. It may be the first time in my medical career that I'm glad I'm on call."

"At least all the ranch kids are gone and out of our hair today. That's one less thing to worry about."

"True." She checked the time. "I've got to run." After

refilling her mug for the drive into town, she kissed Travis. It was just a brush of lips, but that tug in her gut was strong. "Later."

Travis stayed on her mind all day. In all the time she'd known him, been around him, this was maybe the first time she'd seen him so high-strung. So far, a couple of fistfights and Olivia's last-minute wedding changes were the worst events of the week. Maybe the week would play out better than it started.

About ten that morning, as she was leaving a patient consult room—another patient who'd come bearing a gift wrapped in festive *Congratulations* paper—the front-desk receptionist paged her.

"Dr. Graham. You have a call on line three."

Caroline stepped into her office to answer. "Caroline Graham."

"Hi, Caroline. This is Jackie."

"Good morning, Jackie. What can I do for you?"

"You can have lunch with me."

Caroline glanced down at her schedule. Booked solid with patients. She really liked Jackie Montgomery, and Jackie had done nothing but welcome her with open arms from the day she arrived. But still, she hated to keep lying to her about the faux marriage. Maybe a little distance...

"I'm so sorry. I'm slammed today. With the rodeo this weekend, we've closed the office for Friday so we're seeing a week of patients in fewer days."

"I didn't make myself clear. I want to have a Montgomery women's lunch. Just you, me, Olivia and Lydia. I've talked with Lydia. Since the office will be closing at noon tomorrow, we'll have time for a nice long lunch."

Caroline looked down again. Jackie was right.

"Now don't start looking for a way out of lunch," Jackie said with a laugh. "I'm calling a mother-in-law privilege."

Caroline sighed quietly. "Sounds like fun. Where should I meet you?"

"Oh, Olivia and I will pick up you and Lydia at the clinic at noon. I'll see you tomorrow." She clicked off.

Caroline set the receiver back into the cradle and leaned against her desk. A soft knock at her door drew her out of her thoughts.

"Dr. Graham. Do you have Mrs. Clark's file?"

Caroline looked at the file she still held in her hand. "Yes. Sorry. Hold on a minute." She quickly marked the CPT medical codes on the patient billing form and handed it to the receptionist.

As soon as she dropped in her chair, her door opened again and Lydia walked in and took a seat. "Lunch with the mother-in-law tomorrow. You got the call?"

Caroline nodded. "Like we have time."

Lydia smiled. "It'll be fun." She stood. "Okay, partner. Back to work."

Caroline followed her into the hall, picked a file off a patient door and looked at the name. "Oh goodie. Mr. Francis is here with his hemorrhoids."

Lydia laughed. "And they say medicine isn't glamorous."

She barely saw Travis Wednesday night. He had meeting after meeting with prospective buyers that ran well into the evening.

Noah had come home revved up from the field trip, so staying in the house with her wasn't on his agenda either. He disappeared outside about seven and she didn't see him again until about ten.

At eleven, she went to bed alone.

Thursday morning went quickly, and Olivia and Jackie

Montgomery were soon waiting for Caroline in Lydia's office.

"What sounds good for lunch?" Jackie asked when Caroline walked in.

"Abe's? The Honey Pot?" Lydia suggested.

"Let's do the country club," Olivia said. "That way, Dad gets the bill."

Jackie laughed. "Sounds good. Okay with you, Caroline?"

"Sure. Any place works for me."

The Whispering Springs Country Club parking lot was crowded. Caroline pulled the Porsche into a spot and waited for the other women to get parked and meet her at the stairs.

At the dining-room-hostess stand, the four women were directed to a private dining room. "Sorry," the hostess said as she pointed toward a closed door. "The dining room had a minor spill so we are using this other room today."

At the door, Jackie stopped to dig through her purse. "Oh, darn. I think I might have left my keys in the car. Go on in. I'll be right in."

Caroline opened the door and walked in.

"Surprise!" a room full of women yelled.

Caroline stumbled back, slamming her hand against her chest. "What the...?"

Laughing, Olivia and Lydia each took an arm. "It's your surprise shower."

Oh crap.

Jackie was laughing as she came in, dangling her keys off her finger. "Surprise," she said, a broad grin splitting her face.

Caroline looked around, recognizing many of the women from church, town and other associations. Her gaze fell on KC Montgomery, who shrugged and gave her a smile.

"I'm shocked," Caroline said. "Truly shocked." She looked at the three women standing behind her. "You shouldn't have done this."

She meant every word. Unfortunately, the Montgomery women and Lydia laughed, sure Caroline's protests were pro forma.

"Come on," Olivia said and began pulling Caroline toward a table at the front of the room. "We really do have lunch coming. Then it's present time."

"But Travis and I don't need anything," Caroline protested.

"We know," Jackie said from behind her. "That's why Olivia suggested a sexy lingerie shower."

Olivia giggled. "My brother will love this."

Caroline felt heat flush her neck and cheeks. "Great," she said. No, no, no is what she meant.

As she made her way to the front, she stopped to hug KC. "Meet me in the bathroom. Now," she whispered in her ear.

KC nodded.

Once the four women reached the head table and took their seats, Caroline saw KC rise and leave the room. She counted to fifty then leaned over. "Gotta run to the restroom. Be right back. Don't hold lunch. Start without me."

Jackie nodded. "Okay."

Caroline hurried from the room and headed toward the ladies' lounge. The door to the housekeeper's closet between the ladies' lounge and the men's lounge was ajar, which was odd. She thought about shutting it as she passed, but she didn't really have much time. She had to get back. Rushing past the closet, she blew into the lounge.

"We alone?" she asked looking around.

KC nodded. "Yes."

Caroline twisted the lock and sagged against the door. "Give me some advice. This is out of control. You're the only one I can talk to. Travis just smiles and says don't worry, but I do."

KC took a seat on a stool in front of the mirror. "I told you your fake-marriage idea was crazy."

Caroline joined her on an adjacent stool. "Except it worked. My grandmother was so happy when she died." She dropped her head into her hands. "What am I going to do? I can't go back into that room and tell all those women Travis and I aren't married. It'd embarrass his whole family. I couldn't do that to him or them."

KC laid a hand on Caroline's shoulder. "So stay married. Travis doesn't seem to be fighting the idea too hard."

"I can't," Caroline said, her voice echoing against the marble counter.

"Why not?"

"Travis doesn't love me."

"Ah," KC said. "But you've fallen in love with him."

Caroline sat up and nodded. Publicly acknowledging her feelings for Travis sent heat rushing up her neck to her face.

"So how do you know his feelings aren't the same as yours?"

"He would have told me. He's always talking about what good friends we are, and things like that. If he felt more, he would have said."

"And of course you've told him how you feel."

"I can't. If I do and he doesn't feel the same, it'll put him in a horrible situation."

"But what if he does feel the same?"

"He doesn't." Caroline sighed. "No, he's being a good friend to me right now."

"Taking Singing Springs Ranch as part of the deal is a great way to show how good a friend he is."

"I gave him that ranch. He didn't take it."

"Whatever. Look, as your lawyer, you've not done anything illegal that I'm aware of. As your friend, I think you're a fool for not telling him that you're in love with him."

"I can't."

KC smiled. "If you could see yourself when you look at him, you'd realize it's written all over your face."

"Oh, God. Do you think Travis knows?"

KC shrugged. "Doubtful. Men can be so clueless when it comes to nonverbal cues. For today, open the presents. Coo over each gift. Make sure the giver's name is well documented. Don't take the tags off the gifts. When you leave, I'll return everything for you."

Caroline hugged her. "Thank you."

"I still say you're a fool. Tell Travis tonight. You might be surprised at his response."

"Yeah, and I might wreck everything. No, I'll stick to the agreement. Remember to process all the title-transfer paperwork for Singing Springs."

"A million-dollar ranch in exchange for marrying you. Hell of a deal."

"It was a good deal for both of us."

There was a knock at the door. "Hello?"

The two women exchanged looks.

"I'd better get back," Caroline said.

They stood and Caroline unlocked the door. Elsie Belle Lambert stood there.

"Is this a private lounge now?" she asked in a huff.

"Just leaving," KC said. "All yours."

They exited and the door closed between them and Elsie Belle.

"Think she heard anything?" Caroline asked.

"No. That door is as thick as your head. Nothing gets through it."

"Ha. Ha."

Caroline had never spent much time thinking about what hell on earth might be like. However, by three p.m., an afternoon bridal shower dedicated to naughty lingerie had made its way to the top of the list. If she saw another pair of thong panties, she thought she might go screaming from the room. But her Southern manners won out. Each gift was opened, cooed over and the giver's name noted along with a detailed description of each item. She wanted to make sure to get Lydia's gift of edible panties back to her.

After the presents were loaded into Travis's car, the other women wandered off to their vehicles. As Caroline was getting into the driver's seat, Elsie Belle walked up.

"That was a nice shower," she said, her Southern accent barely disguising her true feelings.

"Yes, it was," Caroline said. "I admit I was a little surprised to see you here."

Elsie Belle straightened from where she'd been leaning on the car parked in the next slot. "I know your little secret. Either you tell everybody or I will."

Caroline shoved the key into the ignition. "I have no idea what you're talking about." A combination of fear and anger made her vision blur. The sudden rush of adrenaline made her a tad nauseous.

As she began to shut the door, Elsie Belle grabbed it. "I'll ruin you," she said. "I'll tell the entire town about your so-called marriage. You'll be a laughing stock."

"So if you think you know some big secret, why don't you tell everyone?"

"I don't want to do that to Travis. He's a good man, better than someone like you deserves. I swear. Either you tell his family what you've done or I will." Her eyes glimmered with glee. "Jackie Montgomery will hate you. The entire Montgomery clan will never forgive you for what you've done to Travis."

"Let me guess. You think you'd be a better wife for him?"

"You don't understand," she said. "You're just passing through. Travis and I have deep roots here. We belong. You don't. So, yes, I'd be a better wife to him than you ever would."

Caroline shook her head. "Go home, Elsie Belle." She jerked the door from the offending woman's hold and slammed it shut.

"Remember what I said," Elsie Belle yelled through the closed window. "You need to do the right thing."

She steered Travis's car back to Halo M Ranch with shaking hands. Fear about what Elsie Belle knew—or thought she knew—had caustic acid eating the lining of her stomach. She felt her house of cards tilting. Did Elsie Belle have the gust of air necessary to send the card structure flying?

She wasn't sure what, if anything, to tell Travis about the conversation. She knew she should tell him, but with the ongoing ranch rodeo and all the other demands on him right now, she couldn't dump one more problem on his plate. She walked into a deathly quiet ranch house. Travis was at the breakfast bar. At his elbow sat an open bottle of cheap whiskey with about one-third of it gone. Her heart sank at the sight. Ten years of sobriety gone in a flash. She jerked up the bottle, carried it to the sink and began to pour it down the drain. Abruptly, she stopped.

"No," she said and moved back to where Travis sat. "I don't have the right to tell you what you can and can't do. I'm not really your wife. You're your own man." She sat the bottle back on the counter.

The damn man smiled, a sad smile, a tired smile, but a smile nonetheless.

"What are you smiling about?"

"Not mine. In fact, I'm not even tempted to taste it. I've been in that hole and I'm not going back."

"So whose?"

"It's Noah's." He carried the bottle to the sink and finished pouring the amber liquid down the drain.

His words were like a dagger to her heart. "Oh, Travis. No. Are you sure?"

After tossing the empty container in the trash, he retook his seat. "I'm sorry, darlin', but I'm sure. He got it off one of the new cowboys from Riggs & Riggs. Found him sitting with the team around a campfire. From what I understand, they traded it to him for some help around their site."

"I hope you kicked that team off your land immediately."

He shook his head. "Can't afford to. They buy a lot of their cutting horses from me."

She stepped behind him and began to massage the rock-hard muscles in his shoulders. "I'm the one who should be apologizing to you. I haven't been fair. My family hasn't been fair to you. I'm afraid we've dumped a lot on you."

His hands covered hers. "It's nobody's fault. Noah's a little lost right now. Your grandmother did everything she could, but teenage boys need a firm hand." He squeezed her fingers. "I'm happy to be that firm hand, that male role model for your brother. He needs stability right now. He needs to know he's wanted here."

"You're thinking he's pushing boundaries to see what we'll do?"

"He's pushing boundaries all right, but we all did at that age." Their fingers laced. "He has a home here for as long as he wants it. I like having him here."

Before she could respond, her cell rang. The readout showed the call to be from her medical-placement agency.

"I'm sorry. I have to take this." She clicked the answer button. "Dr. Graham."

"Dr. Graham. This is Jeffery Cupps. How are you?"

Dr. Jeffery Cupps was the owner of Cupps Medical Services. As far as she could remember, she'd never spoken with him, only his assistants.

"Hello, Dr. Cupps. I'm fine. What can I do for you?"

"This is highly unusual, but we need you to take a six-week assignment in Key West. Your contract with Whispering Springs Medical Clinic is almost over, so I'm sure you've been taking the usual steps to disengage from there."

Ha! If only...

"The physician we had scheduled for Key West had a serious accident yesterday and will be laid up for some time. You are the only doctor we currently have on retainer who can fulfill the requirements of that contract."

"But I already have another contract after Whispering Springs."

"You'll be done before that contract starts in January. In fact, you'll even have time for a little vacation before January. We'll pay you double your usual rate and buy out the remainder of your contract at Whispering Springs."

"When would you need me?"

"Immediately. Dr. Buggs was already in Key West. He was riding his bike when he was hit by a speeding truck."

"How horrible."

"No kidding. We haven't anyone else with adequate emergency-department experience to take his place."

"I meant the accident."

"Oh, yes. That was awful. Anyway, I would need you to fly to Key West on Saturday. Arrangements have already been made for housing and transportation for the six weeks you'd be there. Can I count on you?"

"That's day after tomorrow."

"Yes, I'm aware of that, but this is an unusual situation. Is this going to be a problem?"

She glanced at Travis who watched her with a puzzled expression. "What about Whispering Springs Medical Clinic?"

"I'll telephone Dr. Henson immediately. Like I said, you were almost out the door there. I'm sure the clinic won't mind the money they will get from the contract buyout."

She picked at a ragged cuticle as she thought about telling Lydia that she was leaving early. Maybe this was for the best, exactly the sign she'd been praying for. It was becoming more and more difficult to not tell Travis how she felt about him. As KC had warned her, she had a tendency to wear her feelings on her face. She needed to put a few hundred miles between them.

"I need to think about this. Can I call you back?"

Dr. Cupps hesitated. "Well, okay, but I need an answer tonight."

Caroline set her phone on the counter.

"What?" Travis asked.

"That was Dr. Cupps. He needs me to take an emergency assignment in Key West. The contracted physician had a bad accident and is in the hospital."

"Can't someone else do it?"

She shrugged. "Right now I'm the only other physician who can take over."

"So this would be in place of going to Montana in January?"

"No. This assignment would start immediately."

"Like how immediately?"

"I'd have to leave on Saturday."

Travis froze in place for a minute. "Day after tomorrow?"

She nodded.

"You're leaving then?"

Tell me not to go. Tell me you love me. Ask me to stay and I'll stay. "I think so. What do you think?" She held her breath, willing him to say what she needed to hear. A sigh. A look of despair. Anything to give her a reason to stay.

"Well, seeing as how we aren't really married, I can't see that I have anything to say about the matter. You need to do what you need to do."

"So you think I should go?" *Say no.*

"I guess that's between you and Lydia."

"If Lydia is in agreement, then I guess I'll take the assignment. It's a lot of money."

"Okay then. It's settled."

"Wait. What about Noah?"

Travis smiled. "He needs to stay here. I like having him here and I think we're beginning to understand each other well."

Caroline wracked her brain for some other reason to stay. Travis obviously didn't need her here. And he was right about Noah. He would do better with Travis. Plus, she would be gone for only six weeks. Surely by then she'd be over Travis.

Now that's pitiful, she thought. *You can't even tell a decent lie to yourself.*

"Are you going to call Lydia?"

"Yes, right now. I have to call Dr. Cupps back tonight."

Lydia had been expecting her call. Apparently, Dr. Cupps had already talked with Lydia before Caroline got the chance.

"I really hate to see you go," Lydia said. "I do understand Dr. Cupps's situation. It's only six weeks. What about Travis?"

He doesn't care if I'm here or not. "He was really understanding about my going. Noah's going to stay here. The company will continue paying the rent on my house, so I'll be able to come back and pack up after the assignment."

"And move everything to Halo M?"

"Um, yeah. Dr. Cupps did tell you that he would buy out my contract with Whispering Springs, right? I mean, that's a chunk of money the office could use."

"He did and, yes, the timing is perfect. The portable ultrasound died this morning."

"Again?"

"Yes, but this time I won't have to try to patch it up or rig it. I'm buying a new one."

Lydia's voice was high-pitched excited, and Caroline was happy her friend viewed her early departure in a positive light.

"Thank you for everything, Lydia. The last twenty months have been the highlight of my life."

Lydia laughed. "You talk like you're leaving. Don't be so melodramatic. It's only six weeks and you'll be back. Oh. I've got a great idea. I bet Travis could meet you there for a late honeymoon. What a perfect spot. I know his parents would help out with Noah."

Caroline didn't correct Lydia's assumptions. She wouldn't be back. There wouldn't be a delayed honeymoon. There'd be no more Travis in her life.

She'd arrange to have a moving company pack up her house. Historically, she would have sent everything on to the next project location without giving it much thought or maybe back to Mamie's house if she didn't need it for the assignment.

Right now her mind couldn't process everything. She wasn't sure where to send her personal belongings. Shipping everything to Key West wouldn't work. She wouldn't be there long enough and it was too soon to ship it to Montana.

"Caroline? You still there?"

"Oh, sorry. Yes. I was just thinking about everything I've got to get done tomorrow."

"What about Olivia's wedding?"

She didn't want to be at Olivia's wedding, and especially didn't want to be *in* Olivia's wedding. She was a fraud, a fake sister-in-law. Olivia—and probably the rest of the Montgomery family—would despise her if they ever found out she'd made Travis fake marry her to get Singing Springs.

Plus, watching Olivia and Mitch say their wedding vows, seeing the love they had for each other, would probably kill her on the spot.

"I'll probably not make it. I'll call Olivia and let her know." In fact, while she was talking to Olivia, she'd plant the seed that things between her and Travis weren't going well. It was time—past time—to let him off the hook.

She redialed Dr. Cupps. "It's Caroline Graham. I'll take the Key West assignment."

"Excellent. I knew I could count on you. There will be an electronic ticket waiting for you at the ticket counter. Thank you again, and enjoy Key West."

"I'll try."

She clicked off her phone. It was a done deal. She was leaving for Key West. Texas, Whispering Springs and Travis Montgomery would simply be where her brother was living. Not her.

UNTIL THE MOMENT she stepped on the plane for Key West, she hoped he'd call, ask her to come back to Halo M. Hoped he'd say he loved her. Tell her he couldn't live without her. But as the plane lifted into the air and the ground fell farther and farther away, she saw her hopes and wishes fall with it. He'd been the friend he said he would be. He'd been the lover she'd never imagined existed.

He'd never promised more.

She let the one teardrop fall before closing the door on her emotions. Now that Mamie was gone, she didn't have anyone to lean on. She'd been on her own for years and been fine. She'd be fine again...one day.

Nineteen
~~~

By Sunday night, Travis was glad the rodeo was over for another year. Halo M Ranch had had the best year yet for sales and orders. His cousins' ranch crew from the D&R hadn't won, but for a first-time ranch, they'd made a good showing and that had pleased him greatly.

Noah had taken Caroline's departure with the normal teenage shrug, too involved with all the rodeo activities to be too concerned. Besides, he'd said, she'll only be gone a little over a month.

But now Travis sat in his office stunned by the conversation he'd just finished with Caroline. She'd arrived in Key West without a problem. The condo overlooking the beach was lovely. Her new job was fast-paced and interesting. And she'd decided she wouldn't be returning to Texas.

The wedding presents needed to be returned with a short letter explaining that, unfortunately, the marriage wasn't going to work out. KC would be by to pick up the wedding presents in the dining room and return them. She would also pack any of Caroline's personal belongings and ship them to Key West.

Travis leaned back in his chair, his heart leaking into his gut.

She isn't returning to Whispering Springs. Or Halo M Ranch. Or to me.

Caroline hadn't just taken a short assignment. She'd used it to get away from him.

How the hell had everything gone to shit so fast?

Where had their relationship gone off the track? How had everything gone haywire without him noticing? It was all because of that damn phone call from her agency. Of course, he hadn't told her not to go. He didn't have that right. But how could she not realize he was crazy in love with her?

He'd tried to tell her so many times, but every time she'd made some comment about their good friendship and he'd backed off. If being friends meant keeping her in his life, then fine. She could call them friends, even if he wanted more.

When he couldn't say the words, he tried to show her with kisses and touches and even song lyrics. Either she never got the message or—even more likely—she had gotten the message and had decided not to acknowledge it. That way she didn't have to tell him that all she felt was friendship.

"Hey! Anyone home?" KC's distinctive Southern voice echoed through Travis's house.

"I'm here."

"Where?"

"Kitchen."

KC walked into his kitchen, up to his side and whapped

him upside the head. "You are a fool, Travis Montgomery. I can't believe we are even related."

"What?" Travis rubbed the throb in his head. "What'd I do?"

"You let the best thing in your life fly off to Key West."

"Don't hit me again. And I didn't let Caroline do anything." He shrugged. "She's a grown woman. She does as she likes."

"Then get on a plane and go down there and get her."

"No." He shook his head. "If she didn't want to go, she could have turned down the assignment, but did she? No, she did not. She left me. I didn't do anything."

His cousin snorted. "You got that right. You did nothing."

"What do you want, KC? You here just to rack my balls?"

"Nope. We're here to get her stuff and haul back all those wedding presents."

"Oh, right. Well, Caroline didn't waste any time getting her stuff moved out, did she? What the hell. Who's with you?"

"The twins will be here in a minute." Her statement was accompanied by the sound of two door slams. "And I believe they're here now."

The front door slammed. "Where's everybody?" Reno called.

"Kitchen," KC called back.

"Hey, cuz," Darren said when he and his brother walked in.

"Hey, Travis. Can't you keep a wife?" Reno said.

KC slapped the back of Reno's head.

"What?" Reno rubbed the spot. "What'd I say?"

"God, help me with clueless men," she replied. "Would

you two take all those presents in the dining room and load them into the back of my SUV?"

"Don't I even get to say hi before you put them to work?" Travis asked with a smile he'd forced on his face. A smile he didn't feel anywhere in his soul.

"Fine. Say your hi's and then we need to get busy. I'd like to get Caroline's clothes shipped first thing in the morning."

Her words were like a slap to his face. It was all happening too fast. Caroline had just told him she wasn't coming back, and suddenly his cousin was here to remove every trace of Caroline from his house? For a brief moment, he thought about hiding something of hers, anything that would make Caroline have to come get it, anything that would make her face him again.

But, no. Caroline had made herself clear many times. She and he were friends, and apparently that was good enough for her.

"I've got something I want you to send to Caroline when you mail her stuff."

"Not a problem. Where are all her clothes?"

"In my room. Head on over. I'll show Reno and Darren where the stacks of gifts are and then meet you there. I wouldn't want you to miss anything," he said sarcastically.

After leaving his twin cousins working in the dining room, Travis headed to his office and pulled the unfiled marriage license from his desk drawer. He studied it, remembered how beautiful she'd looked that day, how strong she'd been when her grandmother died. Their signatures were bold in dark-blue ink. Her grandmother's was thin, barely legible. This last memento of her grandmother would mean a lot to her. He'd meant to get the license framed for her but just hadn't had time. Now, time had run out.

When he got to his room KC was folding a pair of Caroline's jeans to put in a shipping box on the bed.

"Put this in there, would you?" He handed her the license. Letting go of the paper was letting go of Caroline. Inside, his heart ached. On the outside, he maintained his don't-give-a-shit composure.

KC dropped the jeans in the box to study the piece of paper. "You guys had a marriage license? I thought this was all a ruse for her dying grandmother."

"It was. Her grandmother was a retired judge and wanted to do the ceremony and sign the license. Caroline didn't want to disappoint her, so we got a marriage license that morning. We just never filed it. Send it to Caroline as a keepsake from her Texas assignment."

"Interesting," she said with an eyebrow lift.

She studied him as though waiting for a reaction on his part. Well, she'd be disappointed. He wasn't going to fall apart, if that's what she was waiting for.

"Okay," she continued. "I'll send it. By the way, I found these as I was packing what little jewelry Caroline had." KC passed him the wedding-ring set. She folded up the last shirt and laid it on top of the jeans. Pointing a finger at him, she said, "You. Are. An. Idiot."

"What are you talking about?"

"You. Caroline. Hell, man. It's obvious you're in love with her. Why the hell didn't you ask her to stay?"

"I don't beg any woman to stay when she wants to go."

"You are a bullheaded fool, Travis Montgomery. You two were perfect for each other, and you just let her walk out."

"Damn it, KC, I did not just let her walk out. She left. What did you want me to do? Hold her clothes hostage until she came and got them?"

"That'd be better than what you're doing."

"She doesn't love me."

"God, save me from men in love," she swore. "Think about it, dunderhead." She waved the license in his face. "If you loved her, you could have filed this, you know."

"I'm not going to trick her into being married."

"Idiot. Must run in the Montgomery male chromosomes, because we Montgomery women don't have that stupid gene." She put the license in her purse and picked up the box. "When you realize how stupid you are and you want to call her, or better yet, go see her, call me. I'll give you her new address."

After the Montgomery cousins left, Travis picked up his phone and called his brother.

"Hey, bro," Jason said. "Lydia told me that you and Caroline were splitting. Tell me she's wrong."

"I wish I could."

"What happened?"

"Let me tell you the story." Then Travis told Jason everything, from start to finish.

The next week he did one of the hardest things he'd ever done. He broke the news to his parents that Caroline had left him. They were crushed. His mother even cried, which just about killed him.

He held off saying anything to Noah just yet. The teen had been on his best behavior since the incident with the whiskey. His school work was excellent. His attitude couldn't be better. He worked around the ranch without a word of complaint. Now that Noah currently seemed to be on the right path, Travis didn't want to land another devastating blow in the teen's life. Caroline might have to come back to Texas so they could talk to her brother together.

After she'd been gone a couple weeks, Travis found

himself fighting a deep depression about his current love life, or rather the lack thereof. He simply wasn't sure what he should do, or not do about Caroline. He sat in the cedar swing on his deck, studying the orange, yellow and pink streaks in the sky as the sun dropped below the horizon. He sighed as he thought about his past and his future.

He had loved his first wife as only a young, first love can. A love so pure, so innocent, so naïve that it would have had to change over time.

What he felt for Caroline was so different. This time, the love was between two established adults with life histories. This love was different. Not better. Not worse. Just mature. A love based on an understanding of what he wanted in life.

And what he wanted was Caroline Graham Montgomery. In the swing beside him. At the dinner table talking over meals. In his bed, making love for years to come.

KC was right. He was an idiot. He needed a plan to—

"Hello? Anyone home?"

"Oh, damn," Travis muttered and thought seriously about not responding, but Southern manners being what they were, he couldn't do that. Thank goodness, Noah was over at the Websters'. "On the deck."

Elsie Belle Lambert flounced around the side of the house, a wicker picnic basket in one hand. "Oh, Travis. I just heard." She practically danced up the steps.

"What did you hear?"

"Well, first that your rodeo this year was a huge success, and second, that Caroline Graham has moved to Key West."

"Both true. Now, what can I do for you?" *Besides boot you off my deck?*

"It's what I can do for you," she said with a flirtatious wink. She held up the basket. "I brought dinner. It's such a lovely evening I thought you might like to share it with someone."

He would, but that someone wouldn't be her. However, her father had just purchased two expensive geldings from Travis, and he couldn't afford to offend the Lambert family.

"That's thoughtful of you, but I'm not really fit for company tonight."

"Oh, Travis. You say the silliest things," she said with a giggle. She set the basket on the patio table, opened it and pulled out a couple of stemmed crystal wine glasses and a bottle of chardonnay." Since the cork had already been loosened, she pulled it out and filled both glasses. "Let's drink to your successful weekend."

"You know I don't drink."

"Oh, pooh. What will one little drink hurt?" She pushed a glass toward him.

"You don't understand. I can't drink that wine."

"One little drink, Travis. Just to celebrate." She drank her glass in one gulp.

"I'm not drinking with you. Now what do you really want, Elsie Belle?"

She sat in the swing next to him. "You know what I want, Travis. You and I are perfect together." She wrapped her arms around his neck. "Daddy would be so pleased if we married." When she leaned in to kiss him, he pulled away and stood.

"That's not going to happen."

She stood and glared at him. "I know your little secret, the one you don't want the whole world to know."

His heart slammed against his chest. "What secret?"

"I know that Dr. Graham paid you to marry her. Paid you with Fitzgerald's place." She flipped her hair over her shoulder, a smug smile on her face. "If you want to keep your little secret of how you sold yourself for a piece of land, you'd better start seeing a future with me in it."

A little too close to the truth to be comfortable. "Where did you hear that?"

"From the bride herself."

He shook his head. "First, the story is a crock of bull. And second, no way Caroline would have confided in you. So try again."

She slammed her hands on her hips. "I'm not lying. So maybe she didn't tell me directly. I overheard her telling your cousin about your deal."

"How?"

She huffed. "My brother and his buddies used to hide in the housekeeper's closet next to the ladies' lounge and listen to the girls talk."

He spit out a harsh laugh. He and Jason had done that too. "I'd forgotten about that trick. Doesn't matter. What you think you heard, you didn't. Caroline and I married because we loved each other. End of story."

"I don't think so. A wife in love with her husband wouldn't be moving thousands of miles away if that were true."

"You need to leave. There's nothing here for you. I love my wife, whether she's standing right beside me or helping a fellow physician in Key West." As he said the words, he felt the truth in the core of every cell in his body. How funny he could say the words to Elsie Belle when he'd never said them to Caroline. He was going to remedy that.

"Go away."

"Well!" she said in a huff.

"And take that booze with you."

Once he'd gotten the pain in his side on her way, he called Jason.

"I need some help."

"What can I do?"

"I'm going after Caroline. Next time, the marriage vows will be for real. Can you follow up on all the sales from the rodeo?"

"Sure, but can you hold off running down to Key West just yet."

"Maybe. Why?"

"KC told me about the marriage license you both signed. She said there was something about it that was bugging her. She put in a phone call in to a lawyer friend in Arkansas this morning asking about Arkansas marriage laws. Since we're both licensed in Texas and the laws can differ from state to state, she thought we should clarify any possible legal ramifications. Her friend hasn't called back yet, and since it's almost quitting time on a Friday, it could be Monday before we hear anything."

"I'll give you until Monday and legal crap be damned, I'm heading down to Key West."

The longest weekend of Travis's life passed at a snail's pace. He filled the weekend with every ranch task he could think of, including mucking the stalls on Sunday. Finally, at eleven a.m. on Monday morning, the call he'd been waiting on came. When he saw Montgomery Law Offices on the readout, he grabbed the phone.

"About damn time you called back," he growled.

"Good morning, Travis. It's KC. Jason is here with me. We've got you on speakerphone. Is that all right?"

"Sure, sure. Whatever. What did you find out?"

"First, sorry about the delay. My friend's husband surprised her with a limo and a night on the town on Friday and she didn't get back with me until this morning. Here's what she told me. Arkansas statutory law requires any person obtaining a marriage license must return the license to the clerk within sixty days from the date the license was issued or pay a 160 dollar late fee. In 2001, the Arkansas Supreme Court said that failure to comply with licensing statues, like not returning the license within the sixty-day period, does not void an otherwise valid marriage. Specifically, the Supreme Court said that failing to return the license within the required time frame did not render the marriage void where the parties involved had solemnized the marriage by a wedding ceremony and the minister signed the license. Their decision was based on the fact that the statue didn't say that failure to return the license voids the marriage, only that failing to return licenses means paying a fine. The case the decision was based on was Fryer versus Roberts. I looked it up after she and I spoke and read the entire judgment."

"So in plain English for this lay person, please?"

"It doesn't matter that you and Caroline didn't return the license. You had one. You took vows in front of a person recognized by the state to perform weddings. You all signed it. Plus, you had witnesses."

"What we're trying to tell you is that you're legally married to Caroline, big brother," Jason interjected into the conversation.

ALMOST THREE WEEKS had passed since Caroline had arrived in Key West. The promised housing was a third level one-bedroom oceanfront condo with a balcony overlooking the water. Her transportation was miniature Smart car. As promised, KC had shipped her clothes. KC had made sure that her Rolls, the Shadow, was secured inside the Whispering Springs rental house garage and promised to check on it often.

The sun dropping beneath the horizon made her adjust her sunglasses to block the glare. Picking up the glass beside her, she took a long drink of her non-alcoholic Flamingo Travis had taught her to make. It was silly, but when she made one each evening, she felt closer to him.

Pressing the palm of her hand against her stomach, she felt the elation as it rolled through her. One in a million chance. She laughed. Those damn fertility masks her parents had sent must have worked. Holy cow. She'd almost fainted when she saw the double pink lines on the urine test. No surprise when the blood test confirmed her pregnancy.

She wished Mamie was still alive. This would have thrilled her. On the other hand, maybe Mamie had twisted a few heavenly arms. She chuckled at the mental picture of her grandmother twisting arms to help Caroline get pregnant.

But pregnant and not married would not have set well with her conservative relative.

And Travis. What in the world would he say? She had to tell him, of course. God. He'd probably think she did this on purpose.

She rubbed at the twitch at the corner of her left eye. Poor guy had been sucked into situations he'd never agreed to. Noah. The public outing of their marriage ceremony. And now a baby he hadn't bargained for. She didn't even know if he wanted children. After Noah's outrageous behavior, he'd probably be concerned about her gene pool.

But a baby changed everything, didn't it? She couldn't continue this nomad existence. A child deserved a home. Roots. A set of friends. A family.

A father.

Where to plant those roots was the immediate question. Lydia had made her a standing offer to return to Whispering Springs Medical Clinic, regardless of her situation with Travis. After all, Lydia had reminded her that she still had the rental house there in town. And Whispering Springs would be a great place for Noah to grow up. He knew so many of the teenagers there now. He seemed to like it.

The big question was how would Travis take her moving back?

Her doorbell chimed, startling her. She didn't know anyone in Key West. Heck, she hadn't even met the neighbors. With this assignment, she was on twelve and off twelve.

"Coming," she shouted through the open sliding glass door. She hurried through the small condo and flung open the door. Her heart dropped into her stomach. The breath left her lungs in a rush.

"Travis. What's wrong? Has something happened to Noah?"

"Noah is fine. In fact, he's doing great. Can I come in?"

She stepped back on shaky legs. "Sure. Of course."

The living room, which never seemed large to begin with, shrank to a tiny box when he walked in. She should have been able to smell the cherry from the plug-in air freshener. Instead, Travis's woodsy cologne scent filled the air. Her gaze traveled from the top of his silver hair down to the tips of his polished boots. Her heart climbed from her gut, lodging like a boulder in her throat.

"Nice place," he said, looking around. "Kind of small." He walked to the opened glass doors and looked back at her. "Beautiful view."

Quivering legs carried her across the room to stand beside him. "If you like oceans."

"Don't you?"

She shrugged. "Why are you here?"

"I've been having chest pains." Travis pointed to the middle of his chest. "It's right here. Do you want me to open my shirt so you can see?" He jerked the snap shirt and it popped open.

Caroline licked her lips. "I always did love a snap shirt," she muttered. Talking over her racing heart, she said, "Seriously. What are you doing here? There are lots of doctors between Texas and Florida."

He smiled, deepening those crinkles around his eyes she loved so much. "Well, Doc, you see, I don't need any doctor. Only a specialist will do."

Caroline looked up at him with a lift of her eyebrow. "A specialist? What kind of specialist?"

"One for my heart. It's broken, Dr. Graham. Totally in pieces. I can't eat. I can't sleep. All my guys tell me I'm an ass and they're going to go to work for someone else if I don't get it fixed."

"Really?" A tornado twisted inside her gut.

"Really." Travis grabbed her waist and pulled her to him. "Come home, Caroline. Back to where you belong. With me. My bed's too big. Nobody laughs at my jokes like you do. I need you. Come back."

"You need me?"

He brushed a kiss across her lips. "That's right. I need you. Come home."

His kiss scrambled her ability to think rationally, so she pulled out of his hold and turned away. "No, Travis. Need isn't enough."

"How about this then? I love you."

Fat, heavy tears began to fill her eyes. Her heart swelled so large it made breathing difficult.

"You love me?"

"I do. I swore I'd never love again," he said, his voice so quiet she could barely hear him. "I didn't want to fall in love with you." She turned to face him. "I liked you. Hell, you drove me crazy just by walking in the room. The sex was unbelievable. I found myself wanting to be with you all the time. When I wasn't with you, I was thinking about being with you." He sighed and ran a hand through his short hair. "Somewhere I got in my mind that if I fell in love with you, then I was being unfaithful to Susan and what we had. I know that sounds nuts, but..."

She waited for him to continue. He sounded as though each word was dragged from deep in his soul. Soul-deep words could be hard to reach and harder to say, so she didn't rush him or try to finish his sentences for him. He had to do this himself.

He looked at her. "I loved my first wife, but what I feel for you is different and I think that scared me. It's deeper, richer, more ingrained in my soul. I love you, Caroline. I love you so much that sometimes it hurts. Without you, I don't feel whole. It's like you're the other half of me. I wasn't lying. I do need you. I love you. Please come home and build a life with me." He took a step toward her. "Say something, damn it." He smiled. "I know you are rarely speechless."

Caroline flew across the room and threw herself into his arms. "I love you so much, Travis." She began spreading kisses all over his face. "I've missed you more than you imagine."

He wrapped her in his arms. "I don't have to imagine. I know. I've missed you that much too." He kissed her, taking the simple press of lips into a deep soul-searing experience.

She took his hand and led him over to the sofa. "You might want to sit down. I've got news too."

He sat on the couch and pulled her into his lap. She kissed his wonderful mouth, sucked on his luscious bottom lip. "I've missed these lips," she said against his mouth. She felt the movement of his lips as he smiled.

"I have more news too," he said. "But I'll let you go first."

"Do you gamble?"

He drew his head back and looked shocked. "Gamble? No, not really. Why?"

"You probably should. Or, maybe I should say, *we* probably should. We've beaten a one in a million chance."

She watched as he considered her words and then the wide opening of his eyes as he realized what she was trying to tell him.

"You're pregnant?"

"I am. Are you upset?"

He laughed and hugged her so tightly she struggled to breathe.

"I can't breathe," she said on gasps.

"Sorry," he said and hugged her again.

"So you're not mad?"

"Mad? I'm thrilled. I'm going to be a dad."

"What would you think about getting married for real?" Her gut churned with fear. What if he said no?

He chuckled.

She slapped his shoulder. "Don't laugh."

"Honey, that's the piece of news I need to give you. Prepare yourself. Seems your grandmother was a little smarter than I, or maybe you, gave her credit for."

"How so?" When she frowned, he kissed the wrinkles in her forehead.

"We had a marriage license, a person legal to marry us and we went through a wedding ceremony. In Arkansas, that's good enough."

"I don't understand. We never filed the license."

"Don't have to. There's a 160 dollar penalty for filing outside the sixty-day window when we were supposed to return it. But the state says we're married."

She rested her head on his broad shoulder. "You're kidding."

"Nope. You're mine, fair and square."

She sighed. "And you're mine."

"That I am. What about Montana?" he asked as he nibbled down her neck.

"Canceled. I've been offered a long-term contract with another medical clinic," she said, running her hands up the hard contours of his chest.

He grabbed her wrists and pulled her hands off. "You signed another contract? Where?"

She leaned forward and ran her tongue along the rim of his ear. "Not yet, but I'm going to. It's a little town in Texas. You've probably never heard of it. Whispering Springs. There's a medical clinic there that made me an offer I couldn't refuse."

"What was that?"

"Life with the man of my dreams."

New York Times and USA Today Best-selling Author Cynthia D'Alba was born and raised in a small Arkansas town. After being gone for a number of years, she's thrilled to be making her home back in Arkansas living on the banks of an eight-thousand acre lake.

Photo by Tom Smarch

When she's not reading or writing or plotting, she's doorman for her spoiled border collie, cook, house-keeper and chief bottle washer for her husband and slave to a noisy, messy parrot. She loves to chat online with friends and fans.

Send snail mail to: Cynthia D'Alba PO Box 2116 Hot Springs, AR 71914

Or better yet! She would for you to take her newsletter. She promises not to spam you, not to fill your inbox with advertising, and not to sell your name and email address to anyone. Check her website for a link to her newsletter.

www.cynthiadalba.com
cynthiadalba@gmail.com

Other Books by Cynthia D'Alba

WHISPERING SPRINGS, TEXAS
Texas Two Step – The Prequel
Texas Two Step
Texas Tango
Texas Fandango
Texas Twist
Texas Hustle
Texas Bossa Nova
Texas Lullaby
Saddles and Soot
Texas Daze
A Texan's Touch
Texas Bombshell
Whispering Springs, Texas Volume One
Whispering Springs, Texas Volume Two
Whispering Springs, Texas Volume Three

DIAMOND LAKES, TEXAS
A Cowboy's Seduction
Hot SEAL, Cold Beer
Cadillac Cowboy
Texas Justice
Something's Burning

DALLAS DEBUTANTES
McCool Family Trilogy/Grizzly Bitterroot Ranch Crossover
Hot SEAL, Black Coffee
Christmas in His Arms
Snowy Montana Nights
Hot SEAL, Sweet and Spicy

Six Days and One Knight

Carmichael Family Triplets Trilogy (coming soon)
Hot Assets
Hot Ex
Hot Briefs

SEALs in Paradise

Hot SEAL, Alaskan Nights
Hot SEAL, Confirmed Bachelor
Hot SEAL, Secret Service
Hot SEAL, Labor Day
Hot SEAL, Girl Crush

Mason Security

Her Bodyguard
His Bodyguard
Mason Security Duet

Other Books

Backstage Pass

Read on for more
Whispering Springs, Texas books
by
Cynthia D'Alba

Texas Two Steps

WHISPERING SPRINGS, TEXAS BOOK 1 ©2012
CYNTHIA D'ALBA

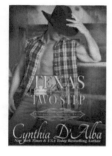

Secrets are little time-bombs just waiting to explode.

After six years and too much self-recrimination, rancher Mitch Landry admits he was wrong. He left Olivia Montgomery. Now he'll do whatever it take to convince Olivia to give him a second chance.

Olivia Montgomery survived the break-up with the love of her life. She's rebuilt her life around her business and the son she loves more than life itself. She's not proud of the mistakes she's made—particularly the secret she's kept—but when life serves up manure, you use it to mold yourself into something better.

At a hot, muggy Dallas wedding, they reconnect, and now she's left trying to protect the secret she's held on to for all these years.

Texas Fandango

WHISPERING SPRINGS, TEXAS BOOK 3 © 2014
CYNTHIA D'ALBA

Two-weeks on the beach can deep-ened more than tans.

Attorney KC Montgomery has loved family friend Drake Gentry forever, but she never seemed to be on his radar. When Drake's girlfriend dumps him, leaving him with two all-expenses paid tickets to the Sand Castle Resort in the Caribbean, KC seizes the chance and makes him an offer impossible to refuse: two weeks of food, fun, sand, and sex with no strings attached.

University Professor Drake Gentry has noticed his best friend's cousin for years, but KC has always been hands-off, until today. Unable to resist, he agrees to her two-week, no-strings affair.

The vacation more than fulfills both their fantasies. The sun is hot but the sex hotter.

Texas Twist

WHISPERING SPRINGS, TEXAS BOOK 4 © 2014
CYNTHIA D'ALBA

Real bad boys can grow up to be real good men.

Paige Ryan lost everything important in her life. She moves to Whispering Springs, Texas to be near her step-brother. But just as her life is derailed again when the last man in the world she wants to see again moves into her house.

Cash Montgomery is on the cusp of having it all. When a bad bull ride leaves him injured and angry, his only comfort is found at the bottom of a bottle. His family drags him home to Whispering Springs, Texas. With nowhere to go, he moves temporarily into an old ranch house on his brother's property surprised the place is occupied.

The best idea is to move on but sometimes taking the first step out the door is the hardest one.

Loving a bull rider is dangerous, so is falling for him a second time is crazy?

Texas Bossa Nova

WHISPERING SPRINGS, TEXAS BOOK 5 ©2014
CYNTHIA D'ALBA

A heavy snowstorm can produce a lot of heat

Magda Hobbs loves being a ranch housekeeper. The job keeps her close to her recently discovered father, foreman at the same ranch. She is immune to all the cowboy charms, except for one certain cowboy, who is wreaking havoc on her libido.

Reno Montgomery is determined to make his fledging cattle ranch a success. Dates with Magda Hobbs rocks his world and then she disappears, leaving him confused and angry. He's shocked when he learns the new live-in house-keeper is Magda Hobbs.

When a freak snowstorm cuts off the outside world, the isolation rekindles their desire. But when the weather and the roads clear, Reno has to work hard and fast to keep the woman of his dreams from hitting the road right out of his life again.

Texas Hustle

WHISPERING SPRINGS, TEXAS BOOK 6 ©2015
CYNTHIA D'ALBA

Watch out for chigger bites, love bites and secrets that bite

Born into a wealthy, Southern family, Porchia Summers builds a good life in Texas until a bad news ex-boyfriend tracks her down. Desperate for time to figure out how to handle the trouble he brings, she looks to the one man who can get her out of town for a few days.

Darren Montgomery has had his eye on the town's sexy, sweet baker for a while but she's never returns his looks until now. He's flattered but suspicious about her quick change in attention.

Sometimes, camping isn't just camping. It's survival.

Texas Lullaby

WHISPERING SPRINGS, TEXAS BOOK 7 ©2016
CYNTHIA D'ALBA

Sometimes what you think you don't want is exactly what you need.

After a long four-year engagement, Lydia Henson makes her decision. Forced to choice between having a family or marrying a man who adamantly against fathering children, she chooses the man. She can live without children. She can't live without the man she loves.

Jason Montgomery doesn't want a family, or at least that's his story and he's sticking to it. The falsehood is less emasculating than the truth.

On the eve of their wedding, Jason and Lydia's well-planned life is thrown into chaos. Everything Jason has sworn he doesn't want is within his grasp. But as he reaches for the golden ring, life delivers another twist.

Saddles and Soot

WHISPERING SPRINGS, TEXAS BOOK 8 ©2015
CYNTHIA D'ALBA

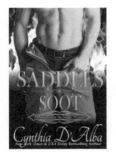

Veterinarian Georgina Greyson will only be in Whispering Springs for three months. She isn't looking for love or roots, but some fun with a hunky fireman could help pass the time.

Tanner Marshall loves being a volunteer fireman, maybe more than being a cowboy. At thirty-four, he's ready to put down some roots, including marriage, children and the white picket fence.

When Georgina accidentally sets her yard on fire during a burn ban, the volunteer fire department responds. Tanner hates carelessness with fire, but there's something about his latest firebug that he can't get out of his mind.

Can an uptight firefighter looking to settle down persuade a cute firebug to give up the road for a house and roots?

Texas Daze

WHISPERING SPRINGS, TEXAS BOOK 9 ©2017
CYNTHIA D'ALBA

A quick fling can sure heat up a cowgirl's life

When a devastating discovery ends Marti Jenkins' engagement, she decides to play the field for a while. A ranch accident lands her in the office of Whispering Springs' new orthopedic doctor, Dr. Eli Boone. And yeah, he's as hot as she's been told.

Dr. Eli Boone is temporarily covering his friend's practice and then it's back to New York City and the societal world he's lives. He's not looking for a wife, but he wouldn't say no to a quick tumble in the sheets with the right woman.

Due to ridiculous challenge, Eli has to learn to ride before he leaves town. He turns to the one person who can help him win the bet, Marti Jenkins.

As he learns to ride a horse, Marti does a little riding of her own...and she doesn't need a horse.

A Texan's Touch

WHISPERING SPRINGS, TX BOOK 10 (C) 2023
CYNTHIA D'ALBA

From NYT and USA Today bestselling author Cynthia D'Alba comes a steamy romance with a hot cowboy, a smart heroine and two meddling mothers who scheme the perfect meet cute.

Army Major Dax Cooper's life blew up with the IED that took his leg and most of his Delta Forces team. Medically retired, nightly dreams torture him, not only forcing him to relive the explosion time after time, but also the loss of the future he desired and is now denied. Unfocused and adrift, he follows his brother to Whispering Springs, Texas to lie low and think.

Psychologist Cora Belle Lambert understands what it's like to be an outsider. Sandwiched between two gorgeous and successful sisters, one a former Miss Texas and the other the current high school homecoming queen, and blessed with a stunningly beautiful mother, she considers herself to be the ugly duckling in her family. Determined to prove her worth, she takes on broken kids who need an avenging angel on their side. Kids. Never adults and definitely not an ex-military alpha male with sexy hard edges and mesmerizing azure-blue eyes.

Forced together on a mercy date set up by their mothers, each recognizes untapped promise in the other. Can these two broken people overcome the cruel hand of fate or will they allow their demons within to gleefully dance on their dreams?

Texas Bombshell

WHISPERINGS SPRINGS, TX BOOK 11 (C)2023
CYNTHIA D'ALBA

What happens when fate blows your life to hell?

From NYT and USA Today bestselling author Cynthia D'Alba comes a steamy romance with a hot cowboy, a smart heroine and two meddling mothers who scheme the perfect meet cute.

Sheriff Marc Singer isn't looking to remarry. Widow Dr. Jennifer Tate is focused on her career and raising her genius daughter. Thrown together sixteen years after their divorce, Marc and Jenn must face the reality that one night of passion after their divorce left them with a lifelong connect. Will they find that time heals all wounds and give themselves a second chance? Can a divorced couple go home again?

If you like relatable heroes, plenty of wit and charm, and small-town backdrops, you'll adore Cynthia D'Alba's tale of beginning all over again. Tap the link to buy the book today!

Made in United States
Troutdale, OR
01/21/2024

17046746R00196